Rune's Magik

Mel D. MacKenzie

To Anna
Keep following your
dream!

Mel D. MacKenzie

DEDICATION

In Memory of Charles Payne
Best friend, companion and soul mate
For always believing in me even when I didn't.

Special Thanks to:

Sylvia Berg

for taking the time to help iron out the wrinkles

Duncan Berg
Vanessa Berg
Elaine Levesque

Thanks for your help and for keeping me motivated!

Cover art by Johannes Plenio

CONTENTS

PROLOGUE

Her petite bare foot touched cold stone in the icy water of the fast moving, shallow creek and her little body suddenly felt cold. Now awakened from her daze, she cast her widened, golden-yellow gaze anxiously around the unfamiliar and shady forest surroundings. Very little light broke through the high canopy above, born of massive ancient trees with extensive and immense branches holding leaves larger than any man's hand.

Pulling her foot free from the water finally, she shivered as she wondered where she was and how she got there. Her eyes darted over her surroundings as her mind strained to conjure the lost memories. Tears filled her eyes, but before she could cry out, she gasped at a strange scuffling noise nearby. Quickly, she looked in that direction, but saw nothing aside from trees and sparse bush. Daring not to breathe, she listened carefully for any more signs of movement. All that could be heard was the faint rustling of the breeze through leaves and branches, carrying with it nothing but the faint damp forest scent. She let out a slight whimper, hugged herself, and grasped onto the thin sleeves of her simple cloth dress as she shielded herself from a sudden burst of cold wind that shifted the blanket of fallen leaves on the ground.

Turning her fearful gaze up into the crowded canopy, she could now see the sun's light trickling in as the wind pushed the leaves aside, but this only heightened her fear. "Mimi!" she yelled out, her little voice squeaking nervously. She heard only wind and the rustling of leaves in response. "Mimi, where are you?" she called out again as tears crawled down her face and she listened intently for any sign of another person. "Mama?" she called out finally, before beginning to sob.

A scream then burst from her lips as she heard movement coming from a gnarled tree behind her. She cautiously backed away from it as she nervously twisted her long blonde hair. While peering fearfully into the dark gaping hollow, she became certain that there was a large pair of dark, red eyes staring back out at her. "Mimi!" she shrieked and turned to run but was halted by a calming voice.

"Hush now sweet child, there is nothing to fear." The smooth, womanly voice soothed and warmed her instantly and she looked ahead in a daze. "That's a good girl. Now come to me, you want to see your father, don't you?"

With a tired smile, she moved toward the pacifying voice.

1

CHAPTER 1

The colossal waterfall violently cascaded down onto the deep water below and sprayed its refreshing mist over the cliffs and through the air. A light breeze carried the mist a short distance, wetting the nearby rocky surfaces and sparse plants, then danced its way over the short grass and scattered bushes, finally tickling the branches of the nearby dense forest. Inside the forest, a chorus of song could be heard as many birds sung happily at the radiant blue sky. Abruptly, a flock burst from the trees and flew off as a figure sprinted down the forest path, huffing and puffing.

Milla cursed at a branch that slapped her face as she sped by. Her swiftness caught many creatures by surprise as her small and delicate feet, encased in soft, brown leather boots made very little sound as they launched her thin frame over the rough forest path. Her short-bow, full quiver and large sack fastened securely to her back didn't seem to impede her speed at all. At last reaching the edge of the dense, green, forest - she stalled, heavily gasping at the warm sweet air. She cast her light green eyes over the low, even grasslands and down the rocky road. The wide roadway had been carved out by many years of repeated travel by foot and cart. Her gaze followed the road until it disappeared into the next wall of trees. A disappointed sigh left her lips and her shoulders dropped as a look of defeat overtook her features. Finally, her nostrils flared with a long outward breath and she swallowed hard as she continued her run, turning off the path and heading toward the high, river cliffs.

"Omi!" she called out as she reached the edge of the tiered cliffs and looked for the faint pathway down. A refreshing breeze shot up from the cliffside, carrying with it the waterfall's invigorating mist. Her eyes caught dense, thick smoke coming from the cliff wall below, and she smirked. "Omi Lieve!" she yelled again now spotting the steep pathway and beginning to cautiously trot downward toward the pungent smell of burning wood and herbs. Finally reaching the entrance of the smoke-filled cave she called out again, "Omi! Are you in there?"

A hoarse cough emitted from inside the cave, then the voice of the ancient woman, "Milla, is that you?"

Milla waved her thin hands at the aromatic smoke as she entered, passing the worn curtain door that had been tied open with handmade rope, as she resisted coughing. Her eyes moved around the small cave. The familiar rough cave walls were methodically fashioned with many shelves, all filled to the brim with clay jars and small burlap sacks. Spoons and rods of different sizes hung on the wall to the right and old drawings and paintings hung above the simple wood and hay bed to the left. There in the near center, sitting on an old wooden stool, was Lieve. Next to her was an oversized clay pot on a large tripod above a fire. Milla shook her head and smiled, then moved her long flaxen braid over her shoulder as she asked, "Omi, why do you burn fire in here? It's not safe."

Lieve let out a raspy laugh as she used her gnarled staff to heave herself off the old stool and gave Milla a tight hug as she approached, "I know what I'm doing child. Come, I want you to try my new stew. It will heal-"

Milla embraced her grandmother only for a moment but pushed away and held her hand up to interrupt, "I can't Omi, there's no time. Lorelei is missing."

The small elderly woman raised her tangled white eyebrows as she looked up at Milla. Her green eyes, the whites heavily darkened as with many women her age, closed and she nodded, "Yes I saw," she said solemnly, "Fetch me my stirring rod, will you?"

Milla obediently complied, grabbing the rod that was standing against the cave wall below the spoons, and handed it over with a perplexed look, "You saw? When? You didn't have time to come tell us before it happened?"

"These old legs of mine have a hard time making the journey at any pace, child. And even if I could, you are correct, I would not have made it in time," Lieve said as she took the rod and wiped it off on her dirty burlap robe. She made her way back to the clay pot, her body swaying with a slight limp and her dirty, tangled, gray and white hair swayed with her.

Milla's shoulders dropped and she let out a sigh, "If only you could live closer. If you lived in the village we could have stopped this from happening."

"You know what they think of my type of magik," Lieve snarled as she sat back down and began to stir the thick stew.

Milla nodded as she watched the chunky soup churn and bubble, "I know but it's not magik, you said it yourself."

Lieve pulled the rod from the stew and tapped the excess fluids from it as she answered. "What matters is that they do not understand it and they fear it. You've heard the old stories. If I wasn't your omi you would fear me as well."

"I hope I would never be so foolish," Milla growled in return then blinked as her mind refocused on her task, "But none of that matters right now, I have to rescue Lorelei."

Lieve turned a look up to Milla and sighed, "I know you mean well child, but it is too late for Lorelei-"

"I am not a child Omi, and how can you say that?" Milla snapped, "Would you give up on me so easily as well?"

Lieve let out another breath and placed her stirring rod across her lap as she gave an understanding smile. "My sweet Milla, you know very well I can see the paths of the future. Lorelei has been taken by something far more powerful than you or I-"

"Don't try to protect me from the truth Omi, I know about Lorelei's real father now. Mother told me." Milla puffed and rested her back, cushioned by her over-sized pack, against the abrasive cave wall. Lieve remained silent and the silence grew long and uneasy. Milla smoothed out her slim fitting, green leather tunic before she finally explained, "I came in late from gathering herbs and mother was at the table crying horribly. She was in a panic and when she finally spoke she kept saying 'he took her,' and 'he took my sweet Leilei'. I kept prodding her to tell me who and that's when she said it was Lorelei's real father. She said he was a lord from the east." Tears began to fill her eyes as she continued, "Everything suddenly made sense. Father's depression and then... killing himself. He knew Leilei wasn't his and knew mother betrayed him... and it explains why mother avoided taking care of Leilei and had that guilty look in her eyes every time she looked at her."

"Milla perhaps you should not jump to conclusions. You don't know-"

"Don't lie to me Omi! She also told me you knew," Milla scolded, wiping away a falling tear. "It's her fault father killed himself. I hate her."

"You should not say such things about your mother," the old woman said sternly, "You do not know-"

"How dare you defend her!" she barked back, "After what she did. My poor father died of a broken heart! She's a murderer!"

"She is my own blood! You will not make such accusations without knowing the facts!" Lieve's hoarse voice growled as she stood and wiped down her stirring stick angrily.

"Then tell me the facts Omi, tell me the truth that will excuse her betrayal," Milla said with an angry tone.

Lieve shook her head and looked away, "I cannot."

Milla stared at her grandmother indignantly then looked away as well, "The facts don't matter anymore anyway. All I care about is finding Lorelei, that's why I came to you. I know you can point me in the right-"

"Absolutely not Milla. I have already lost Lorelei. I will not lose you as well."

Milla remained silent for a short time as her large green eyes began to tear up. Her lips quivered as she choked out her question, "Then she's dead?"

The old woman shook her head, "No, she is alive. But she is lost to us. You must accept that and go home. There is nothing we can do."

Milla snarled, "I have never seen you give up this easily. You've told me many times that a new way can always be found, that no path is certain. You-"

"Milla! It is too dangerous," Lieve snapped then sighed as she calmed, "You must return home and comfort your mother-"

"Never! I'll never go home to that- that whore ever again!"

"Hold your tongue Milla or I will tear it out!" Lieve warned as she forcefully put her stirring rod back in its place.

Milla snorted and looked to the cave exit, "I won't go home, and if you don't help me find Leilei then I'll do it myself. She told me he lives somewhere east of here. If that's all I have to go on, then that's where I'll start."

The old woman took in a slow breath then nodded, "Then... if you will not be swayed..." she turned and began looking through her empty, dark clay pots. Finding a suitable one, she lifted it and handed it to Milla, "Take this to the river and bring it back full of water. I will see what other paths can be found."

***

When Milla returned, she helped Lieve remove the hefty pot of boiling stew from the fire and replace it with the smaller pot of river water. Lieve went about the cave gathering dried herbs and small clay jars of oils and strange smelling fluids. After mixing them with little care for measurements into the pot, she placed the last container on the ground and stood close to the pot. A moment of pensive silence passed before she began to chant rhythmically and move her hands above the water, swaying them to and fro. Her eyes rolled back showing only the yellowed white of her eyes as they remained open. After several minutes passed, and the cave air was infused with the fragrant aroma of the ingredients, Lieve stopped chanting and looked down into the churning water. Milla stayed back, as she was very familiar with this ritual and knew stepping too close would distort any image her omi would get.

Lieve finally shook her head, appearing solemn as she continued to peer into the murky water, "All paths lead to death."

"I won't accept that," Milla said indignantly, crossing her arms, "I will find Leilei. No person or magik can stop me."

Lieve sighed and jerked her view away from the pot, seeming disturbed by what she had just seen, "There is a darkness to the east that is blocking any path you take to your sister. As long as that darkness exists, you cannot reach her alive."

"Then tell me how I can help get rid of the darkness."

Lieve frowned at Milla's request then heaved a sighed and investigated the water again. After staring long and hard, her eyes squinted as if focusing on something, "I see... a path," she finally said, "But it is blurry and unsure."

"But it could help me remove the darkness, so I can find Leilei?"

"Yes, but even if you do succeed, your path to Lorelei is unsure, and it will be so until the darkness is lifted."

"Then tell me where to go and what to do. When I'm done, I'll return to you to find the path to Leilei." Milla declared as she pushed herself from the wall.

"Milla," Lieve started very seriously, "Do you know why those with powers such as mine are feared?"

Milla frowned at the question, "Because of old stories and stupid superstition."

Lieve shook her head, "There is basis for the fear. The Great Seer was a real man. The stories told may be partly exaggerated but there is truth to them."

Milla let out a loud sigh, "You're nothing like him Omi. You are kind and giving and loving."

"You assume he was not?" Lieve said sharply, "You assume all he did was to spread fear and gain power? You assume his intentions evil?"

"What are you getting at Omi? And what does this have to do with finding Lorelei?" Milla said, her voice thick with confusion.

"What I am saying, my dear Milla," Lieve started as she moved to Milla and took her hand, "is often the acts of great evil, are done with the most loving intentions. I would do anything to keep you and Lorelei safe. Even if it destroyed the rest of our world. Fate and Destiny are not always clear, but some strands, once pulled, can unravel the tapestry. I may not have the powers of the Great Seer Milla, but I can see these strands clearly."

"Please just tell me what you're saying Omi. I don't understand. How does this help me find Lorelei?"

"Let me ask you one question Milla, and then we can continue," she took in a steady breath as she turned and moved back to the churning pot, "What would you risk to save Lorelei?"

"I would risk anything," Milla said with fire in her words.

Lieve looked disheartened as she began to focus on the water again.

"Then so be it." Her eyes looked distant as she stared into the pot and she spoke. "You must follow the main road east of your village. Do not stray from the road or take any turns. Stop only to rest and gather supplies. Eventually, after some time, you will see a seemingly impassable river. From a small distance, you will see a humble village near the river with a thick forest to the south. You must first go to that village and offer to purchase the services of a magik user. You must take the one offered to you no matter who they are, do you understand?"

Milla quickly nodded, "And then?"

"Continue east across the river with the magi and allow this one to guide you further east. Your path will then be set."

"That's it?"

"That is it." Lieve said sadly then let out a long breath.

Milla nodded and smiled brightly as she moved in for a hug. "Thank you so much Omi. I'll leave right away."

"Wait," Lieve said as she turned her eyes to Milla and took a step back, "You must know that once you cross the river with your magi, you will no longer be in control of your path, for the path will no longer be yours. Our fate will be that of your new traveling companion. You must trust in it to survive. You should not return until your task is complete, as there will be no need to return."

Milla thought this over a moment then nodded, "Alright. Is there anything else?"

"I have some things you will need." Lieve pulled a pouch out of her hidden pocket, "Take these dregs to purchase whatever you need," As Milla took the pouch thankfully, the stone dregs clanged together noisily, and her brows raised as she tested the weight. Lieve then pulled out another pouch and began to move around the cave to fill it with herbs, describing their uses as she placed them inside. "Dried lubjo, treated with krobjo bark. Chew it or stew it in hot water to help in healing wounds quickly. Or, grind it and place it directly on a wound. It will sting." She grabbed a satchel, pulling out more herbs as she explained, "Lustu for an upset stomach. Kulor boiled in fermented nectar then dried. Grind it and add to your food or drink to help you sleep. But not too much," she said, raising a finger, and turning to Milla, "or you will sleep for a very long time. And let me see," she said as she continued, now rummaging through the far back of a top shelf. She eventually pulled out a clay pot with a tattered cloth cover tied on with thick twine. After carefully opening it, she ripped a piece of her apron off and used it to pick out a small blackened mass of what seemed to have once been a fruit of some sort, "This is an ancient okoko cryuh. Avoid touching it with bare skin and keep it away from your other herbs. It can cause coma and if enough is used, it could lead to death."

Milla scoffed, "What would I need that for?"

"That is like asking what you need a rope for," Lieve reprimanded, "Its use is obvious, though you will need it most when you do not have it," she explained as she finished wrapping it and placed it inside Milla's pack. She then rummaged around in her oversized pockets until she found a tough leather string and pulled a strange gold and black stone from the pocket as well. She tied the stone securely to the center of the string, then tied the makeshift necklace around Milla's neck, "You must keep this on at all times. Promise me." Milla smiled and nodded then embraced her grandmother, "Promise me!" Lieve said more insistently.

"I promise. Thank you, Omi, I'll never forget this," she said as tears filled her eyes again.

Lieve fought off her tears and held Milla tight, "Sweet child, do not forget you are still young and not world wizened. There are many who enjoy stealing the innocence of the young. Keep the magi with you and trust him. He is more than he seems. He is the light through the darkness. Leaving his side before your task is done will leave you alone and vulnerable in the dark. Do you understand me? You will be alone."

Milla gave another tight squeeze, "Yes Omi, I understand." She wiped her tear-filled eyes, "I love you Omi and I promise I'll come back as soon as this darkness is gone. Tell mother I..." she stopped and looked down at her hands then back up, saying carefully, "Tell mother that I'll be safe and not to worry about me."

Lieve forced a smile as Milla turned to leave, "I will. Remember that your mother and I love you and Lorelei more than life itself. Stay safe my sweet Milla and remember what I said. Keep it on at all times!"

Milla turned a smile back to her omi as she answered, "I'll remember. Stay safe Omi, I will be back before you know I'm gone," and she made her way out of the cave.

CHAPTER 2

Milla stumbled slightly from a small pothole hidden by a blanket of large multi-coloured leaves as she trudged along the old, well-used forest road. She was on her seventh day of travel and had seen several villages, three rivers and many acres of forests - but none fit her grandmother's description. The first few days she spent speeding down the road as fast as her legs could carry her, but by now her body was tired, her feet were sore, and her pack felt like a sack of rocks.

Despite it being a bright and sunny day, all of her remaining energy had been sapped by the coldness of the forest she now passed through. The massive trees blocked almost all of the sunlight from reaching below the high canopy. As this area also lacked moisture, it allowed for very little growth of other plants in the forest, aside from meager bushes and prickly ferns and moss. She emerged from the edge of the old, shady forest and guarded her eyes from the unanticipated glare of sunlight. Closing her eyes, she stopped and raised her face to the sky, taking in the warmth of the sun. Turning her head down now, she opened her eyes and looked off to the side of the road. The ground dropped off into a clearing, thick with matted down, flaxen grass that looked extremely comfortable after a long stretch of travel. She removed her pack then tossed it into the clearing, following quickly behind it, then falling to her knees. She was long overdue for a good long rest and a snack. Casting a drowsy gaze over the yellowed and dry grassy plains ahead, a twinkle in the distance caught her attention. Shielding her eyes again from the bright mid-day sun, she tried to focus on the glimmer and saw a wide canyon dividing the land to a depth unseen. The gleaming mist raising from the canyon had her suspecting that it was, in fact, a fast-moving river. Her brows raised with surprise, as never in her life had she seen a river so wide. Her gaze traced the rocky cliffs south until she saw a tiny village which also happened to be very close to a nearby dense forest just a short way further south. Her heart jumped into her throat and she fought tears of relief as she quickly gathered up her pack. Forgetting all fatigue and pain, she rushed towards the village enthusiastically.

***

"A spoon woods wark jist a' weel ye ken," Feagan called out mockingly as he sat a safe distance away on an upper shelf across the cozy, sunlit cottage kitchen. He then took a quick swig of his drink skin which looked oversized in comparison to his tiny body, which was not much taller than a man's hand.

"Using a spoon would defeat the purpose, Feagan. Now quiet! I need to concentrate," Rune barked, and his eyes blinked several times before refocusing on the bowl atop the simple wooden table in front of him.

"'At is nae toy ye wave aroond. It coods be dangerous if ye-" Feagan interrupted himself with a hiccup followed by a burp.

"Would you shut your gaping hole! It's hard enough to concentrate without you blabbering your constant warnings! I know what I'm doing!" Rune roared as he eyed the mangy faerie with a glare, "I swear, you've a mouth bigger than a Turly and you're not even the size of their heads."

"Rune, ye knaw whit happened lest time. Ah-"

Rune grabbed a nearby clay cup off the table and threw it at the scruffy faerie, knowing Feagan could easily dodge it despite his inebriated state. And he did so, buzzing his brown and orange wings rapidly while flying up to the decrepit ceiling. The cup whizzed past and shattered on the wall. He flew back to the warped, high shelf then dusted off his makeshift old burlap tunic absently as he snorted, "Braw, be stubborn," then began to lift and maneuver a clay bowl over himself, "But Ah warned ye." The burp that followed echoed in the little bowl.

After directing a threatening look toward the hiding Feagan, Rune turned his attention again back to the mixing bowl, pointing his crude wand at it with great intent in his eyes. He suddenly stopped, realizing he hadn't added the powdered nectar yet, "You'll see, Feagan," he said distractedly as he reached below the table for the heavy sack underneath, "in a short time my magik will be just as powerful as my father's and this entire town will be begging me for forgiveness and they'll start treating me with the respect a magi deserves." He grunted as he lifted the sack onto the table and began to measure out the nectar into the bowl.

"Respect!? Hah!" Feagan's muffled voice crowed, "Only th' amoont ay respect due when attendin' yer death pyre," he said dramatically. He held back a hiccup as he lifted the bowl slightly and continued, "They'll hae tae scrape yer remains intae a pot tae be able tae pit ya up there!"

Rune growled as he pointed the wand at the mixing bowl, "They won't be scraping my remains into any pot Feagan. Some friend you are."

"Ah teel ya whit, young Rune," Feagan said with a slight chuckle as he peered out, "If Ah am wrang an' ye successfully make yer sweet cakes wi' 'at wand an' yer magik, Ah will unlatch th' closest windae shutter an' shaw myself tae th' first passerby. Ye can chomp oan yer treats an' watch me gie chased aroond by shovel an' broom tae yer hearts content."

Rune laughed and looked up as he lowered the wand, barely able to see Feagan's black and brown eyes peering out, "And if you're right?"

"'En, if th' spirits will it an' thes bowl protects me, Ah will scart yer remains aff th' walls myself an' feed ye tae th' Turly brothers in a stew." Feagan ended his statement with an exaggerated, hearty laugh, broken by a hiccup and lowered the bowl back down as he downed another swig.

Rune, still grinning, rolled his eyes then raised the wand and pointed it, again, at the mixing bowl as he said firmly, "Fitting. Make sure to wait until after they've eaten the stew to tell them I was the main ingredient. Now quiet." He took in a slow breath, closed his eyes, then opened them again, focusing intently on the bowl. He began to chant the words, "Blett, auka loger. Skilja. Baka." The bowl began to shudder as he spoke, and his light-yellow eyes darkened as his pupils grew. He then narrowed his eyes with greater focus as he repeated the chant over and over, sounding increasingly intent with each encore. A slight smirk formed on his lips as the bowl wobbled violently.

***

Milla panted heavily as she finally reached the wide town entrance between the short, simple stone wall. She slowed her pace and caught her breath as she moved forward, while looking over the nearby stone and mud buildings. They weren't much different than the buildings in her home village, though here, they used very little wood around the structure, and a lot more grass for the roofs. The area here was also far drier than what she was used to. The grass more yellow and the dirt road, despite being well packed, dusted her boots thoroughly as she walked.

A very large woman, by height and girth, stood next to a large nearby home. The woman busied herself by beating the smithereens out of one of several woven rugs hanging on a line from the wall of the home to a thick wooden beam planted deep into the ground. Her frame, features and nose were broad and the lines on her face seemed to indicate a woman that frowned often and deeply. Milla gulped and pondered as she studied the angry looking woman. The lines on the woman's face might have even been deeper if her hair hadn't been tied back so tightly into a bun. Milla then glanced down the dusty town path wondering if she should find someone friendlier to ask directions of.

"Who are you?" the woman growled as she stopped beating her rug and moved her large frame towards Milla.

Milla gulped again and steadied herself, "My name is Milla, I'm just passing through-"

"Then turn back down the path and pass," the woman growled as she lifted her trunk of an arm and pointed Milla back the way she came.

Milla licked her dry lips and hugged herself, "I-I was hoping I could stop here for a night's rest and a meal before I continue."

The woman's dark eyes scrutinized the newcomer a good long time as she rested the polished wooden stick on her shoulder, "There is an inn down the road that has rooms for strangers. If you can pay that is."

Milla nodded quickly, "I can."

"Then off you go, but don't expect any other hospitality. Pay for what you need and leave early. We are not keen on strangers around here," the woman snarled then turned to head back to her rugs.

Milla stood a moment, not moving as she regained her wits. "Thank you," she finally called out before turning to head down the road again. She turned back to the woman as her anxiety almost caused her to forget her task, "Oh! I have need of a magik user. Do you have any in town that I could hire?"

The hulking woman turned abruptly with an irritated look on her face and she stomped back toward Milla, "A magik user?" she echoed, "What for?"

"To help with my travels further east," Milla explained as she absently motioned to the east.

The woman's expression quickly changed, now offering Milla a sinister smirk, "I'm afraid we have only one magi here and we can not spare him."

Milla sighed and looked down as confusion overtook her features.

"Unless of course," the large woman continued slyly, "you pay some extra coin to the town to make up for his absence. There are many bandits and trolls about. We would have to pay for extra guard shifts. I can't guarantee he'll accept your offer though."

Milla looked back up and narrowed her eyes, "Trolls?" she then quickly asked, "How much extra?"

The woman crossed her large empty hand across her girth with a pleased smirk and held on to her opposite elbow, "No less than two long dregs I would say."

Milla failed to hold back a show of relief, "I'm sure I can spare it. Who should I pay it to?"

The husky woman seemed annoyed that she hadn't asked for more, then answered, "I am the mayor's wife, Bera. I will be sure it gets to the right hands. You might as well pay it now. If he doesn't agree, come back to me and I will return it." She watched attentively as Milla nodded, removed her pack, placed it on the ground, then reached in for the dreg pouch being sure not to jingle the stone chips overmuch as to not give away how many she held. After pulling out two long dregs, she handed them over quickly. Bera offered a pleased smirk and roughly yanked them from Milla before saying, "The magi you're looking for lives in the last cottage at the end of this road. You can't miss it. His name is Rune," she then turned and walked away.

"Cottage?" Milla asked but Bera continued to walk away, giving no response.

It was an odd thing to hear of a magi living in a cottage. In all the stories one would hear in the far west, magi lived in secure towers and were paid handsomely for their services to the town. It was feared that if one with magik wasn't treated well, they would eventually turn their powers against the town.

Milla sighed quietly then called out, "Thank you!" before gathering up her pack and hurrying down the road.

After only walking a short way, she turned her attention to a large wood and stone building coming up to her right. The sign above the wide front double doors had a symbol of a lush tree with many branches, commonly used as an inn sign. A considerable amount of noise came from within consisting of music, singing and shouting. She hesitated in front of the inn, then turned her eyes back down the road as she thought over her next move. Turning her eyes once more to the inn for only a moment, she continued down the road and hurried her pace. A smile slowly grew on her face as she rushed toward the home of the magi. This would be the first time she had met a magi face to face. She had only stories to base her expectations on, but most of them were fantastic. Regular looking people with the power to conjure fire, wind and other things with a simple chant and gesture. A powerful magi was considered to be something rare. Terrifying and breathtaking all at once.

She came to a sudden stop as the small ugly cottage, at the end of the road, came fully into view. Standing mouth agape with confusion, she shook her head and looked to see if there was perhaps another that she had missed further down the road. Seeing nothing but the road passing through the bordering wall and toward the hills and distant forest, she looked back at the cottage in front of her. It was small – the size of one large room at a glance and was in dire need of repair. Holes in the wall were patched with old wood and cloth, and the grass roof needed urgent repair or replacement. Of all the buildings she had passed in this town, this was by far in the worst condition. She gulped and steadied her nerves. Her omi had told her that she had to accept the magik user offered to her, no matter who it was. Seeing the condition of this shack, it is obvious why someone might turn away to find another. A magi living in such squalor was either extremely bad at what he did or completely mad. Despite her obvious fear, she moved forward. After only taking half a step though, she was blown off her feet with a powerful force. She landed hard on her back, her pack taking most of the force. She lay there several moments in shock, eyes and mouth wide, finally grimacing and groaning before rolling over on her side. A white powdery mist fell all around her as she rolled onto her knees. Carefully, she stood and turned back towards the shack, holding her chest and wincing as she moved. The door and several window shudders of the cottage hung from their hinges and were covered in the white dust, more heavily on the inside than the outside. Milla moved toward the broken door, eyes wide.

"Hello?" she called out as she cautiously stepped into the doorway, looking at the white floors and walls tentatively. She heard a small cough and looked to the center of what appeared to be the main room and kitchen. There stood a thin, white figure with wide light-yellow eyes blinking with a shocked expression. He coughed again, and she asked, "Are you... are you Rune?" then moved into the room's archway entrance.

Rune's eyes turned to her and he blinked several times again before nodding. His shock over the recent explosion, was overtaken by the new shock of seeing Milla, standing in the archway. The dusting of white powder created an aura around her in the sunlight. She stood there in wide eyed silence a moment, looking like a surreal painting. Her long blonde hair flowed in a loose elegant braid over one shoulder. Her snug, green leather tunic revealed a small amount of skin above her high, soft leather boots. And her rosy pink lips were slightly parted in awe as she looked him over with cautious curiosity, "I'm ah, I.." was all he could say.

She stepped slightly closer, gazing now around the scattered and damaged surroundings, "I was told I could find a magi, named Rune, here."

Rune continued to stare blankly at her until a large wooden spoon came flying from seemingly nowhere, hitting him hard on the side of the head with a loud clunk. "Ow!" he howled then cradled his head.

Milla failed at holding back a laugh but quickly covered her mouth to stop. She then asked, "Are you alright?" through her fingers as she looked in the direction that the spoon came from, wondering who threw it.

Rune's face flushed red, but it was hidden well by his powdery white mask, "Uh, yes. I'm fine," he stuttered then bent down and picked up the spoon, getting Feagan's message instantly. "Ah, good... there it is," he said glancing around angrily in hopes to see where Feagan lay hidden.

"Did you summon that with magik?" Milla asked after removing her hand from her mouth, her excitement was obvious by her tone.

Rune turned to her, reading her gaze before answering, "Mm yes, magik. I seem to be uh..." he looked around at his surroundings, his hidden blush deepening, "...having some difficulties with that today."

Milla smiled thoughtfully, "Are you sick?"

Another spoon came flying toward him which he quickly dodged before answering, "Erm, yes! I do seem to have caught something." Rune's gaze hunted Feagan again. He finally saw him slipping behind a clay jar while reaching for a spoon hanging on the wall. Rune quickly raised the spoon he held and tossed it at the jar creating a loud clang that made Feagan let out a small yelp, "I should be rid of it soon though."

Milla watched his curious actions then eyed him a few moments before finally saying, "I have some herbs for most common ailments if you need-"

"No, no. It will pass quite soon," he cleared his throat and made a small, futile attempt to dust off his tunic. "So, what brings you to Skera Braka and my door?"

"I require the services of a magi for my journey. I will pay of course." Milla explained quickly.

"And you came to me because..." Rune returned, confusion thick in his tone.

Milla mirrored his look of confusion, "I was told you're the only magik user in town. Are you not?"

Rune sighed and dusted off his legs a little. As he tousled the powder from his brown hair he finally spoke, "Who was it that told you that?"

"A woman... a rather large woman I met at the entrance of town. Bera was her name. Are there other magi here?"

Rune sighed again and turned his head to look out the window, but his focus turned to the broken shudder that appeared to be moments from snapping and falling, "No, there isn't. How exactly do you want me to help you on this journey anyway?"

"Well..." Milla stopped and thought, "Whatever is required. I'm looking for help with a problem to the east and I was told I should take someone with magik with me." She paused, "So, what can you do?" Rune's eyes turned back to Milla and his heart visibly sank. But before he could explain he heard Milla gasp. "Are you doing this?" she asked, but before he could ask her meaning, she removed her pack and it stayed floating in the air next to her.

"I, uh..." Rune blubbered.

"Well that in itself is quite useful!" Milla said cheerfully, "So, what will it cost to hire you?"

Rune stood mouth agape for a moment, then shook his head, "Whatever you see fit. When do we leave?"

Milla smiled gleefully, "I promise I'll pay fairly but for now, I'll leave and let you pack what you need. I'll be staying at the inn tonight. Perhaps we can leave at dayspring?" Rune took in a slow breath and nodded silently. "Good then," Milla dipped her head in a sharp nod, then carefully plucked her pack from the air and the weight slowly fell into her hands. She smiled again, "I'll see you at dayspring then!" She then turned and slipped through the door.

After a few moments Feagan snuck carefully into the door, looking around to make sure no one had seen him, "What exactly are you doing?" Rune growled then licked some of the sweet powder from his lips.

"Gettin' ye oot ay thes unfortunate hole," Feagan said slyly, "An' mebbe getting' ye a coople nights ay," he cleared his throat, "payments frae 'at fine yoong lassie."

Rune smirked, "Right, it might get me out of this hole of a town for a short time, but I think she means to pay in dregs, you degenerate. Just be glad that she was too surprised to notice the faint buzzing of your wings. That was a big risk, Feagan. What will I do when she needs me to actually use magik?"

Feagan laughed evilly, "We can mesmerize 'er wi' simple tricks. She willnae see th' difference."

"I don't like this," Rune finally said with a sigh, "I have to tell her the truth."

Feagan shook his head and dropped his shoulders, "Ay coorse, ay coorse. 'at woods be th' right hin' tae dae, wooldnae it?"

Rune nodded, "Yes. It would be the right thing to do." He then dipped his head as he moved toward the door.

"But," Feagan added, "next daysprin' ye will need tae heed tae the square to pick up mair powdered nectar. It is aye a stoatin honoor seein' th' Turly brothers tendin' their stan' ay rotten fruit." He then flew to Rune, sitting on his shoulder before continuing, "They dae sae enjoy it when ye pass by, dornt they?"

Rune stopped in his tracks looking blankly ahead. He then turned around, "I suppose I could avoid heading to the town square to resupply after I see if I can help her at least. That would be the kind thing to do, wouldn't it? I mean, like you said, she might just need a few tricks to help. I should hurry up and pack then, shouldn't I?" His words mashed together as he hurried to his room to start packing.

CHAPTER 3

A flash of distant lightening lit the dark clouds above. Rumbling thunder followed, muffled by the drumming of heavy rain. The unpleasant scent of wet leather, beast and mud lingered despite the constant gusts of wind.

The large wooden gate, secured soundly to the solid stone wall, trembled and groaned as it bent and cracked under the continuous blows of the battering ram. It was the strongest of the four gates into the crossroad city and showed little sign of weakening despite the assault.

Within the city's walls, soldiers stood ready, facing the gate. Their eyes turned now and then to each other for reassurance, as the rain beat down and soaked through their thick leather armour. The flags above bearing the white sun on the light blue background, though heavy with water, whipped violently in the gusting wind.

"Curse this rain!" Major Peleg's gravelly voice rumbled under his dark gray helmet. He then tugged his drenched blue cloak over his shoulders. The shift in weight caused his bay horse to readjust and stamp its front hoof in the mud, "What sort of army continues an attack in such foul weather?" he continued while his well creased eyes remained planted on the gate as it flexed and trembled with each blow.

"Be careful not to curse a blessing, Major," Ethan said as he casually removed his black helmet then slicked back his wet, black hair. His composure was that of calmness, as he too watched the gate. His own mount seemed to mimic Ethan's placidity. Though it much resembled a horse, it was in fact a rare breed of beast called a kir'og. These scarce and costly beasts had remained rare in this land, partly due to their picky nature when it came to their master. Purchasing one was a high risk as there was a good chance it would reject its new owner. As highly intelligent creatures, they were far harder to tame than a horse. At first glance, they looked like any other horse – even with the magnificent mane that continued over the shoulders to the elbows and a tail that appeared to resemble that of a long dog's tail. Any closer scrutiny though, would reveal the beast's fangs and small clawed feet. The creature was as black as Ethan's hair and armour, as was the colour of almost all kir'og. Despite its naturally vicious and carnivorous nature, the only movement the creature made was the whipping of its tail, which was partially hidden, under Ethan's blue cloak that bore the white sun symbol.

"Blessing Captain?" Peleg said with a hoarse chuckle, "There is not a spot on me that's not soaked through. If this war doesn't kill us, sickness will."

"Cursing blessings and tempting fate," Ethan grinned lightly, his pale blue eyes turning a sideways glance to the major, "It's a good thing we don't fall into the old ways as some do or I'd say you've doomed us all." He promptly placed his helmet back on his head and continued, "The rain has put out the fires, and the wood on the gate is now too wet to even attempt to set ablaze. In my mind, that is a blessing."

Peleg spit at the ground then scoffed, "Old ways. Our people are no longer children fearing what is hidden in the dark. It's a time of advancement and learning."

"And yet we still fight over toys," Ethan said dryly as his eyes turned back to the gate. "Or whatever it is this war is about. I-" he was interrupted as a man called out his rank from behind him. He immediately turned to see who it was.

The man's feet splashed over the muddied road as he hurried toward the two. "Captain Ethan, there's a breach at the eastern gate!"

The captain scowled as the sergeant announced his bitter news, "Then contain it!"

"There's too many! We're being overrun!" he said with panic in his voice.

Ethan turned to view the southern gate that he now guarded with most of his men. His eyes danced around as thoughts and tactics sped around in his head. They had all been confident that most force would be directed at this gate and yet, here they stood, wrong. Attacking from the east seemed like it would have been suicide for the enemy. The height and obstacles of getting to the gate alone would have been enough to set most armies against it. They had decided that, even if the enemy succeeded in reaching that gate, getting a battering ram to it would be another great and near impossible feat. Ethan growled before starting his orders, "I will take half the men from here to support the east gate. Give me a mo-"

"With respect Captain," the sergeant interrupted, "We already have reinforcements coming from the north and west gates. We just need you."

Ethan frowned then barked, "Under whose orders?"

"I don't know," the sergeant said with a shake of his head.

Ethan growled, "Lead on," and he pulled the reins of his beast to turn to the east. He called back to Major Peleg, "Hold this gate at all costs!" and urged his mount into a trot behind the sergeant who took to a run, "How many on the other side?"

"Of what?" the sergeant responded through heavy breathing.

"The gate, damn you!" Ethan growled as the road veered toward the wall and out of Peleg's sight, "How many enemies are pushing through? And why was the horn not sounded before the approach?" The sergeant looked toward Ethan for a small moment, but he said nothing as feet and paws continued to splash down the road. "Answer me!" Ethan roared.

"I don't know," the sergeant answered timorously.

Ethan urged his kir'og to speed up then turned it to bump the sergeant and force him to stop. As he did so, he reached down and forcibly grabbed the sergeant's arm, "What sort of unit sends a message to the captain without details? We could be running straight into a blood bath!"

The sergeant only stared up fearfully at Ethan as the sky lit up again. Lightening clawed its way across the clouds and lit the dark surroundings, clearly displaying Ethan's confused face under his helmet. The sergeant yanked himself away as the thunder roared, and he wiped his drenched face as he backed off, "Forgive me Captain," he said as a look of sorrow overtook his features.

Ethan sat up and peered down at the man, his expression set somewhere between rage and confusion, "Forgive you? Forgive you for-" he let out an anguished howl as a sharp pain entered his left shoulder. He looked down to see a blade protruding into sight, having slipped past the edge of his plated armour and under his shoulder guard. He hastily drew his own sword and used leg commands to spin his mount around toward the attacker which caused the pain in his shoulder to become blinding, as the movement yanked the embedded blade from his attacker's hand. As the horse spun, Ethan instinctively lashed down with a fierce cleaving motion. His hefty, razor sharp blade made contact with skin as it carved through the wet leather protection of his attacker. The man shrieked his distress and both of his hands moved to the gaping wound across his chest and stomach. Gore slipped over and through his fingers as Ethan guided his well-trained steed to step back, now seeing the group of five soldiers in front of him with obvious intent to kill. His eyes sped around assessing and processing, trying to focus through the pain of the sword still implanted in his shoulder, the weight of it incessantly pulling him down to the left. He now maneuvered himself to guard against not only these attackers but the perceived threat of the sergeant that brought him here. Then, he noticed that they all wore the armour and colours of his own men, "Traitors, is it? Or are you enemies in hiding?" Without response, the small group attacked as the first attacker now fell, face forward into the mud, succumbing to his injury. The lone sergeant simply watched anxiously as Ethan did his best to defend against his attackers. His mount reared and clawed out at the enemies, knocking them back as it tried to clear a way to escape, but sword soon penetrated the beast's shoulder, causing it to scream and lose footing before it fell forward. Ethan was able to land on his feet as his mount threw him toward his attackers in a well-trained move. They were too surprised by it to respond quickly enough to take advantage of it. Despite his pain, he jabbed his sword toward the closest attacker, piercing the man's chest, though with Ethan's waning strength the wound was shallow and hit bone.

It was easily obvious that Ethan's training was far better, but with only a single arm and the heavy foreign object impaling his shoulder, he could do very little. He deflected what attacks he could but if not for his sturdy armour he would have been already long for the afterlife. After several blows and kicks he was forced against the stone city wall. His helmet flew off into the mud and the blade still protruding from his shoulder was forced in further. He let out an anguished yelp and stubbornly swung out again with undeniable exhaustion. His sword arm then dropped to his side and his body slumped forward.

The group had backed away only slightly to avoid his swing, except for one, who simply dodged out of its way. This man's face was scarred and broken, as if he had fought through far too many battles. He raised his blade to the captain with a triumphant grin, "Now you join your brother," he taunted with a chuckle, then lifted his sword with two hands above his head, aimed to strike down at Ethan's exposed neck. Ethan, with regained vigor, launched himself off the wall into a charge, throwing the unsuspecting attacker off balance and to the ground. The other three swiftly advanced but were all halted as arrows struck each of them at nearly the same moment. They fell to the ground, unable to cry out.

Ethan had yet to notice as with thoughts of this being his final battle, he was madly striking the man's face below him with the rigid hilt of his sword as both of his knees pinned the man's arms down.

"Captain Ethan!" he heard Major Peleg's voice cry out and he stopped. He glanced around and saw the bodies of his attackers surrounding him, too tired to even blink the rain water from his eyes. The archers approached with bows aimed intently at the final two would-be assassins left alive. The sergeant, who had led Ethan into the trap, held his hands up in surrender and the man, below Ethan, recovered marginally from his daze, the dense rain washing away all blood that poured from several newly opened wounds on his scarred face.

Ethan's body began to shake, and he dropped his sword, then fell to his right as the adrenaline wore off and exhaustion and relief set in. He winced and cried out in pain as he struck ground, though several were there quickly to assist him to stand. Through clenched jaw and quivering body Ethan growled down at his attacker, "You and your friend will answer for this."

Upon realizing the attempt on the captain's life had failed, the scarred man quickly drew a blade from his belt, raised it, and stabbed up through his own neck. Blood sputtered from his mouth as he died. Ethan winced at that then looked at the other prisoner as he yelled, "Seize him! Don't let him do the same!" The other was grabbed and held just in time, as his own dagger, raised to his neck, was quickly forced from him. Ethan let out a contented snarl through quivering lips before he collapsed and fell unconscious into the arms of the soldiers.

CHAPTER 4

Rune hadn't slept a wink. Besides the light rain that caused his roof to leak a rhythm of drops into appropriately placed pots, his mind was also tormented with fear and apprehension of the days to come. As the dawn's light broke through his small bedroom's shutters, he stretched and pushed himself to sitting. Looking to his bedroom door, which was hanging from a broken hinge and still covered on one side with white dust, he dropped his head into his hands as he continued to worry. Still, he eventually pushed himself off his bed, threw on his basic thin burlap tunic and wrapped his simple leather belt around his waist. He then began taking time to wander through the powdered home to gather what he thought he might need for the journey. He remained in a dream-like, thoughtful daze, even as he wrapped the last of his food rations in light cloth and placed them in his pack before closing it tight.

"Ye didne lae onie room fur me!" Feagan protested.

Rune sighed, not seeming to take notice of Feagan's protest, "I don't know if this is such a good idea, Feagan. This town and area are all I really know. And what happens if we run into something that requires real magik? Something dangerous. What then? Tricks won't save us."

Feagan fluttered over and unbuckled a large pocket on the side, "Weel," he started as he removed the contents, namely crude bandages, "Yoo've aye bin a guid runner," he smirked, then began stuffing the pocket with soft linen.

"So, if trouble shows up I run and leave that goddess to fend for herself. How heroic." Rune growled as he re-opened his pack and stuffed the bandages into the top.

Feagan laughed heartily, "Goddess, is it? Och, thes shoods be interestin'!" He then stopped and looked up at Rune with a serious expression, "Aw jokin' aside Rune, it's weel knoon 'at most magik users gain

22

their first powers frae need mair than practice. It's nae jist abit th' words an' th' motions, but also feelin' th' intent ay those spells." Rune furrowed his brows and glanced away as he thought that statement over. Feagan hurried himself to remove the bandages just placed back in the pack and filled the small empty space with his favorite brew.

Rune cocked his head to one side as he looked back at Feagan, "I thought you told me I'd never be able to use magik. You said I don't have the gift. Now you're telling me it can happen with the right feeling? Why the sudden vote of confidence?"

Feagan looked away then hopped into the pocket he prepared for himself, "It doesnae matter Rune. We baith need tae gie it ay thes toon."

Rune shook his head then moved off to grab his sandals. As he bent down to tie them he continued, "So you don't actually believe in me, you just want to get out of this town and you know I'm your only way out."

Feagan popped his head out of his new pocket home, "Dinnae be silly. We woods baith benefit, an' Ah coods gang awa' onytime Ah want tae. Ah can tak' caur ay myself."

"Right, you definitely could leave any time. But you can take care of yourself? Are you sure? Aren't you the faerie I found beaten to the edge of his life by a broom," Rune joked as he straightened, then pulled his thick, dark green burlap cloak from a peg on the wall.

Feagan turned amused eyes up to Rune, "A wee lapse in judgment. Bera is far stronger than she looks, an' that's sayin' somethin'. Besides, as I've tauld ye afair, she got th' jump oan me."

"She got the jump on you? She got the jump on a creature with faster reflexes than any of us larger foe?" Rune taunted again, his smile growing, while he loosely tied the strings of his cloak.

Feagan blubbered a protest, "Th' mayor's brew is far stronger than it tastes!"

Rune let out a small laugh, "Right, so you say." The two gave each other playfully taunting glares before Rune continued, "And you wanting us to leave to the east has nothing to do with the fact that we might come close to the dark forest?"

Feagan snorted, "Ay coorse nae!" He then dropped back down into the pocket and covered himself. His muffled voice then spoke up, "Yoo're awaur Ah was banished frae th' Myrkwood. In fact, stayin' awa' is probably a better idea. Th' faeries woods probably kill me if they saw me, an' they hate yer kin'."

Rune moved back to his pack then lifted it and threw it over his shoulder, "I sure hope this is the right choice," he sighed and walked out the front door.

***

Rune stepped through the open double doors of the spacious inn, and a waft of stale mead and spiced meats filled his nose. He hoped Milla would be in the tavern area and ready to go, but she was nowhere to be seen. The tavern was as boisterous as ever and Rune wondered to himself, as he often had, how those staying at the inn could sleep through such noise, which often continued through all hours of the night.

"I hope you don't think I'll serve you anything," the tavern-keep growled loudly when he noticed Rune in the doorway. Rune shook his head nervously and moved toward the side of the dark room, hoping to avoid any more attention until Milla arrived.

"Oh, this must be our lucky day," a gruff voice came from the back of the tavern and Rune visibly shuddered. "Aren't you going to come say hello to us, Rune?"

"Maybe he's too good for us, Helmo," another similar voice chortled, "He is a magi after all, isn't he?"

The tavern broke out into laughter. Rune moved against the wall and kept his head down. Two tall, young, blond men with large noses and blunt features appeared in front of him with impish smiles. "Come on Rune, cast a spell for us," Helmo, taunted as Rune attempted to move away from them.

He was forcefully shoved back to the wall by the other, slightly shorter one, who piped in, "Aw, is the magi scared?" They laughed together.

"Get lost Turly twits. I'm here for business, I don't have time for you," he said, then tried to move away from them again.

Helmo brutishly wrapped his arm around Rune's neck in a manner that almost seemed friendly and pulled him away from the wall. Rune struggled fruitlessly as Helmo continued his taunts, "Come on magi, surprise us with a spell!" He then grabbed Rune by the hair and pulled him to the bar. Rune grunted in pain and moved both of his hands to try to loosen the tight grip but was unable. Once at the bar, Helmo used his free hand to grab the closest mug of mead and splashed it into Rune's face. The owner of the mug seemed not to mind. "Have a drink, Rune! Maybe that will loosen you up!" The tavern erupted in more laughter as Rune spit and sputtered. "Maybe we should take him to the river's edge, Gervas, and see if he can fly!" Helmo yelled out and then spun Rune by his hair toward the door.

Just as he was about to pass a wooden beam at the center of the room, an arrow just missed the tip of his nose and struck the beam. He stopped his movement, after colliding with the arrow shaft, then backed away. The tavern fell silent and all eyes moved around the room, ending at the bottom of the stairs where Milla stood, her eyes dark and fierce. She held her armed bow intently in front of her, with little movement other than slow deep breaths. Helmo's eyes turned and fixed themselves also onto Milla, before he let out an uncomfortable laugh, "Nice shot. I'd watch where you're aiming though, or I might take offense."

Milla continued to aim at him as she spoke, "Let him go or the next one won't miss."

"You found a frail little girl to protect you, Rune? That's the best you could do?" Helmo smiled evilly at Milla, "I'm sure I have much more than he can offer you, pretty thing. But, if you don't drop that bow, I'll have to show you the hard way."

Milla stretched the bow string back, "Last warning."

His eyes moved to his brother, who was edging slowly toward her side. She turned quickly and fired the arrow at Gervas, then swiftly pulled another arrow from the quiver on her waist and restrung it before he screamed out. "My arm!" he wailed over and over, as he fell back and cradled his arm, the arrow sitting steady in his bicep.

"You..." Helmo growled then pulled Rune in front of him as a shield, "I promise, you'll pay for that."

Milla let out a sigh, then snarled as she fired another arrow, striking Helmo in the left shoulder. He shrieked and flung Rune to the side, then fell back. She pulled out another arrow swiftly and moved her aim around the room, assessing other threats, as the two brothers howled in pain. Everyone else in the room just backed away as she eyed them. "Are you ready to go?" she asked Rune, without looking at him.

Rune's eyes, wide with shock, blinked several times and he swallowed hard, "I um, I... yes." he stuttered and stumbled, as he moved to pick up his bag.

She stepped toward him, still moving her aim around the room, "Take four dregs from the pouch at the top of my pack and toss them on the floor for the tavern keep." she ordered. Rune quickly reached for her pack and complied.

"Don't you dare ever show yourself in Skera Braka again, you lunatic!" Helmo yelled as he cradled his shoulder and stood, "You too, Rune. I swear, I will kill you both!"

Milla twitched toward him, and within that motion, another arrow flew, striking him just above the knee, before she quickly replaced the arrow. He let out another shriek as he fell and Milla backed up toward the door cautiously. "Go," she ordered, and they both edged out of the inn slowly. Once outside, Milla lowered her bow and turned to the road. "Run!" she bellowed and began to run toward the town exit to the north. Rune followed right behind, and in no time, they were out of the town and out of immediate reach.

"You are insane!" Rune finally said, through heavy breaths, as they both slowed and turned to see if they were being followed.

Once Milla was confident that they weren't being pursued, she tucked her bow behind her pack and replaced her arrow, "I'm insane? Those two boys were insane. Treating a magi like that? They could have gotten us all killed! Just like the stories!" Rune shut his mouth and lowered his head. "Why didn't you defend yourself?" Milla then asked as she started again down the road.

"I..." he let the word out, then shrugged as he followed behind.

"I've heard of something like this before. In a story my omi told me. You're afraid of using your powers because you're worried you'll hurt someone?" Milla said as she glanced over her shoulder at the town then back to Rune.

"Something like that," he said, then sighed.

Milla slowed to walk by his side and tilted her head as she looked to him, "Did your magik hurt someone or something? Is that why you're so concerned?"

Rune hesitated then nodded, "Something like that," he repeated.

Milla smiled, "Well, you don't have to talk about it if you don't want to. But I hope you won't hesitate when I need you to use it."

Rune nodded and kicked a rock, taking a glance back to town, "I wonder why they're not following."

Milla followed his gaze then looked forward again, "Let's not get too comfortable. They might be gathering up a hunting party and some mounts to catch us."

"The town has no mounts," Rune said, looking at the ground.

"Well, then they won't be able to catch us," Milla smiled playfully at him as she quickened her pace.

Rune returned her smile and his cheeks flushed a little. He hopped as he caught up, to walk beside her, "That was pretty amazing back there."

"Thanks," Milla said proudly, "I've been training with the bow my whole life. I'm the best in my village."

"Why did you actually shoot them though?" Rune asked with a critical tone, "I mean, those were probably some serious injuries you caused, just to stop a bit of bullying."

Milla's eyes widened with bewilderment, as she turned her head to him, "I did warn them. How many times must I warn someone? How many arrows do I need to waste?"

Rune shrugged, "Yes, but..."

"But nothing," Milla interrupted, "What other solutions were there? You obviously intended to let them throw you into the river. You weren't fighting back. Was I just supposed to watch and hope you survive? Besides the fact that it would delay us significantly."

Rune shook his head, "No, but..."

"So, I was right to do something then," she said with a nod and looked ahead, "If I didn't injure them, they would have attacked me for sure. Then what would I do? Do you think I could match their strength?"

"It would be unlikely, of course, but-"

"So, just let them bully me like they were bullying you? I don't think they wanted to throw me into a river, Rune. Would anyone in your town have stopped them? Would they have been punished? I am just a stranger," she stopped walking and turned to him, "You weren't actually friends with them, were you?"

"What? With the Turly brothers? No, absolutely not, but that doesn't mean I wanted them shot..." he said after stopping with her.

"They'll be fine," Milla said with a sigh, "I don't think I hit them anywhere vital. Besides, there were plenty of people around to tend to their wounds."

"But you could have! They-they do labor work for a living. What if they can't walk properly or lift now? What if the wounds fester? You know those two are the only two workers on their crippled father's very large fruit farm? They may not get enough at harvest to feed themselves because of you."

"Their father is a cripple?" Milla said, with sudden concern in her eyes.

"Well, no, but imagine if he was?" Rune said as he crossed his arms and looked at her accusingly.

Milla's glance turned ice cold, "Are they, at least, the only two workers on their farm then?"

Rune tapped his foot and looked away, then back, "Well, no, they have plenty of servants that do the work for them. But that's not the point! These are things you should consider before hurting someone!"

Milla looked up to the sky in frustration, "Look, if you're so concerned about them go back and check on them. I have better things to do then listen to you whine about it. Just be sure to catch up."

"Whine?" Rune barked, "Do you have no grasp on right and wrong at all?"

Milla growled as her eyes narrowed, "I don't have time for this. Are you coming with me or going back?"

Rune stared at her a few moments then glanced back to the town. He then let out a short breath, "Well, you haven't given me much of a choice now, have you? They'll kill me if I go back."

"Kill them first then!" Milla said forcefully.

"Where do you come from to think that life is so easily snuffed without consequence?" Rune's voice raised in pitch with his frustration, "Where are your morals?"

Milla stepped forward, as she pointed a finger at Rune, "Where I come from we defend ourselves when others wish us harm. Where I come from, we take another life freely if it means protecting our own. Where I come from, we do whatever it takes to survive, and where I come from, we don't stand around talking when we have work to do. Now are you coming or not?" she roared, then turned and stomped down the road. Rune watched her walk away, then let out a growl, and chased after her. Milla turned her head and smiled as he approached, "Good. Now how do we get across this river?"

"There's a bridge a bit to the north." Rune answered in a quiet mumble, as he adjusted his pack, "But, there might be trolls at the bridge so, we'll have to be careful."

"Trolls?" Milla quickly stopped and turned to him with wide eyes.

"Well, that's what we call them. They're men that camp under and around the bridge, who demand payment for crossing. But I suppose you can just shoot them too," he said sneeringly, as he passed her.

Milla rolled her eyes and followed beside him, "How many at a time usually?"

"Could be three, could be fifty. It's a very large bridge."

Milla puffed, "We'll worry about that when we get there then. Maybe you can use your magik?"

"And do what?"

"I don't know, you're the magi. Whatever spell you have that can stop thieves from taking our money and killing us," Milla answered dryly.

"Like you said, we can worry about that when we get there." Rune said, now getting even more worried. A silence fell between the two for several moments before Rune spoke again. "If you're such a good shot, couldn't you just have shot through a baggy part of the shirt, or maybe-"

Milla let out a loud, frustrated roar, "Look, Rune, I get that you're upset, but this complaining is getting us nowhere! How about you just drop it and not speak until I ask you to, alright? I'm not paying you and bringing you along to whine," she then stomped forward at a quicker pace.

Rune stopped a moment as anger built up inside him. He let out a slow, calming breath, then continued following her.

CHAPTER 5

Ethan's body wrenched upward partially as he woke. It was clear that in his disoriented state he was unable to make sense of his surroundings. He tried to sit up, but the gentle pressure of a hand pressed him back down. "You're safe," a woman's soothing voice cooed, "Lay back. You need to rest."

Ethan's dazed eyes shifted around the small, dim room as he slowly complied and laid back fully. While he attempted to focus his vision, the pain in his left shoulder began to emanate. Grunting his discomfort, he cast his recovering sight to the woman tending him. The thick gray robe, apron, and hair laid back with a healer's cap, made her role clear. Her round, plain face softened into a comforting smile as she watched him process his thoughts. He then looked over the canvas ceiling and confusion set in. "Why am I in the skera's tent?" He inquired, his voice strained through his dry throat, "Was there no room in the city?"

A familiar gravelly voice explained plainly, "We had to retreat." Ethan turned his head to see Peleg, still in full muddied armor and his helmet carried casually under his arm, "We're beyond the ridge to the north. Our position is easily defended from here, there is nothing to be concerned about."

"Major," Ethan said, with a sigh, now relaxing fully and closing his eyes a moment, "What happened? We should have been able to hold the city for weeks."

"You two can discuss the war another time. The captain needs his rest," the healer spoke again firmly, directing her comment towards Peleg.

Peleg seemed to not even notice her presence as he continued, "After you fell, another larger attempt was made on you. We were able to get you to safety, but by then, it was obvious that many of our men had turned on us. There was fighting in the streets, no one knew who to trust. It was chaos. Even now, the men look at each other with suspicion and stick to tight trusted groups."

"To what end?" Ethan growled as he opened his eyes and attempted to sit up but was forced back down from the pain. He squeezed his eyes shut and stiffened, speaking through a clenched jaw, "They risk all simply to kill me? It doesn't make sense. Why, when they fail, would they rather die than be captured?"

"Regardless of their motivation, it has won them the city." The major explained sternly.

Ethan stiffened again as the pain intensified, "They gain nothing through this. When my brother was killed, those who supported him rose up and won us three important battles. Our enemies work against themselves in this. The only one they are helping..." he cringed again at the pain that was now strong enough to muddy his thoughts. "My mother..." he continued through clenched teeth, as he grabbed hold of his shoulder, his eyes now squeezed tightly closed as he braced through the anguish.

"Enough now, Major Peleg, he needs rest!" the healer's voice was now stern. "I think the soldiers have mourned enough as of late, do you not agree? Leave him rest and see they mourn no more," she hinted strongly.

The major eyed her a moment then turned his gaze to Ethan. It was clear he was in far too much pain to focus on any more details. With a quick salute and a, "Captain," Peleg left the tent.

Ethan's body writhed as he then roared in agony. The healer moved swiftly to a small table nearby and seized a clay flask of milky fluid. She forcefully held his head in place as she poured the bitter liquid into his mouth. He coughed some of it out, but enough flowed down his throat to be effective. Soon after, his body began to relax, and his eyes rolled lightly as he struggled in vain to keep them open. Sleep then captured him.

CHAPTER 6

The sky began to glow a brilliant orange as the sun settled behind the horizon. A chorus of song could be heard throughout the dense forest as birds and creatures of many different species made this area their home. The forest was made up almost entirely of thin, white, multitrunked trees, with leaves ranging from green to red in colour. The tree bark gave off a delicious smell, much like spiced cinnamon, that made passing through the forest pleasant. The leaves smothered the ground below, as they were ever falling and re-growing throughout the seasons.

A gentle breeze picked up the scattered multicolored leaves and they fluttered along the rugged path as Rune and Milla advanced at a sluggish pace. They now approached a small stone bridge, passing over a fast-moving stream, that was flowing toward the massive river a distance to the east. They had lost sight of the river, but could still hear it off in the distance, through the condensed trees to their right.

During the course of the day, they had wordlessly passed several turn offs but continued straight. The two travelers hadn't spoken a word since the argument, but it became a necessity now. So, she asked, "How much further to the bridge?" Her voice was tired and labored. Rune remained silent. "Rune?" she demanded, then stopped and looked at him. He stared back at her angrily. "You're not talking to me?" she asked fiercely, "How childish! How am I supposed to know where I'm going if you don't help me? You're the one that knows the area, not me." Rune continued staring her down, his yellow eyes revealing a glimpse of humor. Milla shook her head, "Look, I'm sorry if I offended you, but it's getting late and I need to know how much further the bridge is." Rune smirked impishly, but still said nothing. She let out a frustrated growl, "You are such a child!" She turned and began to stomp over the small overpass but halted after a few steps. She spun around. "Wait," she said and walked back towards him, "Is this because I told you to stop talking until I ask you to?" Rune's smirk grew, and he cocked his head to one side. Milla's face grew angry as she spoke through her teeth, "I'm asking you to speak now."

"As you wish, dear lady," Rune said, with a poorly mimicked and exaggerated noble bow.

Clenching her jaw still, she asked again, "How long until we reach the bridge?"

"We passed the turn off a long time ago," He answered with a sneer.

Milla let out a roar as she loosened her pack, then threw it to the ground, "You- you!" she kicked her pack, then dropped to her knees and covered her face as she began to rant through her hands, "I'm on the most important journey I've ever been on in my life and yet you play these silly, childish games? This journey could be the difference between life and death and- why? Why was it you I was given?"

Rune's brows raised as he watched her. He waited a while before daring to speak, the silence between them growing with the darkness. "So," he said finally, then cleared his throat, "should we set up camp here?"

She raised her eyes above her hands and grumbled irately, "We don't have much of a choice now, do we?"

"I know a spell that can set the camp up in no time," he bragged then pulled his wand from his pack and moved to the closest clearing. Only her resentful eyes moved to follow him.

A small muffled voice from his pack chided, "Rune, dinnae be a turd."

"I can do this," Rune muttered through his teeth. He steadied himself as he focused on the clearing and began the incantation, "Opinn kyall, samna nest, leggja rúm!" He ended the chant with a raised voice and a final dramatic flick of the wand. Nothing happened. He slowly turned his eyes to Milla who stared back with an irritated expression, "I uh..." he started, "I can do this, I must have just-"

"Just forget it," Milla grumbled, as she stood and picked up her pack. She moved to the clearing, untied the bedroll from under her pack and began to lay it out.

Rune watched silently at first, then continued, "I'm just a bit tired. I can do it if you give me a moment."

Milla gave him an icy look as she laid down and forcibly placed her pack at the top of her bedroll, to be used as a pillow. She spun away from him violently and closed her eyes.

"Right," he said sharply, putting his wand away. He began to untie his own bedroll as he muttered, "This is a safe enough area here, and the nights aren't cold enough to really need a fire anyway. Our bedrolls should keep us warm enough. There's also no wild animals or wandering bandits that I've heard of."

"Good night," Milla grunted.

"Good night," Rune said glumly, then laid out his bedroll and sat on it. For a short time, he stared at the back of Milla's head while he reflected on the day, now passed. After all traces of sunlight vanished, he grabbed his pack, stood up, and moved away towards the thin trees. Once out of view, he opened Feagan's pocket.

"Ugh! It's abit time!" Feagan growled as he darted out of the pack and took in a refreshing breath of the night air.

"Not so loud!" Rune whispered, "She'll hear you."

"Ah need permission tae talk noo tay?" Feagan grunted in a loud whisper.

Rune sighed then sat against a tree, "Not the best start to our friendship, I'll admit."

"'at is a stoatin understatement," Feagan scoffed then continued, "Let's tak' thes chance an' heed back tae toon. Thaur has got tae be a better way tae free oorselves frae 'at hovel than thes tyrannical lassie."

"We can't head back to town. The Turly brothers will kill me now, if I go back." Rune reminded him, "Besides, wasn't it your idea for us to leave with her in the first place?"

The scruffy faerie flailed his arms as he squawked, "'at is besides th' point. An' thes overbearin' harpy will kill ye ur gie ye killed. Th' Turly brothers will jist gie ye a guid beatin'.'"

"Oh, they'll just beat me? Well if that's all..." Rune said then rolled his eyes. "Look, I'm not saying we stick with her for long, but maybe until the next town at least."

"You coods gie thaur oan yer own. Ye dinnae need 'er," Feagan coaxed, as he moved to sit on Rune's shoulder.

"Maybe I don't need her, but she needs me. I can't just abandon her."

"Rune," Feagan said, calming his voice, "Think abit thes. Th' only reason ye care is coz she has a bonnie face. Mony a boy hae dain th' sam thin' an' it ne'er ends weel. She obvioosly disnae shaur yer interest an' honestly mah boy, she's nae worth yer troobles ur yer life."

Rune shook his head, "You're wrong. I'm not doing this just because she's pretty. Anyway, she's obviously just on edge for whatever reason it is she's traveling. It's starting to sound really important. Maybe even dangerous. Besides, you've heard the stories of the young hero earning the heart of a less than interested lady. I just need to prove myself."

"An' sae it starts. Nae jist coz she's bonnie? Ur ye sure?" Feagan said with a roll of his eyes then sighed deeply, "Weel, I've hud enaw air. Yoo'd better gie back tae 'er. Apologize mebbe, if ye dinnae want lae ay th' joorney tae be tay painful."

Rune smirked and nodded as Feagan took his place back inside the pocket, "The journey won't be too painful, I'm sure." He then turned and moved out of the darkness and back to his bedroll to lay down.

"Do you always talk to yourself?" Milla grumbled tiredly.

Rune jumped slightly and tried to think quickly, "No, I... I was just... I mean sometimes I practice before I... My magik that is. It's just I'm not feeling-"

"Calm down magi, it was just a question. Go to sleep, we have a long day's travel tomorrow," she droned, then readjusted herself.

"Right," Rune chirped, "Sleep well."

Milla remained silent.

CHAPTER 7

The rickety carriage bumped and swayed as it sped over the uneven trail. Night had stolen the sky, but the moon offered enough light, through the seams and cracks of the wood, for the passengers inside to discern their surroundings.

Lorelei hugged herself as she looked around at the other young girls riding inside the dark carriage with her. Without sound or expression, they swayed and jostled with the movements of the carriage. All of them seemed to be as dirty and ragged as she was, though most of them had been lucky enough to have worn shoes. She looked down at her own dirty, blistered and bloody feet and wanted to cry, but her eyes remained dry. She had cried and screamed all she could, and now looked as tired and defeated as the girls around her. She pressed her dried and cracking lips together, then let out a cough through her parched throat. All eyes shifted to her, but not a word was spoken, as they all returned to vacant stares ahead. Her eyelids drifted down, as exhaustion took over. Doing her best to rest her head, while the carriage continued to jerk and sway, she slipped off to a restless sleep.

CHAPTER 8

The stars faded as the sun hauled its way toward the horizon. Golden beams slowly reached out and embraced the land, until they finally stroked the faces of the two young adventurers, waking them gently with light and warmth. Little was said as they climbed out of their bedrolls and packed up, other than Rune giving simple directions to the bridge over the great river. The journey, at first, was serenaded by the forest creatures, as well as the crunching sounds of the two chewing on dried rations and stepping on dried leaves as they walked back the way they came over the leaf covered path. The crisp morning soon warmed. By mid-morning the sun twinkled and danced through the motley leaves as they were blown about by a mild breeze. The birds chirped a happy mid-day song and the mood silently lightened between the two.

Finally, they arrived at the desired eastward turn-off and Milla was visibly relieved to now be back on the intended path. It eventually inclined upward to a bearable steepness. As they reached the top of the rise, they both stopped and finally gazed down at the imposing stone bridge. Milla was paralyzed with awe as she inspected the stone structure spanning the colossal divide. It was just over two passenger carts wide but the length, in most cases, would be impossible for a stone structure. The light-colored stone of the bridge seemed polished and well maintained, though with a lack of a wall to stop someone from slipping off the edge and into the deep canyon would give even the bravest soul pause.

"No one knows who built it," Rune began to explain as he patiently waited for her astonishment to fade. He remembered feeling the same awe when his parents brought him here the first time. "It's been there since before anyone can remember, but all the local towns help keep it up. It's a well-used bridge during harvest season."

Milla nodded slowly but remained silent as she continued to scan the view in front of her. She finally turned her attention to the wide crevasse, still unable to see the water below that created a roaring noise and continuous mist between the sable cliff faces, "I really wouldn't want to fall in there," she said with a shudder.

Rune agreed, "I've seen a carriage lose a wheel on the bridge and fall in. It took less than the blink of an eye for it to break into countless pieces and disappear down the river and out of sight."

Milla's eyes widened and turned to Rune, "Were there any people on it? Did the horses get pulled in?"

Rune's head jerked up and down quickly as he looked off, remembering, "There were two men on the carriage. One was able to leap to safety before the fall. The other fell in with the two horses pulling it. They disappeared as soon as they hit the rapids. The funny thing is, if they hadn't been in such a rush and pushing their way past the others on the bridge, it would have never happened. My parents told me it was a lesson learned, for all those watching, in patience. I'll never forget the screaming..."

Milla gulped and remained silent several more moments. She finally spoke, "I don't see any movement. Where do the trolls usually hide?"

Rune shook his head, appearing somewhat confused as his eyes carefully scanned the area, "They rarely actually hide, but they do tend to sleep in the small spot of land on the cliff wall just under the bridge. They usually try to make it obvious that they're there though, so those coming have their purses ready."

Milla nodded and her eyebrows lowered with concern, "I suppose we have no choice but to move ahead then. If anyone pops out from hiding, run back here and we'll regroup and decide how to handle it. If we can't do that, be sure to use your magik and protect us the best you can. I'll solve any problem I can with my bow." Rune gave a concerned nod and they started down the slope. As they approached the bridge their pace slowed to a crawl and they glanced around cautiously. No one jumped out to meet them. Milla stopped fully and Rune stopped with her. Her eyes were wide with fear as the roaring sound of the rapids was nearly as intimidating as the canyon itself.

Rune raised his voice, so he could be heard above the thunderous noise, "It's best to walk down the middle and not look down on your first crossing. Keep your eyes forward."

Milla glanced over at him, her eyes filled with foreboding. Instead of taking his advice she urged herself to move to the side of the cliff. The cold bursts of wind threw off her sense of balance mildly. Carefully, she leaned forward to look down into the enormous canyon. Deep below the wide, white-river rapids clashed and sprayed over dark jagged rocks in a chaotic dance. The spectacle made her queasy and she stumbled back and steadied herself, "We have to cross that?" She loudly protested.

"If you want to go east, then yes, we have to cross that," Rune bellowed as he smiled at her fearful display, "It's really not as bad as it looks. You can hold onto my arm if it will help."

Milla's pupils contracted as she looked ahead at nothing in particular. She turned her attention to the opening below the bridge to be sure no one stirred, then swallowed and straightened, giving Rune a sharp nod. Rune returned the nod and moved himself to the center of the bridge entrance, then offered his arm to Milla. Milla approached him timidly, keeping her eyes on him and not the bridge or canyon. When she reached him, she grabbed hold of his arm and held tight, then turned her eyes to peer across the long bridge.

Rune moved his free hand and placed it gallantly on her arm as he calmly, but loudly asked her, "Are you ready?" Milla gave an unsteady nod and they started forward slowly. As they eased their way down the center, the wind became colder and the gusts were unnervingly strong, but they continued at a steady pace. Milla cursed under her breath at the deafening sound of the rapids below, which could easily mask the sound of any approaching danger. As they reached the halfway point of the bridge, a powerful gust shocked Milla. She shrieked and tried to drop to her knees, but Rune held her up firmly and bellowed, "Almost there. It's not strong enough to blow us in, don't worry!" She let out a whimper and held even tighter to him as they continued across. As they finally approached the end of the bridge, they stopped and took a quick look around for any sign of trouble, but there was none. They quickened their pace and moved off the bridge, then hurried away from it until the noise began to die down to a tolerable level.

Milla finally released her grip on Rune and he allowed her to drop to her knees. She closed her eyes and bowed her head. "It's over," she said, then let out a heavy sigh.

Rune beamed a prideful smile, giddy at having the chance to play the brave hero, "See? Not so bad."

Milla opened her eyes and looked up at him with a relieved smile, "Well, we did it anyway." She pushed herself to stand and her eyes danced over the new surroundings. The terrain was significantly different on this side of the river. The land was near treeless and was almost flat in the visible distance around them. The grass was short and patchy, with few other plants and otherwise, only small boulders and rocks were scattered throughout. "There's no one on this side either. Is that normal?"

Rune shook his head, his face now showing noticeable uncertainty, "No sign of camps. No flags. No burnt ground from fires..."

Milla watched Rune as he spoke, a new sense of foreboding now taking hold, "Is the area being cared for by one of the rulers perhaps?"

Rune shrugged, "I've not heard anything. Our village is so close to the bridge that we are usually the first to hear of change on this side.

Although..." he stopped speaking and moved forward, scanning the distance ahead.

"What?" Milla said as she hurried toward him and grasped his lower arm with a distressed look on her face.

Rune peered down at her hand, then to her face as he smiled triumphantly, "Nothing. Well, it's just that, we haven't heard news from this side since the last harvest. It could be nothing but..." Milla nodded knowingly then let go of his arm as she stared down at the ground and drifted off in thought. "Where to now then?" Rune asked, a little disappointed by the break of contact.

Milla's deep contemplation was broken by his question, and she suddenly looked lost, "I..." she started then looked off and scanned the distant horizon again. "I don't know. I was told to continue east with you once we crossed."

Rune's eyebrows lowered as a fretful look overtook his features, "With me? Why are we traveling this way anyway?"

Milla's gaze dropped to her hands, "It's complicated."

"However complicated, I have a right to know what I'm being dragged in to," Rune replied sternly as he crossed his arms.

Milla shook her head and took a moment to think over her words, "I'm going to see family. But I don't know exactly where they are, that's all."

Rune's expression of uneasiness deepened, "Then how did you know to come this way in the first place?"

Milla shook her head again as she avoided any form of eye contact, "Like I said it's complicated. All I know is that there is something blocking this path that needs to be removed. I'm guessing it will be a little dangerous... maybe."

"You talked to a Seer, didn't you?" Rune accused fiercely.

Milla turned her head toward him, but still avoided eye contact, "And if I did?"

"Do you have any idea how dangerous they are? That's not just simple magik they use. Their powers are primal and evil!" Rune's voice grew louder, "For all you know they sent you on this path to die! They have a cruel sense of humor you know. They can see what will happen to you. Do you have any idea what danger we could be in right now? There's a reason they've been banished!"

Milla growled, her eyes finally meeting his, "Have you ever met a seer Rune?"

"Of course not!"

"Then how do you know that they're evil? From stories?"

"Yes. I've also traveled to the Seer Ruins to the south. Once you've been there you can see the evil powers that they held for yourself. You can even feel it in your bones when you walk around." Rune said with a shudder.

"Many say the same thing about magik users." Milla countered, canting her head, "My town has banned them. We kill any who try to enter."

"A magi is nothing like a seer."

"Oh?" Milla said as she crossed her arms sharply and turned to face him fully, "I've heard the stories though. You know, the stories that warn never to anger a magi. They tell of towns set ablaze with everyone inside burning alive because of one angry magi. And of course, the magi comes out unscathed. It won't be long until your own village bans all magi as well. The fear is spreading. It will be you who is condemned for being alive when that time comes and I who will be reviled for actually speaking to a magi."

"Not all magi are like that!" Rune barked furiously, "There are very few who would cause such harm. The stories just-"

"Slander you and make you all seem like monsters? Much like how seers have been slandered?" Rune let a slow breath out through his nose and turned away. She allowed a silent moment before she continued, "Not all seers are evil either Rune, but they are feared. If my town knew that the person I talked to was a seer, they would hunt her down and kill her as quickly as possible, and that great and powerful seer would have no way to defend herself. She has no powers other than sight." Her arms uncrossed, and she moved to Rune and put her hand on his arm, "She is a good and kind person Rune. In the end, magi will suffer from that fear if it is allowed to spread. You should not be so quick to spread something that might harm you in the future."

Rune uncrossed his arms as he looked down at the contact she made yet again. Gradually he turned. His eyes moved to hers, then he cocked an eyebrow and smiled, "Well then," he paused a moment taking in a deep breath, "Being that you've crushed any argument I could have; do you fully trust that this path won't be the death of us?"

Milla removed her hand from his arm and said slowly, "Well I didn't say that."

Rune's shoulders dropped as his expression became quite obviously miffed.

She puffed as she crossed her arms again and explained, "This was just the only path I could possibly survive. She said my true path is hidden and the only way it can be revealed is if I clear..."

"Clear what?" Rune asked as she fell silent.

She shrugged again and looked away, "I'm not sure. Darkness."

"That's vague, even for a seer," he said with growing concern.

She put a hand to her head in frustration as she explained further, "It's just that something is blocking her sight, I think."

He thought a moment, then asked, "Maybe she's just not powerful enough to see that far?"

Milla shook her head, "No, it's not that. She's told me about distant lands across the water. Her sight is very strong."

Rune turned to fully face her as he clarified, "So, what you're saying is, something is blocking the sight of a seer that's powerful enough to see distant lands?"

Milla hesitated, then nodded, "Some sort of powerful darkness."

"Please tell me this is a joke. Revenge for yesterday?" he exasperated, putting both hands to his forehead. She shook her head slowly with an apologetic look, and he turned to look down the long eastward road. After he took in a slow breath he spoke softly, his tone full of fear, "So, we just keep going and see what happens?" She bobbed her head in a slow nod, her expression matching his as she bit her lips together. "Well then," Rune took in another slow breath. "I suppose we should start. It would be best to get a few hours away from the bridge before the sun sets in case the trolls come back. This area isn't known to be safe," he said, then swallowed hard.

Milla nodded and hesitantly started forward, "Good plan. I think we might just make a good team after all."

Rune blushed and instantly forgot his fears as he quickly took his place beside her.

***

Several hours had passed. The sky was beginning to turn a bright tangerine orange as the sun progressively sunk into the horizon. The terrain was slowly becoming more varied with small hills, thicker grass and a gradually increasing amount of small trees and plants. The walk was peaceful. Besides the random sounds of critters and occasional bird flying above, the only noise that could be heard was the gentle breeze gliding over the land.

In the distance, to the north-east, they could see large black plumes of smoke rising up, though they couldn't see the source. Directly to the east, a large tree filled hill could be seen, that appeared to be in their path.

The sun eventually slipped behind the horizon as they continued down the wide road, turning the world hues of blue and gray. They could now just faintly see that the massive plumes of black smoke were rising from a city in the distance.

"That's not good," Rune said in a hushed tone, "That's Krossbraut. It's the closest trading city to Skera Braka. I wonder what happened?"

Milla's expression was grave, "I can only think of two reasons to see that much smoke coming from a city. War or magik."

"Or maybe someone very clumsy with a torch," Rune added, then offered a discouraged expression, "None of these reasons bodes well for us though. We should go look to see if we can help."

Milla shook her head quickly and examined the road ahead, "I don't think that's a good idea. Let's keep moving east, until that fork in the road, and take the south-east fork. Maybe we can avoid whatever it is that's happening. We can make camp when we find a suitably safe clearing around that hill." With a silent agreement, they moved forward together.

It wasn't long before the road split around the large, steep hill. They turned to the south and began searching in the blue-black surroundings for a place to rest for the night. Seeing a deep depression within the side of the hill, they moved quickly toward it, both very tired and ready for a good night's sleep. The road turned abruptly after the protruding segment of the hill, and as they took the turn, they both jumped at the sight of a large camp of soldiers. Several of the soldiers were kneeling around a large bonfire pit, urging small flames to grow.

"Hey!" a soldier close to the road nearby barked, "Who are you and what's your business here?"

Milla gulped, "We're just travelers passing through."

"That's right," Rune blurted nervously, "We have some important work to the east, so we'll just be on our way."

Milla's eyes widened and she nonchalantly kicked Rune's foot.

"Important work?" the soldier said, moving toward them, "What sort of important work?"

Rune looked at Milla, who seemed to be unable to speak, "I-I just meant we're in a hurry."

"Hurry to do what?" the soldier asked suspiciously, grasping his sword's hilt.

"Nothing," Milla chirped, "Nothing. We're just traveling. He's not right in the head you see, and he has a weak bladder. He's been whining about finding a tree for hours." Several of the soldiers nearby, who were listening in keenly, laughed at her excuse.

"I'm very right in the head thank you," Rune growled, now embarrassed, "And I don't have a weak bladder at all. I just didn't want to distract these soldiers from their job over much. It's called being polite."

"Rune. Quiet," Milla growled as she forced a smile, "It's nothing to be embarrassed about," the soldiers laughed again. "Really, though, I should get him to a tree soon or he'll wet himself." Rune glared at Milla and Milla returned the glare.

"Just stay there a moment," the soldier said after a laugh, then moved to the small group nearby. They spoke quietly together as they watched Milla and Rune.

Rune snorted angrily and whispered to Milla, "What was that for?"

Milla exasperated then explained quietly, "Think about it, Rune. These are soldiers and there is a city burning to the North. Does the word war mean anything to you?"

"What does that have to do with us? We're not on either side of it," he argued with frustration.

"And they would know that, how?" she challenged, her tone thick with mockery.

Rune's face dropped with realization, "Oh. I hadn't thought of that." He then looked to the soldiers who were still talking and raised his voice to them, "Look, we're not spies if that's what you're thinking." Milla smacked his arm several times and he backed away from her.

"What? Why are you hitting me? I'm putting their mind at rest, so we can make camp. I'm tired!"

Milla motioned as if she was ready to strangle Rune, "You are an idiot, Rune! I can't believe you!"

The soldiers promptly approached them with drawn swords and pointed spears. The first who had spoken to them then said, "I think you two should stay here the night."

Rune let out a relieved puff, "Oh, that's kind of you, there's no need for weapons though."

"He means as prisoners, you oaf," Milla barked and raised her arms in surrender.

"Oh." Rune said with distress, raising his arms as well.

They were quickly surrounded by sword and spear and directed into the camp.

CHAPTER 9

A horse drawn cart, carrying three lightly armoured men, edged its way along the southern coastal road at a steady speed. The morning sunlight enhanced the beautiful coastal scenery, as the waves crashed rhythmically against the beaches and rocky shores below.

Wulf, an overly thin man with unkempt brown hair and beard, slouched up front as he drove the cart. His face seemed stuck in an endless frown as he concentrated on his task, and generally stayed that way whether he had cause to concentrate on a task or not. Behind him, sat Milo and Alberic.

Milo, an excessively large man with cropped brown hair and brown eyes, was easily the most imposing figure in the cart. When standing he towered over the other two, and his shoulder span was easily that of two average men. Despite his size, his face showed a simple, kind, gentleness which made him very approachable. It also made him very popular with the children in his area as, despite his age, his mindset remained quite young and he enjoyed the playful mindsets of children far more than the generally serious nature of most his own age.

Alberic, a fit, blond haired and teal eyed man, rested as comfortably as he could as the cart bumped and swayed along the road. Both of his feet rested up on the bench in front of him as he reclined with both hands behind his head. His eyes were ever on the scenery, appreciating the beauty of it. A smile touched his lips as his eyes traced the horizon. The blue of the ocean water was only a little darker than the blue of the sky. Both sported splashes of white; the sky with its sparse clouds and the ocean with its endless crests of rolling waves. Not far from the thin beach, the land turned hues of rich greens and sprinkles of canary yellow, on bumpy and rolling plains. A light breeze drifted his way and he stretched and closed his eyes, enjoying the feeling of it on his warm skin. He then began to draw in a refreshing breath through his nose. Instantaneously, he sat up and coughed, "What is that foul stench?" he complained as he covered his nose with his arm, "It smells like death."

"It wasn't me," Milo said dimly.

Wulf simply scrunched his nose and shook his head as Milo then continued tearing away at his oversized, greasy leg of meat that he had acquired at their last stop. Alberic watched Milo eat for a few moments before finally speaking up, "How can you eat with that smell in the air?"

Milo stopped a moment and seemed to think over the question. He then shrugged his massive shoulders which shook the cart lightly, "I'm hungry."

Alberic shook his head slowly at Milo then blew a long breath from his nose. "I don't like this."

"It's probably just the ocean smell," Wulf grumbled, his voice hoarse and gritty, "These Southerners probably like foul smells."

"Yes Wulf, you don't like Southerners, therefore they must enjoy foul smells. That logic is quite sound," Alberic joked, his eyes full of amusement.

Wulf turned to look at Alberic, "I'm just saying they're not right in the head. Never have been. If it's wrong and foul, they like it. Why do you think they are always at war?" Alberic rubbed his eyes and sat up properly, unwilling to argue. Wulf took the silence as a victory, and he turned back around to concentrate again on driving.

***

Time passed, and they finally neared the large, black stone border gates of the southern capitol city, Regintun. The gate guards remained still, despite the cart's approach, lacking greeting or orders. "Ho there!" Wulf yelled out, beginning his well practiced speech, "Messenger from the Port city of Gottswai, Gem of the West, here to deliver a message from High Queen Erma to King Brandr. Will you let us pass?" A long silence lingered as they crept forward, and no word or movement came from either guard.

"May we pass man?" Alberic snapped as they slowed even further and moved now just between the two guards.

The guard, on the right, then gave a vague motion with his head, seeming to indicate that they could pass. Wulf took the message as such and flicked the reigns to speed up. They continued through the tall black gates. "Damn southerners," Wulf grumbled under his breath, "No sense of duty or tradition." Alberic looked to Milo, neither of the two adding to Wulf's thought, though both shared an uneasy glance.

The sun continued to shine in the distance, but a dark cloud lingered above the city. As they passed through the empty market square, Alberic's face grew even more uneasy as he apprehensively scanned the area, "The market is empty. Doesn't that strike you as odd?" he said to no one in particular. "I wonder if it has to do with this rancid smell." No answer was given, though all faces now shared the same unsettled expression. They continued slowly toward the island castle, through the residential area, but there was little activity in the district. What seemed to be a morning mist hovered in the air, though it was well past mid-day and the ground and buildings lacked the moisture to explain such a mist. The three looked around warily at the few inhabitants who occupied the streets. Their faces were wrought with what seemed to be paranoia and exhaustion. Outside chores were being done at an overly fast pace and constant shoulder glances. The three foreigners were looked at with suspicion and scrutiny by all who glanced their way as their cart moved down the main thoroughfare.

"I don't like this Wulf. I don't like it one bit," Alberic rumbled softly as they moved toward the tall black castle, "I feel like we're passing through a small village, not a major city. They should be used to strangers."

"You'd be a fool to like it, Alby. Let's just get the deed done and get out of this cursed place." Wulf grunted then hurried the cart along.

"If we get that far," Milo grumbled, as he began to suck the last few morsels off the large bone.

Alberic's fingers dug into his leg as his foreboding deepened, "We need to turn around and leave."

Wulf glanced back at Alberic and shook his head, "We can't do that, and you know it."

Alberic grunted before responding indignantly, "Your call, not mine."

They continued through the near silent streets. The sound of their cart echoed down the alleys and passages on either side, and the smell became fouler the further east they traveled, causing them to cough and cover their noses as they continued. They finally reached the bridge leading south to Regintun Castle. The monumental black towers of the castle loomed high above the impassable, sable rock walls. Many more guards than necessary stood watch at the bridge entrance. As the cart approached, Wulf grumbled to the passengers, "This stench will make me vomit my words if we don't get out of here soon." Alberic simply raised his eyebrows with an agreeing glance. Wulf swallowed hard to ease the vile feeling in his stomach and he called out to the group ahead, again announcing himself, "Messenger from the Port city of Gottswai, Gem of the West, here to deliver a message from High Queen Erma to King Brandr. Will you let us pass?"

"What's the message?" One of the guards yelled back scornfully, with little care for procedure.

"The message is for the King, and the King alone," Alberic barked back, his annoyance thick in his tone, "You would do well to know your place. Now, will you let us pass?"

"Obviously, I wasn't clear enough," the guard said as he started toward them threateningly, "Let me rephrase the question. Does she accept, or not?"

"Again, I tell you the message is fo-" Alberic was halted as the guards all pulled sword and spear and aimed them at the passengers of the cart. "Such an act is unheard of!" he thundered as he stood indignantly. "See us slain and you will have a new enemy in this war of yours."

"If her answer is no, we already have a new enemy," the guard said through grinding teeth.

"Have the people of the south lost all honour? This is what you have come to?" Alberic challenged with frustration.

"What is her answer!" the guard shouted far too loud, a tone of madness tearing through.

Wulf then piped in, putting his hand on the hilt of his blade, "High Queen Erma regretfully declines the South King's plea for aid in this war. She will not be a part of your squabbles, but she does wish you well and insists that both sides find a way to peace."

A silence fell over the group. Alberic and Wulf eyed the men, both seemed ready to be attacked. Milo seemed oblivious to the threat, as he continued gnawing on the edges of the bone, searching it for any last bit of flesh. The silence finally broke, as the brash guard ordered, "Take them all to the dungeon!"

Wulf and Alberic both drew their weapons and began to fight off the sudden onslaught. Milo, who was caught completely by surprise, fell backwards off the cart while tossing his stripped bone to the side, and three men quickly swarmed him. Wulf fell from the cart shortly after with a hoarse cry as a spear pierced his leg. He was quickly beat down and bound while the other attackers continued at Alberic. Seeing Wulf fall, Alberic turned and leaped from the back of the cart as Milo roared and raised from the ground, throwing the men, who flocked to bind him, off like wooden puppets. He then followed close behind Alberic, fumbling to pull his mace from his belt. Alberic broke into a run at first, but to slow down the pursuers, he turned, dropped his sword and swiftly and cried out, "Brenna!" as he pushed his hands out ahead of him, past Milo. The front row of men chasing them then screamed out in horror as flames lapped up around them. The rest stopped and hesitated as Alberic eyed them and waited for their next move.

"A magi!" Wulf cried out with anger as he watched through his captors, "You son of a dog! You traitor! You're a magi!" He was then kicked by his captors. Milo simply looked to Alberic with wide eyes, then turned his glance back to the burning men, now smoldering motionlessly on the ground.

"Get him alive!" the brash guard yelled out, "Spread out so he can't hit us in a group!"

Alberic cursed under his breath as he watched his enemies spread out in front of him, though the fear on their faces was unmistakable. Milo moved to Alberic's side and readied his stance silently, holding his mace up and ready.

"Surely, we can talk about this," Alberic forced a smile, "I admit I am not fond of burning men to a crisp, but I will if you force it on me. You have to admit; it helps with the smell."

"You can't take us all down," the guard growled, "You might get a few of us but we will get you in the end. Why not just give up?"

"You hear that?" Alberic laughed as he directed his comments at the men still fearfully spreading out in front of him, "It's alright if a few of you die a horrific death in flames. As long as a couple are left to grab me."

There was an obvious unease spreading with the attackers as they turned their eyes to each other. "Enough!" the head guard barked, "On the count of three, all of you charge!" Milo and Alberic readied themselves as the guard counted down. Just before reaching three, Alberic took in a breath, ready to cast his spell at the first man who moved. But none moved forward after the dramatic call of, "Three!" A silence fell, as both sides eyed each other. "I said three, damn you!" The lead guard yelled out again, but there was still no movement. The guard let out a roar then moved to Wulf and swiftly rested his sword above Wulf's neck. "Surrender or this one dies!"

Milo lurched forward but Alberic put his hand out to stop him. He then spoke up, "I have a counter offer. Let him go and we will leave without another one of you dying. I assure you my friend and I would have no issue taking down at least a majority of you before you could take us. Fire is not my only weapon."

"Sir," one of the guards spoke up to the main guard, but was stopped, as he barked.

"Quiet! This is your last chance. Surrender or he dies!" He declared, as he raised his blade to strike.

"No!" Milo roared as he charged ahead. Alberic's attempt to stop him was flung away, like a fly, as Milo raised his large mace over his head. Wulf took the charging distraction as an opportunity to kick out the leg of the main guard, then struggled to stand as the guard fell over the short stone wall. He was quickly subdued as Milo reached the front line of men, swinging wide as he approached. The few in his way, instead of attempting defense, attempted to run as the giant of a man charged; but they were caught in his heavy swing and sent flying.

"Damn it!" Alberic barked, then moved his arms out wide, and began to gather them in, aiming towards the men nearest him and crying out, "Samna!" The men stumbled and tripped as they were forced to gather together. He then pushed out his hand in a quick thrust toward them, roaring, "Blása vinda!" and, in a gust of wind, the gathered men flew off a short distance. Alberic, then ran towards Milo, and called out, "Milo, we have to get out of here now!" But Milo was lost in a blind rage, roaring and swinging at anything near him, as he made his way towards Wulf. Alberic let out a frustrated noise, which turned into a grunt, as a man charged into him while he was caught off guard. They both stumbled back and fell, then wrestled on the ground, but neither had a weapon handy as the guard had lost his in the force of wind. "You recovered fast," Alberic said with a strained voiced as he tried to push the man off him. The guard simply roared a growl in return as he tried to push his armoured forearm into Alberic's neck. With a bit of maneuvering, Alberic twisted until his leg was well positioned, then swiftly lifted his knee between the legs of his attacker, colliding hard with soft flesh. The man made a noise like a strangled owl and Alberic finished off the assault with a well-placed head-butt to the nose. Blood flowed freely from the broken nose as Alberic pushed the man off him, only to find several men above him aiming swords down at him. "Damn it," he whispered, and raised his arms in surrender, as his head dropped back to the ground.

Milo now stood above Wulf, roaring and flailing at any who approached, and the injured guard struggled to stand, as he held his gushing nose. He forcefully grabbed the sword from the guard next to him as his furious and quivering voice shouted in almost a shriek, "Stop!" Milo's head turned to the shriek for a quick moment, then for another moment, he focused again on defending Wulf. But his expression dropped as he realized what he had seen, and he looked back to Alberic. The shrieking guard spit blood on the ground, then yelled to Milo. "Yield or he dies!"

Milo's head turned to all those surrounding him and all the bodies laying lifeless in his path. The bleeding guard swiftly kicked Alberic three times in the side, and Milo cried out, "No! Stop! I yield!" Alberic coughed and grunted, as he curled to his side and held his ribs.

"I should kill you right now, "the guard said through a nasal voice. Then raised his voice and asked, "Where's the Captain?" The group of remaining guards looked around, not seeing him anywhere. Milo then cleared his throat and pointed over the bridge. A nearby guard moved to the side of the bridge and looked over. After making a disgusted face he looked back to the bloodied guard and shook his head. After another swift kick to Alberic, he ordered, "Just take them to the dungeons!" Milo visibly resisted another charge, then allowed himself to be chained, as he sadly watched Alberic forced to his feet, chained and gagged.

CHAPTER 10

The night was clear and calm. Occasional snaps and cracks could be heard over the roar of the large bonfire at the center of the camp. It muffled the hushed voices of those who sat around it, though Milla and Rune were not among them. The cage wagon that they were being kept in was too far away from the fire to feel any warmth from it.

"Dimwit. Oaf. Simpleton-" Milla muttered slowly as she sat with her back against the cage bars. Her eyes were closed, and it seemed to be that her long string of insults was lulling her to sleep.

Rune drooped forward and stared down at his hands as he listened to her unending barrage. She started not long after they had been locked in the cage, after she had first suggested all the ways of magik he could help them escape. None of them were in his power, and he had used illness and exhaustion as an excuse. It was clear that she was unimpressed by her traveling companion yet again. Trying now to drown out her voice, he attempted to listen to the few soldiers who remained awake, speaking softly around the fire. "...dragon," he only heard the one word in the conversation so far, but it perked his interest even more. He inched closer and turned his face toward them, seeking to catch even more.

"You shouldn't be speaking like that. It could get us killed."

"Look, we have all the cities to the south and east of here, and you've heard the stories of what's happening in Regintun. They're even speaking of crossing the great bridge once we have the North. I respect King Brandr's abilities as well as any man, but th-"

"Magidiot!" Milla said slightly louder and giggled at her own presumed cleverness.

Rune flinched slightly at her outburst then looked her over with annoyance. He then sighed and turned his attention back to the soldiers who were now separating and moving to their tents. One remained and crouched down to tend to the fire. Rune silently cursed at missing the last of the conversation and he worried about his village across the great bridge.

Hearing a familiar warbling whistle, he knew to be Feagan's signal, his body stiffened. He cautiously looked around to see if anyone else had heard. The soldier didn't seem to notice and Milla continued mumbling her insults, not even seeming to care that she had repeated some several times over. Feagan quickly zipped to the cage behind Rune, handed him a large key-latch, then zipped off again. Rune closed his hand tightly over the key-latch to conceal it and resisted a smile as he continued to watch the soldier.

The soldier then stood, pausing his poking and stirring of the fire, as his face turned sour. After a moment, he bent over to continue. Again, after another moment he slowly stood straight and put a hand on his stomach, which then rumbled loud enough for Rune to hear. Suddenly he lurched forward and groaned. Turning his gaze to the cage he growled, "Don't you move," then hurried off into the bushes, one hand on his stomach, the other covering his rear end.

Rune moved to the cage door as soon as the soldier was out of sight. After a quick double check to make sure no one was looking, he shoved the key-latch into the lock then pushed down to release the lock as quietly as he could.

"...pinhead," Milla yawned, "nitwit, bonehead."

"Are you done?" Rune whispered.

Milla's eyes opened and she looked up at him, her expression tired and resentful, "Moron, dunce-"

He tilted his head to the side and faked a smile as he spoke, "Well, you stay here and keep whining if you wish, but I'm going to escape." He then turned while slowly and quietly opening the door, and promptly moved out and toward the nearby forest.

Milla's eyes doubled in size and she floundered before promptly following. As they both moved swiftly toward the thick forest nearby to the east, Milla exuberantly whispered behind him, "How? How did you do that?" Rune remained silent. They broke through the tree line and weaved their way in deeper, stopping only for a moment to listen for pursuit, then continuing. "Rune!" Milla whispered loud as she chased behind him, "How did you open the door?"

Rune stopped and spun toward Milla, his face charged with apprehension and bitterness. He firmly grabbed her arm and whispered sternly, "Just keep running and don't speak until I ask you to!" He then released her, turned, and began to run again.

Milla's expression turned instantly from fury to shame and she followed apace behind.

Finally, they found a drop off in the forest floor with dense roots and bushes surrounding a partially hidden spot. They leaped into the center and both put their backs against the soft earth while panting as quietly as they could. Rune took this opportunity to discreetly toss the key into a nearby bush.

Milla waited a few moments and whispered through her heavy panting, "I'm sorry." Rune turned his head and looked into her large green eyes, trying desperately to stay angry as he also caught his breath. He finally let out a heavy breath and nodded his forgiveness as he closed his eyes and turned away.

"How did you do it?" she asked again in a whisper.

"Magik," Rune answered with a whispered chuckle, his eyes still closed.

Milla nodded slowly as she watched him with unsure eyes. Despite having further questions, she pointed out, "They took our packs and my weapons. We can't survive out here without them."

He opened his eyes and puffed out another breath. Slowly, he moved up into a crouch, looking in the direction they came from. After he lowered back down, he again stared into her eyes with uncertainty. "We'll have to worry about that later," he finally whispered.

Milla bobbed her head in agreement, though her expression was wrought with distress, "Which way should we go? Should we keep heading north-east?"

Rune took a quick look around. He didn't even know that they were running north-east, let alone which direction they should go from here. His eyes again turned to hers as he wracked his brain for an answer. She was looking to him for guidance and, in his own mind, he couldn't let her down again. He then remembered the conversation by the fire, so he shook his head, "They've taken all the cities to the south and east. There was a standard in the center of the camp. It had a blue background with a yellow sword on a black diamond in the center. I think that's the insignia of the south. But whoever they are I don't think they're interested in allowing peaceful travelers to wander through either way," he cleared his throat and looked sheepish, "Even if they don't say stupid things. We'll have to head north and hope their enemies are friendlier."

"How do you know all this?" Milla asked, but before Rune could answer she asked, "Magik?"

Rune's mouth opened and remained that way a moment, then shut it as he just nodded. Opening it again, about to speak, he instead jumped slightly as he heard Feagan's signal yet again. He examined Milla to see if she had heard it as well, but she seemed more curious about how he was acting than anything else. Rune tried to act normal as he turned and crouched again to look in the direction of the sound. There he saw their packs and weapons laying next to large bushes nearby. He sat back down and thought quickly then began a low chant, making up the words on the spot, "Dur sorda nicka suda!"

Milla watched him with awe and great interest but remained silent until he finished, "What are you doing?"

Rune turned again and looked around, purposely avoiding looking in the direction of the packs, "It's a summoning spell," he said nonchalantly, "I just remembered it. I was summoning our packs but I'm still sick, so they didn't show at my feet. They still might be nearby." Turning his glance toward the packs casually he did his best act of being pleasantly surprised, "Ah, there they are!" he declared then hopped over the jutting soil.

Milla followed immediately behind, "That's amazing!" she said a little too loudly, "I'm sorry I ever doubted you!"

"You doubted me?"

Milla smiled kindly at him, but her smile instantly dropped as they heard shouts in the direction they had come from. They hurriedly gathered up their things and continued their escape.

***

Time passed, and they were both beyond exhaustion. The deep darkness caused them to stumble and fall on several occasions and their bodies ached for rest. They had been forced to take many turns around impassable bush, tree, hill, and rock and with the addition of the lack of light, neither knew which way they were running any longer. "We have to stop," Milla panted then grabbed Rune's arm. "Do you know which way we're headed?" Rune gasped for air as he stopped with her, then dropped to the ground to rest. He finally gulped and looked around before he shook his head. She dropped down next to him, "Then we could be running in circles for all we know. Maybe right back into our captor's arms," she complained.

Rune reached into his pack and pulled out some sweet water. After taking a long gulp he looked around again, "We can't just keep running anyway. We need to stop. We need to eat and drink and sleep."

Milla nodded and also looked around the dark landscape. Faintly seeing a nearby clearing within a large group of trees surrounded in bush, she pointed, "We can lay out our bedrolls there. One of us will have to stay awake and watch though. We can take turns."

Rune bobbed his head as he rose up and headed towards the spot, "You can sleep first. I'll see if I can get our bearings with magik." Milla smiled warmly at him as she stood and followed. They laid out their beds and Milla fell asleep almost as soon as her head hit the soft blanket.

Rune settled himself against a tree and struggled to stay awake. His body demanded rest and the struggle to keep his heavy lids from closing finally became too much. His head fell back onto the rough bark and he dozed off.

A short time passed before Feagan showed up. He smiled affectionately at Rune and decided to allow them both to sleep for now. He waited as time passed and the moon drifted above, lighting the sky enough to illuminate the surroundings marginally. Feagan flew over to Rune and jabbed him in the cheek repeatedly until he woke. It took some time for Rune to realize where he was, but when he was aware enough, Feagan motioned him to follow. They both quietly moved away from Milla until they were a safe enough distance to talk.

"Weel 'at was excitin'," Feagan growled sarcastically, " Noo if we coods only fin' a way tae gie uir throats slit ur gie scorched alife, 'en thes trip will be quite complete."

Rune's face contorted into a look of apology and he stretched his sore muscles, "I'd like to avoid getting our throats slit or getting scorched alive if that's alright with you." He let out a hard sigh, "That was my fault. Thanks for getting us out."

"Eh," Feagan answered. He then pointed, "'at way is north. Ye an' arraw fur brains shoods heed it as suin as yoo're rested. Ah led yer pursuers aff in random directions an' they finally gae up, sae yoo're safe fur noo."

Rune smirked very slightly, "Arrow for brains," he repeated then added, "Thank you, at least if they gave up we can sleep safely."

"Aye," Feagan agreed, "Ah will check aheid an' see if Ah can figure it th' best roote an' guide ye frae thaur."

Rune nodded with a dispirited frown, "Alright. Having a guide might be a good idea at this point. We're in deep now friend."

Feagan returned a sage nod, "Ah will swatch tae see if thaur is a safe way back tae yer toon... jist in case."

Rune sighed and rubbed his eyes, "Good idea. Even home might be safer than this. Stay hidden and be safe."

Feagan zipped off without responding and Rune made his way back to Milla. After he arrived, he settled back into his spot and took in a long breath as he watched her sleep soundly. He half smiled to himself as he thought over their daring escape. She would surely be warming to him now, after all, he did save them. At least he hoped that's what she must be thinking. The musings gave him a warm feeling as he settled in. Feeling a little more rested now, he kept watch and allowed her to sleep longer.

CHAPTER 11

Adva stood by the large tower window, her posture straight and proper, hands gently clasped in front of her. It was a posture that came so natural to her now that it was done without thought. Her stiff gowns had helped greatly in keeping her thin form inflexible. As well, her heavy hair that was always kept up in an extravagant style, forced her to keep her neck in line. She could not bend it overmuch, only arch it lightly.

Her orange eyes cast their view across the vast city of Albusinia, spread out below her high tower room. The morning sun spread long shadows from the tall buildings and towers throughout the bustling city, though in a city made up almost entirely of white stone, even the shadowed areas were not very dark. The city was known to be the 'City of Light', after all.

Gazing upon the masses, she watched them make their way through the white cobble stone streets on countless errands and destinations. A frown lightly touched her lips as she heard a light tapping on the door. "Enter Otho," she ordered in a cool tone.

Otho opened the door and entered, his manner as grim as always. He made his way toward Adva purposefully then stood dutifully behind her as he spoke, "My Queen, I have news of the war." Adva remained silent and kept her gaze over the city. After a long silent pause, Otho shifted with uncomfortable annoyance and began again, "Adva, my queen, the death of your son weighs heavily on us all, but you must stay strong. The people need their High Queen now more than ever."

Adva's eyes narrowed lightly but her gaze remained on the citizens below, "Do you know what I see when I look over my people Otho?"

Otho sighed and rubbed his short beard, his frustration apparent. He moved to the queen's side and set his gaze out the window. "What do you see Adva?" He asked with a gentle tone.

"Small flames," she said softly, "Candle flames, each and every one of

55

them. Some will burn until the wax and wick are gone, some will be snuffed out with a breath."

Otho remained silent for a few moments, his mind clearly locked on the thought. He lifted his eyes to watch hers as he spoke, "Your flame burns bright my queen, as do the flames of the rest of your sons. You must know that-"

"I am no mere candle flame," Adva interrupted angrily and looked to him with fury.

"Of course, you aren't, Adva," Otho said soothingly, "You burn brighter than any other and you will continue to do so for countless years ahead, but you must know that your now eldest son was recently-"

"Indeed, I will," she interrupted, her voice thoughtful and calm. "Is there any news of our new students?"

Otho's frown deepened. His displeasure at the change of subject was greatly apparent, "The classes are near full, my queen. There will be no academy to rival it in all the lands."

The queen smiled with contentment as her eyes turned to the city below again and she fell to silence.

Otho allowed the quiet to linger before he spoke again, his voice gentle and soothing, "Adva," he started then put a hand on hers, "There are urgent matters that need your attention, and your sons-"

Adva forcefully interrupted as she looked to him again and raised her hand, smoothing it over the waves of his umber hair, "You worry too much my dear friend. We should not focus on the dead, but on life. I know you miss Lucretia, as do I, but she is still with us even if she has left us. It was her curse, was it not?"

Otho's eyes turned to anger as he responded, "She is not with us, only her madness demanded it be so. This has nothing to do with her, and your sons are not all dead, Adva."

For a time, Adva simply watched Otho's expression that turned to confusion as hers turned to pity. "That will be all," she finally said, then pivoted toward the window again as she returned to her practiced posture.

Frustration rose in his tone, "My queen, forgive me but the war-"

"That will be all, Otho," she repeated in a commanding tone, "You may concern the king with this frivolous war. I have more important matters to attend."

"Adva," he snapped, "this war is turning out to be far from frivolous. We are losing ground and your sons-"

"That will be all!" Adva barked with a fury.

Otho halted mid breath, his jaw clenching in anger. Then, after bowing his head, he said flatly, "As you wish my queen," and he turned, making his way to the door. When he reached the doorway, he stopped and spoke over his shoulder, "Be careful not to succumb as Lucretia did, my queen. I could not bear to lose you the same way," he then closed the door behind him.

CHAPTER 12

Rune groaned as he was gently nudged awake by Milla. As his eyes opened and the realization of where he was, and their situation sunk in, he bolted into sitting and rubbed his eyes.

"It's day-spring," Milla said quietly as she glanced around, "We should head out soon."

Rune nodded and said after a lengthy yawn, "Right. We should head north as soon as possible."

"Did you figure out which way that is?"

He bobbed his head in confirmation, then looked around to gather his bearings. The area seemed quite different in daylight. Seeing that the lush ground had very few clear spots, and the thick branches and ivy hung all around them, he was not surprised they had tripped so often in the night. After standing, he pointed north then began to roll up his bed, "I'm ready if you are."

Milla smiled as she stood and took in a long breath of the sweet forest air. She was already packed up and ready to move, "I was wrong about you."

Rune's tired eyes fleetingly turned to her, full of bewilderment. When he was finished securing his bedroll she started north. He hurried to walk with her and smiled timidly as he asked, "What did you mean? Wrong how?"

She shrugged uncomfortably as she answered, "Well, at first you just came across as some young, oversensitive magi. Maybe not all that bright as well. I was almost certain I had done something wrong, went to the wrong village or something, and got the wrong person. But you're smarter and cleverer than you look."

Rune stopped, looking perturbed, "Is that a compliment or an insult?"

Milla giggled quietly and grabbed his arm to drag him with her as she continued moving, "A compliment." She turned smiling eyes to him and continued, "It's just surprising. You're this scrawny, awkward boy and you still can pull off such amazing things. But I guess it makes sense. Magik requires strength of the mind, not the body."

He stopped again forcing her to stop with him. Annoyance radiated from him, "You're sure these are compliments?"

"Of course," Milla said, turning to face him, "In fact, I think you'll be incredibly powerful once you're a man."

Rune frowned deeply, "I am a man. I take care of myself and I have my own home."

Milla laughed and tilted her head to the side, her eyes beaming with amusement, "You're still a boy Rune, you haven't even grown hair on your face yet."

Rune frowned even further and protested, "I'm not much younger than you."

Milla shrugged as her expression continued, "If you were my age, then you would be old enough to be almost a man."

Rune sighed, and his shoulders dropped. Moving forward again, he continued, "Anyway... thank you I guess."

Milla followed next to him, still smiling, "Now if you weren't so naive we wouldn't have gotten into that situation in the first place, but-"

He interrupted her with a grumpy bark, "Is that a compliment too?"

Milla laughed then tried to mimic his voice as she quietly called out, "Hey soldiers! We're not spies for the enemy, by the way!"

Rune tried and failed to fight back a smirk, his brows still furrowed angrily, "I don't sound like that."

Milla giggled and pinched her lips together as they both continued on. They remained quiet for some time, making their way through the uneven forest terrain. As the sun moved its way to mid-morning, they approached a break in the trees revealing lush green plains. Not too far to the north, they saw a dirt road heading east, then curving north, following the tree line.

"A road! Thank good fortune," Rune said with relief.

"We should avoid it for now. We don't know who's on it. Let's stick to the trees and follow the road from a safe distance."

Rune sighed, as he wasn't happy with this, but showed his understanding with a nod. "Well then, why don't you find us a safe place to rest and eat and I'll quietly run up ahead to scout."

"No," Milla said quickly, "I'm lighter on my feet and I'm a better scout. You stay behind and find us a spot."

"I have magik," Rune argued, then bolted off.

Milla decided not to argue his point, but called out, "How will you know where I am once I've found a spot?"

"I'll find you," he called back and disappeared behind a bushel of trees.

Milla shrugged and began to look for a suitable spot.

When Rune figured he was far enough away from Milla to be out of ear shot and sight, he knelt down and opened his pack, allowing Feagan to fly out. "Ah suppose ye want me tae check aheid fur trooble? Ur hae ye finally wizened up an' decided tae ditch th' lassie an' heed haem?" Feagan said with false annoyance as he buzzed in front of Rune's face.

Rune smirked, "Yes, just see if you can find out if there's anyone on the road. Also, when you're done, we should discuss what you found out last night."

"Is 'at aw yer majesty?" Feagan said haughtily with a laugh.

"Actually," Rune continued with a grin, "If you could also fetch us some ripe berries, maybe a fresh pair of fine clothes and some dregs so we can purchase the best room in the inn of the closest town that would be great too." Feagan's face lost all humour as he stared at Rune. "I'm kidding!" Rune chuckled, "Hurry up, if I'm gone too long she'll suspect something." Feagan scoffed as he zipped once around Rune's head playfully, then hurried off. After watching Feagan fly from sight, Rune made himself comfortable against a tree and rested his eyes.

***

Time passed and Feagan finally returned to a sleeping Rune. He shook his head and let out a small laugh, then moved to wake him, poking him continuously in the cheek, yet again. Rune woke with a start, then calmed when he saw Feagan, "What did you find?" he asked then yawned.

"A spoiled yoong magi sleepin' in th' forest," Feagan said with an impish grin.

"Funny," Rune said dryly returning the grin.

"Thaur seems tae be nae a body travelin' th' road fur noo," Feagan reported.

"Good," Rune said with a thoughtful nod, "If no one is on the road we don't have to keep traveling through this rough forest. So, what did you find out last night?"

Feagan landed himself on a nearby branch and rested casually as he explained, "Thaur is a wee city oan th' way, controlled by th' north. Ye will probably reach it by mid-day on the 'morrow. Fur noo there's nae safe roote haem"

Rune nodded thoughtfully again, "So even if I wanted to go home now I couldn't." He sighed, "Alright, to the Northern town it is then. Thank you Feagan."

"Eh," Feagan replied then moved back to Rune's pack, "Noo rin back tae yer goddess afair she gits leery… Ye spoiled young magi."

Rune let out an embarrassed laugh, "But I need help finding her," he said as he watched Feagan make himself comfortable.

"Ah marked th' trees tae gie ye a path tae 'er. She seems tae hae tried tae hide herself in amongst bush an' cabre. whether she's hidin' frae possible danger ur testin' yer magik remains tae be seen, but ye ken whit mah guess is," he said, his tone thick with accusation as he closed the flap.

"Well, she could be both hiding from danger and testing my magik," Rune grinned, "But since you marked the path, we can do more than pass her test." He could hear Feagan chuckled at that then started on his way.

He easily followed the tree markings, namely Feagan's own style of breaking and twisting branches. Though normally they might be invisible to anyone who wasn't looking for them, with all the extra thin branches and ivy at Feagan's disposal here, they were ridiculously elaborate. Feagan and Rune had a long history of hiding in forests from the town bullies. It came second nature to them now.

As he neared, the smell of a campfire filled his nose. From a distance, he saw what was obvious to him to be Milla's hiding spot. He could vaguely see that there was a clearing beyond densely packed trees and bush. He may not have chosen it himself, as it might be too obvious. He approached discreetly and moved behind a large tree to examine it, checking if he could see her. After a careful scan, he spotted her face, looking out from within, but not looking toward him. Feeling confident that she had not seen his approach, he circled around to the far side and crept in, now making his way into the small, well hidden clearing. He moved in as silently as he could, carefully watching Milla from behind as she continued her watchful lookout. Grinning wide, he tiptoed onto the soft mossy grass, then carefully placed his bag down as he sat next to the small fire she had prepared. He made himself look as comfortable as possible before finally speaking, "I don't think anyone's coming."

Milla jumped and spun around, her eyes wide as she looked at Rune who was grinning and lounging comfortably, "How did you- Where-" she stopped and shook her head, trying not to seem as surprised as she was, "I mean, did you find anything out?"

He nodded nonchalantly, "The North controls the area. We should reach a northern town by tomorrow mid-day. For now, there's no one on the road so it will be safe to travel."

"How-" Milla started then shook her head again, "I caught us some fresh meat. It'll be better than rations I think."

Rune smiled wide, exceedingly pleased with himself, though he played it off as being pleased by Milla's catch and he nodded, "Excellent."

Milla tried her best to conceal her impressed smile but failed as she moved to the fire to prepare their food, "You must be beginning to feel better," she stated simply as she reached for the small, already skinned and gutted carcass.

"Feel better?" he asked as he watched her skewer the meat with a prepared twig.

"You said you were sick. That's why you were having difficulty with your spells," she said then looked up at him.

"Oh," he said, suddenly remembering, "Right."

"You don't seem to be having as much trouble now," she continued, looking back to her task.

"Yes, feeling a little better," he said then cleared his throat, "It must be passing. It's still there a little though."

Milla nodded, clearly overjoyed as she placed the meat over the fire.

CHAPTER 13

The air in the long, dark cave tunnel wreaked of a smell worse than rotting flesh and sulfur. All eyes burned and watered as they eased their way deeper inside, each footstep echoing into the depths of the profound blackness. Alberic had raised his bound hands to cover his nose, though it didn't help at all. The pace was far too slow for the guard, who clearly only wanted to do as he was commanded and leave as quickly as possible. "Get in there!" he barked as he shoved Milo with the hilt of his sword from behind, who in turn bumped Alberic ahead.

"Shouldn't I be gagged so I can't cast a spell?" Alberic called back as he moved, "Some mages can cast without hand gestures you know."

"Then you would have by now," the guard grumbled.

Alberic grumbled quietly in return then turned to look at the guard's torch lit face with a sour expression, "How does this smell not affect you? What foul creature has died in here?"

"Just keep moving," the guard said with another shove.

As the three continued, the humidity increased, as did the smell. The moist rocky surroundings glistened as they reflected the torchlight that did little to make the path ahead much more visible. The tunnel then widened and opened ahead to the left. The guard shoved Milo one last time, then stopped, "In there. Turn around and I skewer you both."

Milo stepped forward to stand at Alberic's side and they looked at each other, hesitating to follow the command. Alberic swallowed and moved forward first, cautiously peeking around the corner. He passed a widened gaze around the massive dark cavern. Very little could be seen in the darkness, save the rocky edges, illuminated by what little light reflected from the single large opening in the cave ceiling which exposed the dark star speckled sky. Milo, being much taller, then peeked his head above Alberic's and glanced around as well. Alberic looked up at him with a cautious expression and they both inched inside, unsure of what to expect.

A deep rumbling voice then emanated throughout the cavern, "I do believe I smell a magi."

Alberic and Milo both jolted then froze at the sound, faces revealing unsure terror. Alberic swallowed hard then called out as he looked around for the source of the resounding voice, "I am. I'm surprised you can smell anything through this stink. Who are you and what do you want with us? And more importantly, is this smell you? If so I suggest a good long bath at the very least."

A low rumble of a laugh was heard throughout the cavern. Behind them, the sound of a torch crashing to the ground and feet running echoed from the tunnel. Milo and Alberic trembled as a deepening sense of fear overtook them both. Alberic then whispered, "I think the guard ran. I don't think that's a good sign," Milo nodded in response and attempted to remove the bindings from his hands.

The thundering voice then began again, "I am your nightmare boy. I am the horror in the night that haunts your pathetic little minds. I am Eilifatli, the doom of this precious realm of yours, and the end of you magi. I will consume your very being."

"This actually isn't my realm," Alberic corrected, the tremble in his voice betraying his false confidence, "We're actually just here for a visit, but if it's alright with you we've had enough of the South for a while," he slowly moved backward toward the tunnel, motioning Milo to follow with his head. "Lovely scenery of course, but the company leaves much to be desired."

Milo shook his head in return and whispered, "They're guarding the exit, remember?"

Alberic cursed under his breath, then whispered in reply, "Let's at least get to the torch and get a wall between us and him." He then spoke up again to the loud disembodied voice, "But I'm from the West and the name is Alberic, if introductions are to be made. Oh, and this is my friend Milo. We were just-"

"Silence!" the surroundings shook as the voice roared and the echo of dirt and rocks falling could be heard throughout the cavern. "I care not for your short-lived story."

"Glad to hear it," Alberic said quickly, backing toward the exit again, "I'll just leave and make my story a longer lived one worth telling then, if you don't mind."

"What do you want from us?" Milo then asked through a quivering voice.

Eilifatli's voice rumbled in a chuckle and rocks began to tumble again. Then, an unsettling silence fell that seemed to consume all other noises. No steps, no breath and no tumbling debris could be heard. This penetrating silence was then broken by the voice, now in a slithering whisper, "You will find out soon enough. Come to me. Your doom lay behind you if you choose to run." Both men looked behind them into the tunnel, now consumed with fear. The torchlight was instantly snuffed out and immediately after, shadows seemed to form then disappear. Blinking red eyes peaked out and disturbing whispers of voices chattered incessantly.

Alberic then sensed something that he had sensed not long before his eastward journey. It was a presence that had visited him in a dream. Words then formed in his head, 'Sooth your mind. Remember your will', and his fear faltered a moment as he closed his eyes and tried to focus. Milo's eyes, on the other hand, widened in horror as he watched the red eyed shadows move closer. He turned to rush away and toward the voice but was stopped by Alberic's bound and shaking hands. "No," he said to Milo, his voice strained, "No, this isn't right. I feel something..." A seething whisper then emitted from the center of the cavern, though the origin was still unseen. A mist crept toward them, the stench nearly unbearable. Both covered their noses with their arms as the mist rose, and Alberic pulled on Milo after he opened his eyes, "Come on, we have to run past them," he urged and lurched toward the tunnel. A shadow whipped by them halting any movement as their eyes both widened with terror. A horrific scream then came from behind them. They whipped around to see the source but saw nothing. Another shadow rushed behind them as a strange moaning from what seemed to be many voices was heard in the tunnel. They both turned again, then slowly backed away from the tunnel as the moaning creature seemed to be dragging itself toward them.

The disembodied voice rumbled again, "Come to me magi, you and your friend both. The shadows will not come this far, but they will tear your insides out should you linger there long."

Milo again made attempt to run but Alberic strained to hold him steady, his eyes wide as he searched the darkness of the tunnel. "You're going to get us killed!" Milo howled and yet again attempted to run toward the rumbling voice, but Alberic braced himself and forced Milo to stay.

Alberic then felt the presence even stronger, distracting him from his fear again. The words formed, 'Fear consumes only when you allow it. Bring light to the darkness and banish your fear.' Alberic yanked at Milo to jar him back as he attempted to pull away, "Stand your ground damn you! He wants us running to him! Why?"

Milo shook his head as he tried to conjure an answer, then looked from tunnel to the unknown depths of the cavern. "What do we do?" he asked, the panic strong in his voice.

Alberic shook his head, his body trembling with dread as he looked deep into the tunnel, now confident he saw some large creature of shadow dragging itself toward them. His brow dripped with a cold sweat and he cried out words repeating incessantly in his mind, "Regin ala lysa!" then pointed to where the creature was. The area lit up for only a moment. His concentration was broken by the high-pitched scream Milo let out upon seeing the creature made up of flesh and lacerated body parts. Grey arms and hands dragged the mass closer to them. Milo dropped to his knees and covered his eyes as he cried out again.

"Do not utter words you cannot possibly fathom!" Eilifatli bellowed fiercely, "The creature will consume you if you do not come to me. You will become one with it after it tears your limbs from you and devours your insides. Come to me and you will be saved from such a horrific fate," his rumbling voice said with far too much humor.

Alberic was frozen in spot for a moment, shaking and clinging far too tightly to Milo's tunic. "N-no," he stuttered with a swallow, "This – I know what this is." More words formed in his mind, 'Control your fear and your will. Only your fear can consume you. Shadows are illusions.'

"Come to me!" the thundering voice boomed with a great rage that rumbled the cavern.

Alberic sputtered a moment as his body convulsed with fear and

Milo screamed out again while covering his head. After taking a hard swallow, Alberic wiped away the sweat from his forehead. He stuttered, "M-m-megin!" and became visibly daunted seeing that there was no affect. The creature dragged itself closer, nearly at arm's reach now, and it let out the horrific cry of many death screams. Alberic cried out, "Regin ala megin!" Then dropped down to his knees, eyes wide with horror. A pulse emitted from his body and the creature disappeared, as did all shadows and fog. The natural cavern sounds then returned and his fear waned. He grabbed Milo and yanked him up. "Run! Now!" he cried out and Milo clambered to his feet and followed behind Alberic as he ran down the tunnel. The disembodied voice from inside the cavern let out a rippling shriek that vibrated through the ground, but they continued to run through the darkness, leading themselves along the walls with their hands, and stumbling over ridge and rock often. After finally reaching the entrance, they skid to a stop to look around. They saw no guards waiting or blocking their path, so they made a break for freedom.

CHAPTER 14

The sun beamed down from overhead while Rune and Milla trudged upon the wide, wagon grooved dirt road. The area seemed to grow greener as they moved along the hilly terrain. The trees grew denser and the hills and gullies of the road became a little steeper, though not so steep as to become a hindrance for the frequent cart travel. Lush, green, hair-like grass flowed down the center and along the sides of the road, though the dark dirt grooves were clear of any greenery.

The two travelers appeared weary from the long trip as they grasped the straps of their packs and pulled them forward to lighten the weight on their shoulders. The meal of fresh meat had given them both the energy to continue with few breaks at first, but the long journey and frequently inclining ground was now getting to both of them. They continued though, albeit sluggishly, without word or complaint until…

"There it is," Rune said with relief. He pointed ahead to the massive city wall of prepared logs, lined up and bound by metal fittings and capped with pointed metal tips that could now be seen above the ridge and around the tree line. It was instantly clear that the city had been there for quite some time, as the walls were quite overgrown by lush green plants that had made happy homes in the grooves and crevasses of those logs. The roofs of some taller buildings could be seen peaking over top. Eventually, as they continued, the massive wooden gate could be seen, opened wide and revealing a broad main thoroughfare.

Milla sighed with relief and smiled, "You were right."

Rune smiled triumphantly and spoke timidly, "Yeah well, magik is handy."

"Yes, you are," she flattered with a grin and gave him a light nudge with her elbow. "Come on," she coaxed then began to trot ahead, " Let's treat ourselves to a real bed for the night before we figure out where to go from here."

Rune felt far too tired to run ahead at this point but for fear of looking weak in front of Milla, just as she was warming up to him, he forced himself into a jog. Now nearing the gate, Milla slowed and then stopped, placing her pack down next to her. As Rune approached from behind she suggested, "We should plan what we're going to say this time," and she reached to the side to unlatch her skin of sweetwater.

Rune grinned at the opportunity to show off, and ran ahead of her, "Tired already? Come on, they're the enemies of the south. They'll happily give us refuge after we tell them what they did to us."

Milla contorted her face in confusion then widened her eyes as she hastily replaced her sweetwater. She lifted her pack, trying her best to replace it on her back as she chased after him. "Rune stop!" she cried out, but he didn't listen.

As he approached the gate, the guards both raised their hands signaling him to stop. He slowed as he called out to them, "It's okay, we just came from the south and-"

"Don't move!" One interrupted as they both unsheathed their swords and approached him.

"You don't understand, I-" Rune tried to continue as they charged at him.

Milla reached him and waved both hands in front of her to try to halt the guards, "No we're not enemies!" she cried out.

"Drop your bags and raise your hands!" the guard ordered and they both quickly complied.

The guards moved cautiously around, then behind them. The first guard poked Rune in the back with his sword and ordered, "Move!" while the other removed Milla's bow and arrows, then gathered their packs. Rune and Milla both, with hands raised began to move toward the city.

"What did you say to them?" Milla whispered angrily at Rune.

"Quiet!" The guard barked and the other followed close behind. Several more guards appeared at the entrance of the city gate, watching attentively as the two prisoners approached. They were led directly down the middle of the main road surrounded by tall stone and wood buildings that had been erected barely a shoulder's width from each other. Most of the buildings were as overgrown with greenery as the city walls, though some were kept clear of the growth. It seemed a thousand eyes were on Milla and Rune as all those on the wide street stopped to watch, and more appeared constantly from inside buildings and alleyways. Eventually, they reached a stone building that housed many guards and a few other important looking people in fine clothing. Some behind tall wooden counters, some in small rooms, and others lingering about in the main entrance area. Once inside, they were led down a long and narrow stone stairwell, that led to a cramped area with several small cells. They were then shoved inside the first small cell ahead of them and locked in.

"We're not your enemies!" Rune yelled out as he shook the barred door. But the guards left them without a word and headed back up the stairs.

Milla let out a long, heavy sigh then sat down on the rock floor and leaned her back on the stone wall.

Rune turned his head and watched her cautiously, then slowly moved to the opposite wall and sat against the bars. He waited a few moments as they eyed each other before he finally spoke, "What, no constant barrage of insults this time?"

Milla clenched her jaw and forced an angry smile as she spoke through her teeth, "I trust you'll get us out of this one just like the last."

Rune swallowed hard and looked to the stairs as he secretly hoped Feagan would figure something out again. He then surveyed the small stone room and grumbled to himself, "Not even a window." He made himself as comfortable as possible as he said, "I'll need time to think. We needed a little bit of rest anyway."

"I would have preferred an inn and a drink," Milla growled and crossed her arms as she looked away.

Rune nodded and they both patiently waited.

CHAPTER 15

The sun gradually made its way toward the horizon as Alberic and Milo sat with their backs against the soft, dark dirt of the bush lined ridge. They were now a good distance away from the putrid cavern. Their eyes remained wide as they stared silently ahead, both replaying the horrific events in their heads. They continued to hide from any possible pursuit, though they had seen no sign of any yet. After some time, Milo finally spoke up, saying dryly, "So, we know where the smell is coming from now. That's something right?"

Alberic flopped his head as he turned to look at Milo, "Do we? I have never seen nor heard of such horrors. Whatever magik is behind this is alien to me."

Milo nodded slowly, "If it's alright with you Alby, I'd rather not find out. We should get out of here and quick."

Alberic bobbed his head in agreement then eyed the sky for some time before speaking, "Our best bet is to head east, continuing away from the cave and then make our way north. I think the northerners would want to hear what we saw in this place."

"East?" Milo protested, "We need to go west first."

"I am aware that duty dictates that we warn our own people Milo, but the information we have could be crucial for the North," Alberic argued, "Besides, they have far more knowledge of strange magiks than any other realm." Milo opened his mouth to speak but Alberic interrupted, "I know what you're going to say. We shouldn't get involved, but our lands are protected by the great river and all those east of it will need to finish with each other before they can turn their sites on us. Even then, crossing the river puts them at a large disadvantage. You also must take our ships into consideration and our coastal defenses if they took another route."

Milo shook his head, "It's just that-"

"I know, I know," Alberic interrupted again, "Our own people are still at risk. Who knows what will happen if whatever is in that cave is set loose, and that has me worried as well. It held a great and terrifying power, and if the North knows nothing of it, then they will be in for a horrid surprise and the war could be over before the West can be warned. But, I believe it is in our best interest to at least try to warn the North. Despite their other oddities, I feel they may be the only ones equipped to deal with such a sinister power. We have no means to defend ourselves from it in the west that I am aware of."

Milo began to speak again, "You're right of course. But there is-"

Alberic interrupted, yet again, "I know there is a great deal of danger Milo and I know you want to go home, have a nice meal, sleep in a warm bed. So do I. But there are greater things at stake here."

Milo looked to the sky letting out a long breath, then finally was able to speak, "There is a large sheer cliff to the east. We need to head west first to go around it."

"Ah," Alberic stated, with a deadpan expression.

"That was a good speech though," Milo said with a cheeky grin.

"West it is," Alberic announced dramatically, "Then we head north."

"After we rescue Wulf." Milo added.

"After we-" Alberic continued as if part of his announcement, then dropped his shoulders and sighed, "That may not be possible. We don't know where he is, or how many watch him, or if he's even still alive," he then added, "It's also still likely that we are being hunted."

"If we don't, he's probably bound for that cave." Milo pointed out.

Alberic cursed under his breath, "We'll try, at the very least. I don't know how happy he'll be to see me though..."

"What do you mean? Wulf is very fond of you," Milo asked with a confused expression.

Alberic gave Milo a dry look, then pointed his hand at a small bush ahead of them as his eyes turned to focus on it, "Brenna," he whispered, and a small flame ignited on the lower branches.

"Oh that," Milo said, staring at the small flame with a dumb expression, seeming to have forgotten, "He'll probably want to kill you I suppose."

Alberic nodded slowly. He then sighed and made a sweeping motion toward the bush while casually saying, "Blása vinda," and the flame was snuffed out.

"I don't want him to kill you." Milo added dimly as he watched.

Alberic shrugged and nodded with agreement.

Milo remained silent a good while, then offered, "Maybe after we rescue him, we send him west to warn the queen and we continue north as planned. He won't really be able to argue, and I won't let him hurt you."

Alberic nodded again and smiled amicably at Milo, "A fine plan, if possible. He will tell the queen of me though. I will not be welcome back in court once she finds out."

Milo frowned at this and they were both silent again for a while. He then shrugged his massive shoulders, "I didn't really like it there anyway. It was boring guarding a room full of people talking about stupid things that didn't matter and prancing around in fine clothes. Maybe we find another place? We can find work, you and I."

Alberic smiled, then laughed lightly, "You do realize that you can go back my friend. You are not a magi."

Milo frowned, "You're my only real friend there. I go where you go."

"What about your sister? She would miss you."

"Bah, she won't even notice I'm gone. Maybe you can write to her for me later, to let her know I'm with you and we are fine," Milo said with a wave of his large hand.

"Unless we're not," Alberic added with an amused grin.

Milo grinned back, "We will be."

Alberic's smile warmed, "I would be thankful for the company then. But I will miss the fine clothes."

Milo let out a breathy laugh, "Even the one with the feathers?"

Alberic frowned as he stood, "You promised we'd never speak of that again." He ignored Milo's dopey grin and continued, "Come, let us see if we can't disguise ourselves and find Wulf before dayspring."

Milo stood as well, but his expression quickly turned solemn as he spoke in a serious, but quiet tone, "Alby..." Alberic turned a questioning look and Milo continued, "I'm sorry I got us caught. I shouldn't have charged in like that. It was my fault that we were captured and sent to that cave. You should have just left me behind. They-"

"Milo," Alberic then interrupted and his expression softened, "You know I would never leave you behind."

"They could have killed us both right there," Milo protested, "Or killed you at least for being magi. I couldn't have lived with that being my fault."

"But they didn't, and here we are, free," Alberic stated simply, "Let's go get Wulf."

A grin took over Milo's face and he nodded. With that, they both headed back toward Regintun.

CHAPTER 16

A commotion from up the stairs brought both Rune and Milla to their feet. They rushed to the front of their cell and tried to see who or what it was. Milla then looked to Rune expectantly, and Rune watched the stairs, hoping it was a plan of Feagan's. The sound of muffled voices and heavy footfalls making their way down the stairwell caused them both to let out a disappointed sigh. Guard boots were the first thing to come into view. As the guard's full frame appeared, he looked behind him while another man, that walked a few steps behind, spoke, "I said, call me Captain. That is my rank while I'm on tour and I will be addressed as such."

"Yes, C-Captain Ethan," the guard said nervously, "The two we captured are just down here."

Milla gulped and backed away from the bars, as the Captain came into sight. He was tall and bore heavy black armour, though he lacked a helmet and gloves. A blue cape flowed from his shoulders to just below his calves and his left arm was held up in an elaborate sling made of blue silk. His face seemed more youthful than one would expect for someone who demanded so much respect. Milla swallowed again and her mouth and eyes both opened a little more, with a clearly smitten expression. His shiny black hair was a little mussed from having been under his helmet, but it accentuated his strong, chiseled features well. As his striking blue eyes turned to her, she froze in spot.

Ethan stopped mid step as his eyes locked on hers. After blinking several times and adjusting the sling on his arm, he turned his gaze to Rune and continued down the last two steps, moving to the front of their cell door. He cleared his throat as he placed his free hand on his hip and bowed his head, looking at the floor as he spoke, "This is them?"

The guard nodded in confirmation, then pointed to Rune, "This one said they are from the South."

"I misspoke," Rune clarified promptly, "That's just the direction we came from."

"Quiet you!" the guard barked.

The Captain looked back at Rune, then to the guard, as he held out his right hand, "Latch," he demanded, and the guard quickly put the key latch into his hand. "Leave us," he then ordered, and the guard bowed his head and turned to hurry up the stairs. Captain Ethan took in a long breath and turned his eyes to Rune. He finally spoke, "What's your name boy?"

"Rune," he said and swallowed, "We're not from the south. We're both from the west. We were just traveling east, and we were captured by the south. We escaped and came north."

Ethan listened carefully then spoke, "That's a lot of directions. Why head north? Why not head back west? It's obviously not safe for travelers to be roaming the roads right now."

Milla answered, "I have important business in the east. We hoped it would be safer to head north first, to make sure we didn't run into the south soldiers again."

Ethan looked toward her, but not at her before looking back at Rune, "Surely you would have known you'd run into North soldiers at some point. We're in the middle of a war. All travelers would be viewed with suspicion. What business is it that you two have in the east that's important enough to risk your lives?"

Rune motioned to Milla, "It's not my business. She just hired me to help."

"Hired you?" Ethan said, then smirked, "To do what? Not as a guard, surely."

"I- um..." Rune stuttered.

"As a guide," Milla answered, "I'm from far west and I know nothing of anything east of my lands."

Ethan finally looked to her, his eyes locking on hers again. Her fair cheeks turned a shade of pink and she looked down, "I'm sorry if we caused any sort of commotion over nothing."

Ethan watched her a moment then spoke, "It seems to me this war is causing the guards of Silvius to overreact a little. Though, who can blame them when the war draws so near to their borders. I will speak to them in any case." He then looked back to Rune, "You say the south captured you?"

Rune looked at Milla, wondering if she'd tell about his embarrassing slip up but she remained silent. He then explained, "I'll start from the beginning. Milla here approached me in my village to hire me. On our way here, we noticed the bridge trolls weren't around and thought it was strange. As we continued we noticed a city in flames and became even more worried, so we tried to avoid whatever it was, but ran right into the south soldiers. I said the wrong thing and they thought we were spies for the enemy... sort of like this time, so they imprisoned us. We escaped and decided to head north to what we hoped was safer territory, so we could continue our way east."

"Krossbraut," Ethan quietly confirmed, with a nod, as his features turned somber. It quickly changed to curiosity as he asked, "So, how did you escape?" Rune looked at Milla, but she was still not looking up or speaking. He swallowed as he thought of something to say. "Did you pick the lock? Kill your captors? Use magik?" Ethan asked, as he began to grin.

Rune looked to Ethan with a panicked expression and Milla finally raised her eyes, her expression similar. The two then looked at each other, neither really knowing what the North thought of magi.

Ethan sighed, still grinning, "Magik then? Well, that is quite unfortunate. You understand that I now have no choice but to burn you alive on a pyre?"

Rune's eyes widened even further, "No, I swear I can't even cast a simple spell."

"I'm sorry, it's too late for that now. It's better to be safe you see," Ethan sighed again, forcing back a smile. He looked up in thought, I suppose we can use the fire for cooking a large feast afterwards. I'd hate to waste all that wood."

Milla spoke up fearfully, "No, he's not, really. He's just a guide and he... he stole the cage latch from the soldier's pocket when he wasn't looking. I swear."

Ethan began to laugh and shook his head, "I was only teasing. I had heard that you westerners have some odd views on magik. We don't fear it here as you do in your land. In fact, we have the greatest schools dedicated to the advancement and safe practice of magik. I was simply curious how you escaped, but no matter."

Both Rune and Milla sighed heavily, and Rune quickly asked, "Schools of magik?"

Ethan nodded but quickly changed the subject, "Did you happen to overhear anything from the soldiers that may help us?"

Rune stopped and thought a moment then shrugged, "They said they had all the villages from the south and east of there, Krossbraut that is, and that they planned on going north. They were pretty confident that you'd be defeated and even spoke of crossing the great river once they had."

Ethan looked indignant at that and shook his head, "That seems a little overconfident. I find it doubtful that they have already occupied that much of the east on one hand. And on the other hand, our armies are far greater in number and in arms. That is not even taking into consideration that we have far more magiks on our side." He shook his head, "They must have a potential advantage we are unaware of. Did they say anything else?"

Rune shook his head, but paused before he added, "Well, one of them mentioned a dragon."

Ethan's eyes widened a little and his face became serious, "Dragons haven't been seen in this land for a very, very long time. The wards would have stopped one from entering... wouldn't they?" He asked no one in particular.

Rune looked at him curiously, then shrugged, "I don't know much about the wards, save from hearing of them in stories. But the stories do say they were designed to stop dragons from entering our continent. If the wards even exist anymore that is."

Ethan nodded, moved the latch to the cage then pressed it inside and pushed down. As the latch bent at the hinge and the heavy spring released the lock he answered, "They do. I will send word of what you have told me and let the rest of the captains deal with it. There are far more with greater experience than I in such matters. Until then-" he opened the door wide, "Please accept my apology for the misunderstanding. I will be sure the local inn gives you the best rooms available and you will be well fed and stocked for your continued journey to the east."

"Thank you!" Rune said excitedly then patted Ethan on the arm in a friendly manner as he passed. Ethan winced and backed away as his injured arm was struck. Rune's eyes opened wide as he realized what he did, "Oh! I'm sorry."

"Think nothing of it," Ethan said through a grunt then motioned toward the stairs, "After you. I will show you the way." Rune nodded and skipped to the stairs and Milla moved shyly through the cage door, looking up at Ethan sideways. "My lady," Ethan murmured gently as he continued to motion to the stairs, "After you."

Milla blushed deeply as she nodded and hurried ahead.

As the three emerged into the bright main room of the jailhouse, they were eyed curiously by every guard in the room. Captain Ethan casually spoke as he gestured at the nearest guard, "Their things, if you don't mind."

The large woman grunted as she moved off to a side room, then emerged again shortly after with their packs and Milla's bow and arrows, "We'll give her the weapon as she's leaving town."

"No, you will give it to her now," Ethan corrected. The woman made a sour face as she clearly was unhappy with the order, but she did as she was commanded. As she handed Milla the bow, Ethan asked, "Are you any good with that?"

Rune quickly checked the pockets of his pack as Milla shyly smiled at Ethan and answered as she pushed a few strands of hair behind her ear, "I'm okay. I mean, yes. I'm good," she cleared her throat, "With the bow."

Ethan smiled kindly at her then motioned to the exit, "It is not a skill that I was ever able to pick up," he explained, as he started toward the exit. Rune frowned slightly as he gave up his search and followed the two outside. Ethan continued speaking as he stepped out onto the sidewalk and into the sunlight, "My father tried-," he stopped as he was interrupted by a swarm of several men and women of different ilk asking hurried questions, "One at a time," he said as he raised his hands to hush them.

Rune and Milla stopped a moment, unsure if they should find their own way, or wait for Ethan to finish as a man with a pot belly and fine clothing spoke first, "I do hope we can count on your protection of the outlying lands, Captain. A great deal of our income-"

"We should find the Inn," Rune said quietly to Milla as he looked down the street.

Milla shook her head and watched Ethan speak with confident authority to those around him. "I assure you we are doing our best to protect all the lands, but you all must keep in mind that we are at war. Our focus must be stopping our enemy's advancement and pushing them back. We all must-," He was interrupted as several in the group began to raise complaints.

"He said he would show us the way," Milla then whispered to Rune as she watched Ethan try to listen to all the complaints at once.

"He meant out of the jail. We can find our own way to the inn. He's obviously a busy man," Rune said idly as he inspected the wide cobblestone boulevard, trying to ignore the faint smell of horse dung. He shifted to look beyond a horse drawn cart that passed slowly, to check the opposite side of the street, then after getting a sense of where they were and the direction they came from, he began walking opposite of that. As they didn't pass an inn when they were first escorted from the west gate to the law house, he thought it would be a safe bet.

Milla hesitated then turned to follow, "We should at least wait to ask him where it is."

Rune let out a mocking laugh as he shook his head, then called out to a man nearby, "Sir! Which way to the Inn, if you don't mind?"

The man pointed down the road in the direction they were headed, "Just down a few blocks, you can't miss it. There's a big sign in the shape of a tree."

Rune waved with a smile, "My thanks!" He then turned to Milla and said, "We don't need an important and busy captain to guide us. He did enough already. Let's not tempt fate."

Milla frowned and continued to follow, "I only meant he offered. It's only polite to wait."

"We shouldn't over-" Rune stopped as he was interrupted by a voice from behind them.

"My apologies. It seems there is always work to be done," Ethan said as he hurried down the sidewalk to catch up with them, "I will walk with you."

Milla smiled brightly, "That is very kind of you, Captain."

Ethan chuckled lightly, "I need to head this way anyway. Besides, with the luck you two have had on your journey thus far, I would fear that, without an escort, you'd be back in the jails again before the day's end."

Milla giggled lightly, but Rune's expression made it obvious that he found it less than amusing. "If you have more important things to do, we would understand. I'm sure we will manage to stay out of jail from here on."

"Of course. I was only making light. Nevertheless, I am to head to the inn myself, and would prefer the company," Ethan countered with a charming smile, "One can only be surrounded by soldiers and men of rank for so long before going mad."

Rune shrugged and quickly said, "It's the price you pay for your position, isn't it? You're lucky to have it. I hear it's the only way us low born can be heard or do anything beyond scraping by and making babies to serve the upper classes."

Ethan only nodded slowly.

"Have you ever met a lord or lady?" Milla asked Ethan.

He smirked and nodded, "Far too many I'm afraid."

Milla smiled brightly, "I hear they are all beautiful people who wear extravagant clothes. And when they speak it is either as soft as a song bird or as powerful as a dragon."

Ethan laughed rather loud at that, then cleared his throat, "You listen to many stories, I assume?"

Milla looked down with embarrassment and blushed, "I do. I love stories. Mad seers, evil magi and the great heroes that save the world. My favorites are the stories of the Wardens of Light, saving the world from the tyrannical rule of the dragons."

Ethan raised a brow as he smiled, "Well, I am afraid the reality of nobility is far different than in the tales. The lords and ladies are no more beautiful than the commoner. In fact, if you remove the elegant clothing and fine hair styles, you could not tell the difference. And their voices are as any others, though they are trained to speak and act a certain way. It is all an illusion though."

"Jealous?" Rune joked.

Ethan shook his head and grinned as he pointed ahead, "The inn isn't much further."

The wooden sign of the inn was large and conspicuous. It was in the shape of an elaborate tree with many branches, leaves and roots. It was clear that at one point it had been skillfully painted with intricate lines and patterns, but most of that had now faded. Ivy and other greenery had made itself at home on the sign, though it seemed that an effort had been made to keep most of it within the branches of the sign and away from the trunk and roots. The building itself was a sight to behold as well. A large portion of it sat on their left, beyond the large, fragrant stables. The wooden beams crisscrossed above the stone foundation that also formed the large steps that reached the edge of the street's walkway, passing below the large tree sign. But that was not the extent of it. The building continued over an archway formed above the main road and continued to the other side, where the rest of the inn lay; a long three-story structure, of the same design as its twin on the other side of the street.

As the three made their way up the stairs, they were greeted by a middle-aged man in full gray armour. The lines around his eyes deepened as he smiled. "Picking up strays, Captain?" his gravelly voice called out with a chuckle.

Ethan smiled at that, "Major Peleg, it's about time you got here. You must give me an update once we're all settled. I'd like you to meet my two new friends, Rune and-" he stopped short as he turned his head to Milla narrowing his eyes in thought.

"Milla," she answered for him.

Ethan smiled at her, "Forgive me. Our introductions were far from proper," He then looked back to the major, "They are visitors from the western empire."

Peleg laughed lightly, "As oblivious as ever to all struggles east of the great river I'm sure. Did either of you even know of the war before you entered our lands?"

Rune and Milla both looked down sheepishly as Ethan answered, "They hadn't a clue. They've already been captured by the south and now us. Thankfully, we are far greater hosts." He beamed at the two, who exuded embarrassment. He then continued, "Major, would you mind securing them the best rooms available as our official apology? We cannot have them heading off thinking we are as savage as the south, can we?"

Peleg chuckled and thumped his armoured hand against his armoured chest in a salute. He said no more as he made his way back into the inn.

"You're making fun of us," Milla said sadly, with a frown.

"My dear lady," Ethan said, still beaming a smile, "Of course I am." She continued to frown for a moment, but a smile overtook her lips as his own smile was contagious. He then added, "There will be a feast in the main hall tonight. You two should settle in, then after nightfall, I would like you to join me there as my guests."

"I won't turn down free food!" Rune piped in, "Thank you."

Ethan dipped his head to Rune, then Milla, his smile never leaving his face, "I will see you both tonight then." He turned on his heel and made his way into the inn.

Milla watched him walk away, a smitten grin touching her lips, "He's very kind."

Rune watched her a moment, "Right," he finally answered. "Let's get to our rooms. I'm exhausted." After a nod, Milla followed Rune into the inn.

CHAPTER 17

Lorelei's eyes opened gradually as she slowly breathed in a rich floral scent. Blurred vision cleared as her gaze danced around the small, dark room. Her brows furrowed as she glanced over the walls of light stone, decorated by small, intricate tapestries. She noticed a small desk and chair against the wall, opposite of the bed that she lay in. An elegant four drawer dresser was against the wall, next to the lavish wooden door, that was decorated with over-sized and intricate metal hinges.

After sitting up slowly, she cringed at the stinging pain coming from her feet. She examined them and noticed that they were now cleaned and bandaged with care. Confusion and reality finally set in causing her to stiffen and look around again in a panic. She placed her feet on the soft rug below and forced herself to stand. Painfully, she limped to the window to her right, which was covered in metal bars formed in the shape of ivy and painted white. Her little fingers grasped onto the bars as she peered through. Beyond lay a large, moonlit courtyard. White marble pillars, overgrown with ivy, surrounded a grassy area lined with flowered bushes. Benches and tables, also made of white marble, were placed evenly in the grass, closest to her window, just beyond the stone walkway. She noticed several other windows lining the walls surrounding the courtyard, the pattern only broken by beautiful, arched, blue doors trimmed with gilded metal decorations.

Her lips quivered as she wanted to cry for her mother or sister, but she didn't. Now turning from the window, she limped to the door and pulled at the handle. The door would not open, so she desperately continued her attempt, shaking and tugging, while her right hand braced for strength on the wall next to it. It rattled with her effort but would not budge. Frustration took over and her face reddened as she switched hands and began to slam her fist on the door violently, now crying out, "Help! Let me out!" She saw fire-light beam from below the door and heard footsteps outside. She took several labored limps backward and her eyes widened in fear and anticipation of who or what might be on the other side. The door handle rattled as latchkey was set to it from the other side, and she swallowed hard as the door opened. After guarding her eyes a moment from the lantern light, she tilted her head in confusion. Before her stood a woman, covered head to toe in white with only her face showing. Her white dress went so low as to even hide her feet. "What is it, child? Can you not sleep? Are you in pain?" The woman asked in a soft and comforting voice.

Lorelei was unsure of how to respond at first. She then asked in a soft stutter, "Wh-where am I?"

"Why, you are in The Reisa Academy of course. Do you not remember?" The woman cooed with a smile, showing pity and amusement.

Lorelei shook her head and her lips quivered again as her eyes began to tear, "I want my mama," she said, "Where is Mimi?"

The woman knelt down and smiled, "Your mother has sent you here, child. You do not remember? She wished you a better life and education. Do not worry, we will take very good care of you and you will see your mother soon, alright?"

Lorelei swallowed and didn't answer, as tears continued to drop from her eyes.

"Come, you must rest. You must heal from your long trip here. Why did you not wear shoes, poor child?" the woman said as she entered and directed Lorelei to the bed.

Lorelei followed the lead but looked to the door for escape as she answered, "I don't have shoes. Mimi was making me a new pair because I lost mine."

The woman smiled warmly at that, "Well, little mistress. You shall never want for shoes again. Tell me what color you like most, and I will have a pair made for you in that color." Lorelei simply looked at the woman with confusion and didn't offer an answer. The woman giggled lightly as she tucked Lorelei into bed, "You do not have a favorite color?" Lorelei shrugged, and the woman smiled warmly again, "Well then, let me see your eyes," she said as she raised the lantern up to have a good look. "Yellow eyes? Gold perhaps? How very unique, my dear," she said as her smile faltered only a moment. "Gold then. I will have a golden pair of slippers made for the golden eyed girl. Would you like that?"

Lorelei nodded slowly and asked after a yawn, "Do you promise my mother will see me soon?"

The woman smiled kindly and stood, making her way back to the door, "What mother would not come to see her daughter in such a fine place? Now, get your rest and I will wake you in the morning with the finest breakfast you've ever tasted." She then made her way out the door and locked it behind her.

Lorelei frowned, not feeling reassured at all, but fatigue took over and she soon fell asleep.

CHAPTER 18

The sun had just slipped beyond the horizon when Rune and Milla emerged from their rooms, both thankful to have been able to wash up and have a short nap. The smell of the feast had woken them both and they were now very hungry. They eagerly made their way down the wide, candle lit hallway and stairs towards the main hall. A large group of people were gathered in the area in front of the large hall doors that were still shut tight and guarded. The tapestry lined area was dim, having only been lit by tall candelabra placed in each corner, but it was light enough to be comfortable on the eyes. Rune frowned as they walked amongst the others together, "It looks like we're early."

Milla sighed and put her hand on her stomach, "I'm starving."

Rune nodded in agreement and opened his mouth, ready to add to her statement, when the large doors began to open. He instead said happily, "I guess we're just in time!"

The two made their way inside the main hall with the group. The main hall was much brighter, as two large chandeliers, with many candles, glowed above them while several elaborate looking, tall candelabra surrounded the entire room. Rune and Milla moved off to the side, staring in awe at the central long table covered in delicious looking foods of all sorts. Long, simple tables were set up around the room, though the table at the far end of the room was covered by a fancy looking light blue tablecloth, elaborately decorated with golden suns and swords. Milla bit down on her lips with anticipation then whispered to Rune, "Where do we sit?" Rune shrugged dramatically, then drifted distraught eyes around in hopes for a clue.

"Ah, you've made it," Ethan said, through a wide smile as he approached them from the side. He was no longer in his black armour, instead sporting black leather pants and a blue brocade tunic, edged with golden stitching.

"You both look as though you've never been to a feast before."

They both shook their heads in unison, looking lost and anxious. Rune motioned to the head table, "I suppose that's where the nobility sits?"

"Nobility and anyone of import, yes," He answered.

Milla's eyes drifted to the table as Rune motioned to it, and then to the women standing near it. They wore finer dresses than she had ever seen, and their hairstyles were more elaborate than she had dared ever dream to attempt on her own. She self-consciously played with her braid as she watched them laugh and chat, then looked down at her plain, green leather tunic. "If I'd known this would be so fancy I would have..." she frowned instead of finishing her thought.

Ethan smiled at her after following her gaze, "You don't need fine clothes. As you can see, most others in the room do not." He beckoned a cup bearer over and took a goblet of wine with his usable hand, passing it to Milla as he then explained to Rune, "Tonight, the lord of the land, Lord Felix, sits up there with the Mayor of Silvius and a few others who hold positions in the lord's designated territory." He took another goblet and handed it to Rune before taking one for himself.

"Will you be sitting up there then?" Milla asked quickly.

Ethan hesitated, masking it with a long drink of wine, "Yes, I will be."

"The perks of being a Captain," she stated with a smile.

Ethan returned her smile warmly.

"And where do us low and unimportant sit?" Rune asked, though Milla smacked his arm quickly after.

Ethan frowned lightly and said, "Displays such as this are not truly a measure of a man's importance; only his influence. Every person in the realm is important in their own way. But you may choose any other table."

Rune scoffed, "You're an idealist. That's not how the world works. The nobility thinks of us as beasts of burden to do their bidding and run out to die, when commanded. If we grow too powerful or important, they snuff us out. We raise their food and fight their wars while they sit at the heads of tables and eat better than we will in a lifetime."

"Rune," Milla growled.

Ethan forced a smile and said, "You're quite bitter for one so young." He took another sip of wine.

Rune frowned, as he looked directly at Ethan, "My parents were Weiland and Nertha."

Ethan almost spit his wine back into his goblet as his eyes widened and blinked rapidly. He swallowed and appeared speechless for a few moments. He finally said, "I was not aware they had a son."

"Most people aren't," Rune said flatly, "But they did. Their little secret."

Milla looked back and forth between the two, utter confusion written on her face, "I'm sorry, who?"

Ethan winced at the question and mulled over the explanation, but Rune quickly obliged, "My father was a powerful and famous magi. He and my mother were killed by the Northern royalty for not sharing the knowledge they acquired. You see, when royalty wants something, they either get it, or make sure no one else does."

Ethan winced again, "That's not... well, that's not the story I heard."

"Of course not," Rune growled, "You're from the North. They twisted the story to make sure they themselves seem like the heroes for destroying an evil magi. That's the story everyone likes to tell. It's much more entertaining than hearing the story of a corrupt royal family killing a magi and his scholar wife for knowing more than they should."

A silence grew between the three, as Rune frowned and looked to the floor. Milla and Ethan both took sips of their wine, though Milla scrunched her nose at the foreign taste. Ethan finally spoke up as Major Peleg walked over to join them, "Perhaps a discussion for another time."

"Did I miss something interesting?" Peleg chuckled hoarsely as he approached the awkward looking group.

"Thankfully yes," Ethan said with a laugh, "How goes your preparations, Major?"

Peleg smiled questioningly as he looked over the group, "They go well, of course. Commander Ronen has already set out with the bulk of the men. I do require your attention on the matter before the night is over, being that you can't join us."

Ethan frowned and looked to his injured shoulder as if he had forgotten about it, "Right. We should discuss your positioning on the ridge. We need to avoid further surprises." He looked to Milla and Rune again, offering a small bow of his head, "If you will excuse me. I will be sure to speak with you again before the night is through."

Rune and Milla both bowed their heads in return and watched him and Peleg walk away. Milla then turned her eyes to Rune. She spoke cautiously, "I'm sorry, I didn't know that about you."

Rune continued to frown as he shrugged, "How could you have? There's a lot about me you don't know. Why do you think Bera was so eager to get rid of me and the whole town hates me?"

Milla said nothing for a while, deciding instead to sip at her wine. She took in a slow breath before saying, "I'm sure they don't hate you. Besides, if they wanted to get rid of you so bad, why not do it sooner?"

Rune shrugged and mumbled, "I'm not sure."

"Maybe you can tell me their story sometime," Milla said softly, "Before I hear it from anyone else." Rune simply nodded in agreement. "Let's find a place to sit," she suggested, and the two moved off to a nearby table.

Not long after, the main doors closed, and the entire room was seated. Servants began to move in through side doors and make their way to the central table of food but touched nothing. Instead, they waited patiently, their backs facing the food. The side doors, at the far end of the room, then opened. A round and well-dressed man entered from the far left and made his way to the front of the grand table. "Please rise," he announced after a quiet took over the room, and all who were sitting stood. One by one, he announced those who entered from the far doors, starting with Lord Felix. The tall, lean, and sophisticated man, with jet black hair and a finely trimmed beard, made his way towards the center of the table as those who followed behind, were announced. The portly Mayor came next, then a small succession of important men and women in the community. Lord Felix moved to the largest central chair as if to sit in it, but instead took the chair to its right, as the portly mayor took the chair on the left. The remainder of those entering moved to either side of the two important men.

Major Peleg was then announced, followed by a long pause. Peleg took his seat at the far end of the head table, leaving only the large center chair remaining. "Finally, it is my great honour to announce Captain Ethan. Though just passing through our humble city, he has agreed to grace us with his presence." Those at the lower tables began to stomp a foot in the same rhythm as those at the head table pounded their fists down, causing a metallic clanging noise as utensils bounced with the beat. Milla and Rune mimicked those around them with wide eyes, surprised to see Ethan move into the room and take the large seat in the center between Lord Felix and the Mayor. As soon as he sat, those still standing finally took their seats as well, including Rune and Milla, as they looked to each other with confused expressions.

The servants began taking food from the central table and serving it to all, always beginning with Ethan, Lord Felix and the Mayor, then the rest of the head table, before moving to the rest of the room.

"I didn't know Captains were that important," Milla said quietly to Rune as the hum of conversation overtook the room.

Rune nodded, then shrugged as he watched a servant place a small plate of food in front of him then Milla. "He must be the guest of honour or something."

"That must be it," Milla said, an enamored smile touching her lips, as she watched Ethan speak to those around him. She placed her elbow on the table and rested her chin on her hand, "He's probably a hero then. Maybe that's how he was injured."

Rune had already begun digging in to the small plate of chilled, salted meats and cheeses. He looked up at her. After shifting the contents of his food to one side of his mouth so he could speak, he said to her, "Maybe. I thought you were starving."

Milla's eyes fluttered as she returned to reality and she looked down at her plate. Her stomach instantly knotted with hunger, so she quickly began to dig in.

***

The night continued, filled with the constant hum of many conversations, while the servants busied themselves filling drinks and periodically changing small helpings of food with others. Finished or not, if the time came for a new flavor, plates were replaced with a new dish. Ethan remained in constant conversation with those around him, hardly seeming to have a moment to eat.

The last dish was finally served. The bowl consisted of small citrus fruit pieces mixed with balls of multicolored melon, lightly drizzled with a spiced, sweet syrup. Milla, being well beyond full only picked at the new dish while Rune continued to stuff the final bits of food into his mouth. He was clearly full as well, as it took him some time to swallow the food, but he continued to eat anyway.

The main doors were eventually opened. It was a polite sign, to all those in the hall, that the night was coming to a close. Ethan stared down at his final bowl of food as Lord Felix continued speaking at him. Milla turned her eyes up toward him as she continually poked at a melon ball. He seemed to feel her gaze as his own eyes raised to meet hers. She blushed lightly and offered him a look of pity. He smiled in return, offering a small shrug then turned to answer the chatty Lord. "Poor Ethan," she said to Rune, who now sat back with a full mouth, chewing slowly.

He scoffed, as best he could without losing food from his mouth. After swallowing, he finally spoke, "Yes, poor him. He had to sit at the head of the room and get served first while the rest of us wait."

Milla shook her head, "You haven't been watching, have you? He barely touched any of his food. He's been too busy being talked to."

Rune scoffed again, "He could eat and still talk."

Milla turned an annoyed gaze to Rune, "He could, but it's not polite."

After a sheepish shrug, Rune replied, "I'd rather be full and thought rude than hungry and thought a gentleman."

Milla laughed lightly at him and shook her head. Turning to look to Ethan again, she noticed he was gone and Lord Felix was pushing himself up to stand. She sat up straight, as she looked around, trying to see where Ethan had gone.

"You must both forgive me," Milla jumped lightly, as she heard Ethan's tired voice behind her, "I would have liked to speak with you both further but there are still matters that require my attention. Perhaps I will be able to catch you at dayspring?"

Milla and Rune both turned in unison while Ethan spoke to them. Milla answered quickly, with a smile, "Of course. We understand. Make sure you find something to eat though, you look hungry."

A wide smile grew on Ethan's face and he leaned down in between them as he spoke quietly, "Lord Felix is quite fond of explaining, to all around him, how trying his duties are and how superb he is at attending to them. The man is confident, if nothing else."

"Maybe, next time, you should sit with us lowly servants of the realm then," Rune said, with a grin, after leaning back further to ease the fullness in his stomach, "We know the value of a good meal."

"Tempting," Ethan laughed, "Have a good night. Both of you."

"You too!" Milla said, with far too much enthusiasm.

Still smiling, he bowed his head to the two of them and turned to make his way out. Milla watched him until he was out of sight, then let out a sigh. Rune, in turn, watched her, then rolled his eyes, "You can stop drooling now."

Milla blushed deeply, as she turned to look down at her hands which she placed on her lap, "I'm actually glad you got us captured this time," she said as she smiled, "We should probably head to our rooms. I'm tired."

Rune shook his head, then rubbed his full belly, "My best failure ever." He slowly turned, moving his legs over the bench, then stood.

Milla laughed, then sighed, as she stood as well, "I wonder if they'll tell stories about him."

Rune grunted, "I'm sure they will. The heroes are always tall and strong in the stories, right? Maybe that's why they couldn't tell the stories about my father being a hero. He wasn't tall enough or strong enough. And magi are almost always the villain, aren't they?"

Milla frowned lightly, "You can tell the story then."

"Maybe," Rune said with a sigh as he started to the door, "Who would really want to hear it, though?"

"I would," Milla said as she walked next to him.

Rune smiled at that, "You don't mind the heroes being less than perfect?"

"Of course not!" She said gleefully, as they moved up the stairs, speaking in an inspirational tone, "A good story has all sorts and catches you off guard with twists and turns. Heroes come in many shapes and sizes. If all heroes were the same, stories would get boring." The smile on Rune's face grew. As they reached the top of the stairs she asked, "Do you think Captain Ethan is much older than me?"

The smile dropped from his face and he shrugged, now speaking quieter as they made their way down the hall, with bedroom doors on either side of them, "Well, he's old enough to be a Captain, so probably."

Milla shrugged again, "Well, he does look pretty young to be a Captain. Maybe there's something special about him?"

Rune didn't like where the conversation was going, so he forced a yawn and said tiredly, "I'm tired, so I think I'll head to my room. I'll see you at dayspring."

Milla nodded, still smiling and looking off, as she strolled towards her own room, "Alright, good night, Rune."

Rune let out a sad sigh, as his shoulders slumped down, and he moped to the door of his room. As soon as he closed it behind him, a candle lit in the room. "Thes is much better than campin' in th' wilderness!" Feagan said happily, "Much better than uir auld shack an aw."

"Yes. Also, much better than a jail cell," Rune added, as he moved to the plush bed and fell backwards on it, looking defeated.

"Is she still mad abit 'at?" Feagan asked, fluttering over to Rune's side.

"No. She's not mad at all," Rune answered, then turned over to face Feagan, "She's too busy drooling over the Captain to care about anything else."

"Eh," Feagan said with a pitied frown, "Want me tae poison his bevvy? Ur mebbe Ah can fin' a speel tae make heem mah size an' steal heem awa' frae 'er. He's a mighty sexy laddie."

Rune rolled his eyes at Feagan, "Steal him from her?" He shook his head, "Even if that were possible, I don't think you're his type." He then collapsed to his back again, "I just need to face the facts. We'll finish our journey, she'll leave back to wherever she's from and I'll head home with my pay."

Feagan thought on that a moment, "Ur, we coods stay in th' North."

"Why would we stay in the North? I don't know anyone in the north. I don't have any skills to make a living. At least I have a place to lay my head in Skera Braka," Rune said sadly then sat up to remove his sandals.

"Thaur is opportunity in places loch thes Rune," Feagan said then moved to sit on Rune's shoulder, "Yer new Cap'n friend micht hae an idea ur tois. They also accept magik haur as a gift, nae a curse."

"You mean the magik I don't have?" Rune growled then tossed his sandals across the room.

Feagan sighed, "They hae academies. Ye coods tak' th' payment ay thes trip frae th' lassie an' -"

"Just stop," Rune interrupted then sighed, "After this trip, I stop pretending. I go back to Skera Braka and I live out my life as a powerless nobody there. The North would never accept the son of Weiland and Nertha either-"

"Dinnae teel anyone 'en!" Feagan protested, "Lae 'at in yer pest, start anew!"

Rune let out a frustrated breath, while he laid down and Feagan moved next to his head on the pillow, "It's who I am Feagan. I am the son of a hated man. I am nothing. I am nobody. I have no magik and no skills. But I do have a home."

"Rune ye-"

"Just, stop," Rune said, as he covered himself with the blanket and turned to his side, "One thing I am, is tired. Good night."

Feagan frowned deeply. Deciding not to bother Rune further on the matter, he made himself comfortable on the pillow and remained there to rest.

CHAPTER 19

Milla and Rune walked out of the inn and into the bright morning sun together, both feeling well rested and refreshed. Rune stretched out his arms and let out a contented rumble as Milla took in a long breath of morning air, immediately scrunching her nose as the city's smell wasn't very pleasant. A young man approached them, holding the reins of two bay horses who followed behind him. His clothing and skin were covered in what looked to be several day's worth of filth and he walked with his shoulders and head down. As he neared he lifted the reins towards them and bowed his head, "I was told to give you these as soon as you left the inn. Compliments of Captain Ethan," he explained.

Milla and Rune accepted the reins with surprise in their eyes and Milla spoke cheerfully, "That's very kind of him! Please give him our thanks."

"My lady, you will be able to pass that message on yourself, as he has also asked that you both meet him at the east gate," the young man said as he pointed them in the right direction, then gave a curt wave and ran off.

Milla beamed a smile then quickly removed her pack and moved to secure it to the horse. Rune, on the other hand, moved slower to his horse. He eyed the beast then watched Milla mount, "I don't know how to ride," he grumbled as he removed his own pack and searched for the place to secure it.

"Don't worry, it's easy," Milla said in a chipper tone, "Just do what I did."

Rune gave her an exasperated look as he finished securing his pack then awkwardly tried to copy her as he took hold of the cantle and struggled to get his foot into the stirrup.

Without a word, Milla watched him move his free hand to different places on the saddle to find a grip. He then hopped several times before finally being able to throw his leg over and seat himself. The horse turned its ears towards Rune but otherwise seemed to take the struggling well, remaining still even as he shifted to make himself more comfortable. When Rune completed his tedious repositioning, Milla finally spoke as she smiled, "Well, you're halfway there. Just follow my lead and do what I do. Pull back like this to make him stop." Rune nodded hesitantly as he watched her demonstrate, then copied her after she clicked her tongue and lightly kicked both heels into the beast's sides. Following the directions of the dirty young man down the cobblestone road, they both moved towards the east gate through the plant invaded streets. Milla continued to beam happily as they advanced, "I wonder what he wants," she pondered aloud timidly, "Maybe he'll show us a bit of the land before we go."

Rune shrugged and muttered, "I'm sure he just wants to wish us safe travels. Besides, don't you have something more important than a tour to attend to?"

Milla's heart visibly sank, "I suppose you're right."

As they finally approached the gate they both took note of Ethan adjusting himself on his blue roan horse as a soldier held the reins for him. His movements were a little awkward, having only one arm to adjust with, but it didn't take long for him to settle.

His armour was different than what they had last seen him in. It was mainly blackened leather with dark gray amour plates on his chest and back. It also donned elongated plated shoulders, bracers, and leg guards. As he was handed the reins he looked up to see the two approaching and smiled, "Ah, you're earlier than I thought you'd be."

Milla's spirits seemed to instantly lift as he spoke, "I hope that's alright."

"Yes, quite alright," he said returning a warm smile. His glance turned to Rune, "I hope you both slept well. The journey to the east border is not a short one, but we should reach it within two or three days. It will be much faster than if you would have gone on foot at the very least."

"We?" Rune asked quickly, "You're joining us?"

Ethan turned an amused grin toward Milla, "I had thought, with your current luck, having another escort that knows the land would not hurt you. I'm afraid I'm quite useless as anything else right now," he said motioning to his arm.

Milla had a hard time controlling her joy as she smiled wide, "That's wonderful. We'd be honored if you joined us."

"Well," he grinned at her playfully, "It was either escort you or continue my journey home, and I must say the former seems far more alluring."

Milla blushed and looked down at her hands.

Ethan's smile faltered, and he studied her reaction. "What I mean to say is," he cleared his throat, "I would enjoy making myself useful more than heading home while the war still rages."

Rune frowned heavily at the exchange "Just to the east border?" He asked quickly.

"I'm afraid I can go no further," Ethan responded then took the leather strap of a large satchel that was handed to him. He secured it to the saddle before the weight of it was released to rest on the saddle's extra long flap, "My place is in the north." Rune let out a relieved sigh and Ethan took note of his reaction. His eyes moved from Rune to Milla, then back to Rune and he smiled as he dipped his head, "I am ready when you are."

Milla looked back up, her smile still wide, "I am very ready. Let's be off."

The three headed out the west gate with Rune, lagging behind.

***

Several uneventful hours went by as they journeyed down the wide dirt road in a row, with Ethan leading at the front and Rune continuing to follow at the rear. The mane of rich green grass on either side of the road flowed like waves in the gentle, warm breeze. Sunlight glistened on the scattered yellow weeds as their heavy and waxy berry heads flopped back and forth. The trio had passed by and politely greeted all those walking by on their way to Silvius, but otherwise there had been an awkward silence for the duration. As they passed a fork in the road that cut around a large jagged rock covered in moss and leafy plants, Ethan looked to the sky then spoke loud enough for all to hear, "We should let the horses rest soon and get some food in us."

"Good, my bum hurts," Rune called back as he shifted in his saddle.

Milla turned a frown to Rune then urged her horse ahead to ride at Ethan's right side. He uncomfortably shifted his left arm and winced at the pain. She asked, "What happened to your arm?" as she nodded toward it.

Ethan shifted it again. "I took a sword from behind during an ambush," he explained through a strained voice, "I'm lucky to be alive." He grunted as he allowed the arm to settle and his voice returned to normal, "In fact, I would likely not be if the ambushers had followed their plan. I had later found out, after the survivors were questioned, that there had been a lookout posted who was to distract any aid who might come. But they had either ran in fear or gained some integrity. If it weren't for Major Peleg's gut feelings and our skilled battlefield skera I would have been naught more than a cautionary tale of blind trust now."

Milla winced at the thought. "And yet you now trust two strangers to travel alone with." Ethan grinned at her then looked off, examining the scenery. She continued, "I have some herbs that might be able to help, if you'd like," she said, looking to him attentively.

He turned smiling eyes to her, "I would appreciate that, thank you. The skera had recommended that I head straight home to get rest and better care, but it seems my plans have changed, and I could not bring her with, even if I wished to. I admit, the pain is getting rather bothersome."

Milla looked to the road that now began to incline toward a hill as they continued, "You didn't have to risk your comfort and healing like this for complete strangers," she regarded him again with a look of great esteem, "You are truly an honourable man and we are very grateful for the help."

Ethan turned remorseful eyes to the ground and graciously dipped his head at the compliment, "It is no trouble, really."

She beamed at him then asked, "Where should we stop to rest?"

He then nodded eastward, "There is a bridge crossing not far from here and a perfect clearing for us to rest just beyond." Milla nodded and the three ascended silently.

Finally reaching the peak of the hill, Ethan reined in his horse to stop, and his expression quickly grew worried as he focused on the bridge at a distance ahead. Milla watched his expression as she stopped with him, then turned her gaze to see what had him so concerned.

Several armed men waited at the mouth of the bridge closest to them. Some rested at the side of the road and others stood on the bridge, leaning on the side walls as they idly conversed. As Ethan silently assessed the situation, Rune rode up on his left side, following both of their gazes. Ethan then let out a frustrated puff, "I can see twenty-three. I'm not sure what to make of them. They don't appear to be soldiers or guards. There is no uniform to them, yet they are well armed."

"Trolls," Rune stated simply.

"Trolls?" Ethan mimicked questioningly, "Trolls are not permitted in the North."

"Well," Rune said with a sarcastic grin, "You should go down and tell them. I'm sure that will go over well."

Ethan looked to Rune sideways and grinned, "Point taken. Well then Rune, being that you are more knowledgeable about these sorts than I, what do they wish of us? Payment?" Rune nodded slowly, and Ethan continued, "How much do they generally expect?"

"It depends," Rune answered, "Sometimes it's as low as a long dreg, sometimes it's much higher."

"Well," Ethan stated, seeming to have made a decision, "Then we shall pay what they ask and continue our journey."

"Sometimes," Rune continued sharply, "they want more than dregs."

"More?" Ethan asked cautiously.

Rune took in a slow breath, "Sometimes a fine healthy horse, sometimes rations," he paused, "sometimes a pretty girl."

Ethan quickly looked to Milla, his concerned deepening as she returned a doe eyed stare. He shook his head, "And we are only three. We wouldn't be in a position to argue price."

"Is there another way across?" Milla quickly asked, looking up and down the wide, fast moving river.

Ethan thought it over, "There is another bridge to the south, about a day's travel, but it is possibly in control of the enemy. There is also another several days to the North, but we would have to backtrack and take the other road, or we would be forced to travel through dense tree and bush."

"North is our only option then," Milla said with a sigh.

"I think our best bet is to turn back. I can secure a company of men to clear the bridge," Ethan said as he turned to look in the direction they came from.

"One of us can run ahead and ask them their price, "Rune suggested quickly, "It can't be too bad. We've seen a few others coming from this direction. I'm sure they would have warned us if the trolls were especially unfair. I volunteer. I've done it before. Let's not make all these hours of travel a waste."

Ethan glanced at Rune for a moment then turned his eyes to the bridge as he thought that over.

"He does have magik," Milla added, "If things go poorly I'm sure he can save himself." She then looked at Rune accusingly, "That is if he is capable of turning his magik on others."

"Magik? You are a Magi?" Ethan asked quickly, offering Rune a look of disbelief.

Rune looked off as he answered, "I don't need it for this. They're usually reasonable when negotiating price for passage."

Ethan watched Rune suspiciously for a moment, then shifted his left arm carefully as he placed his right hand on the hilt of his sword, "I still think securing soldiers to clear the bridge is our best option."

Rune frowned and looked over the dangerous men at the bridge, suddenly feeling the urge to run back home. He then turned, looking back in the direction they came, "You mean repeat what we just did twice more?" He growled, "I'm tired and I've just about had it with this journey as it is. I'm not going to throw away hours of travel over a few trolls."

Ethan thought that over then shook his head, "Your plan is too risky. If you-"

"No, it's our best option," Rune interrupted, "And I have to be the one to do it. You look too much like a soldier and Milla would be too tempting as a prize. I'm the best one to do this, and I'm going to do it. We don't need to debate about it more."

"Rune," Milla said with a sigh, "I appre-"

"Let's just get it over and done with," Rune said as he spurred his horse forward.

Ethan reached out to stop him but was unable to reach far enough to his left due to his injury. Seeing Ethan's failed attempt, Milla quickly urged her horse forward, but Ethan jolted his hand over and grabbed onto the reins of her horse to stop her, "It's too late. Let's hope he knows what he's doing."

Milla shook her head with worry, "Damn it Rune, not again! Both times he's talked to men in our path he's gotten us captured. He's such a fool."

"I have faith in him," Ethan said as he watched Rune gallop down, though his face betrayed his worry.

They both watched intently as the men saw Rune's approach and prepared to block his path. Rune stopped just ahead of them with arms raised and began to speak with them as the archers on the bridge prepared themselves. "Ho there! My friends and I are looking for passage across the bridge. What is the price?"

"That depends," one of the men said as he walked towards Rune, idly chewing a piece of grass. "Why do you and your friends want to cross?"

"We're traveling," Rune answered simply.

"Where?" the man asked, placing a hand on his sword.

"East," Rune answered simply again.

The man spit out his piece of grass and looked back to the others with an exasperated look, and the group laughed lightly. "Look boy," he started again. "We won't charge a single dreg if you just answer the questions clearly. It is very important that we know who travels this way and that. Now tell me. Who do you travel with, and where in the east are you headed?"

Milla and Ethan could only watch and wait as Rune explained his story to the dubious group. He answered happily, "Oh! Well I travel with a girl named Milla who is traveling east to see family and our escort Captain Ethan of the north army."

It became clear quite fast that his story was not taken well as a few of the shady men approached him with hostility, "Is that so? And who are you to be traveling with this Captain? Are you a personal servant perhaps? A messenger?"

"Get out of there Rune!" Ethan growled under his breath as he watched the scene. It was obvious that Rune did not see the movements of these men as threatening.

Rune shook his head in answer, "No. He's injured so he's helping guide us to the east border."

"Injured you say?" the man said with a grin as he looked up the road. "Is that them up there?"

"Oh no," Milla said quietly as she watched helplessly, "He's gotten himself killed or worse."

"He still has his magik, right?" Ethan said hopefully.

Milla nodded as they continued to watch. Both of their faces dropped in horror as one of the men violently grabbed the reins of Rune's horse, as he turned to look up toward them, causing it to rear up. Rune was able to hold on, but he was quickly surrounded and soon had many hands pulling him down.

Milla began to move forward, "We have to help him!"

Ethan stopped her again, "There's nothing we can do. We can only hope they don't-"

A thunderous boom interrupted him and caused both of their horses to rear up and squeal. They looked to the site as they regained control of their horses to see the bodies of the bridge trolls flying away from Rune, many into the fast-moving water. Rune's horse was also blown away from him and it skid along the grass and dirt before rolling once and coming to a stop on its side. Ethan and Milla both urged their horses forward into a gallop to get to Rune's side as quickly as possible. As they did, Rune's horse came to and kicked out in a panic before struggling to stand. It then galloped away to the north. Rune had cowered from the sound but as his friends approached, he watched in horror as several of the men, that just attacked him, screamed horribly for their lives as the river's current dragged them away. The bridge itself was now clear and the few men that didn't hit the water now writhed in pain from broken bodies a distance around Rune. Ethan and Milla both dismounted and moved to check on Rune, but as they approached him he widened his eyes and ran toward the screaming men. "We have to help them!" he yelled as he ran.

"It's too late Rune," Ethan called out, "they're gone."

Rune stopped as he could no longer see or hear the men in the river, and he swallowed hard. He then looked to the men around him and ran to the closest who held his chest and groaned in pain. Milla and Ethan followed just as the man coughed and spewed blood from his mouth and nose. "Do something!" Rune barked as he moved to him, looking down with helpless panic, "Help him!"

Milla rushed to the man but it was obvious his time was short, "Rune, there's nothing I can do." She looked the man over and made a face as she saw the problem, "His ribs are crushed."

"No, no, no!" Rune yelled, "You have to help him!"

The man's struggled breathing soon stopped, and Rune shook his head with wide eyes, "What have I done?"

"Nothing they wouldn't have done to you," Ethan said and moved to put his hand on Rune's back.

Rune bolted away from Ethan and Milla and quickly checked on the others. Seeing far too much blood and no movement from any, he dropped to his knees, "I killed them. I killed all of them."

"Rune calm down. You did the right thing," Milla urged.

"The right thing?" Rune barked and stood, then walked toward her furiously, "The right thing? We could have gotten past with no death! They would have come around. I got- I was scared. I didn't mean to-"

"Rune!" Ethan barked in a commanding voice and Rune jolted, then looked over, ready to listen, "I know taking a life is difficult. Trust me, I know. But you did what you had to do. Like any soldier, you defended yourself. You need to calm down."

Rune hesitated, then nodded, dropping to his knees again.

"We need to get across the bridge," Milla said as she moved back toward her horse. "We need to get away from this and give Rune some time to rest."

"My horse," Rune said abruptly, "Did I kill it? My Pack! Where's my pack!" he yelled as he quickly stood and looked around frantically.

"Your horse ran to the North. I'm afraid that's the last we'll see of it. I hope you had nothing of great value in your pack, your horse carried it." Ethan explained as calmly as he could.

Rune's face went pale as he worried about what had happened to Feagan. He looked around frantically hoping to see a sign that Feagan had gotten out to safety but saw nothing.

"It's alright," Milla explained, "He can summon it once we cross the river. I've seen him do it before. Why don't you and I share a horse Ethan, and Rune can have the other."

"Not everything can be solved by magik!" Rune roared at her then walked around with both hands on his head as he tried to think of a solution.

Milla jolted back at his outburst and Ethan watched him curiously for a few moments. He then shook his head, "Rune, you get up onto my horse and I'll walk. I need to stretch my legs anyway and the constant bounce of the horse has been nothing but outright agony on my injury."

Rune did his best to fight off tears, then looked to the north again before nodding at the suggestion. He moved slowly to Ethan's horse, still looking around hopefully, as he mounted awkwardly.

The three slowly made their way across the bridge and eventually found their way to the clearing to set up camp. Rune simply laid out his bedroll and laid down, being sure to stay turned away from the other two.

Milla and Ethan gave him his space and avoided talking higher than a whisper in case he was trying to sleep. She prepared herbs and bandages to treat Ethan's wound and made a small fire to boil water for tea. The evening remained warm and so they allowed the fire to die down for the night. The medicinal tea quickly put Ethan to sleep, so Milla decided to take the first watch, as there was little choice in the matter.

CHAPTER 20

Eilifatli's golden eyes burst open and he raised his head. "What... was that?" he grumbled to himself. He closed his eyes again, using his mind's eye to search for the source of his nap's interruption. "I have felt you before, haven't I?" he murmured, still searching. Finally, latching onto the source, his eyes reopened, "Such power for someone so young." He lowered his head, returning to his rest, and smiled as his eyes drifted closed, "We will meet soon, young stórrhugr."

CHAPTER 21

The sun had already settled into the horizon and darkened the area around the small camp. They had set up near a large boulder, their bedrolls surrounding a small dirt patch with their fire set up in the center. Their day of travel had gone slow as Ethan remained on foot for the most part, though after a great deal of urging, he eventually switched places with Milla. Rune's gloomy mood seemed to have been highly contagious as all three had trekked along quietly, save for required idle communication now and then.

Rune now sat, with his back against the boulder and his arms around his knees, a short distance away from the other two. Milla had just finished setting up makeshift tents over their small beds as the clouds threatened rain, and was now attentively cooking a freshly killed cervidae on a spit over the large fire. She didn't complain that no help was offered by Rune or able to be given by Ethan. In fact, she seemed to enjoy showing off a little to the handsome Captain.

Rune's thoughts had remained distant and filled with concern as he had still not seen any sign of Feagan. His mind was tortured with the thought that he may have killed his best and only friend. Milla and Ethan gave him space and silence, allowing him the time to mourn the loss of the men he had killed and come to terms with it.

Another thought scraped the back of Rune's mind though amongst the worry for his friend. In truth, he had no idea what he had done to cause that explosion of force. He had not tried to cast a spell when the men tried to apprehend him. The one thing he knew for sure; the fundamental rule of magik written in every magik tome and told to him by his father and Feagan both, was it required focus and words. It doesn't simply happen from will. All the other times that this had happened, he had been attempting a spell and had assumed it was a failure of that attempt. Now, he had no idea what it was, and that scared him.

"Here," he heard Milla's soft voice and lifted out of his stupor a moment to accept her offering of freshly cooked meat. He nodded a thank you and placed it on his cloak next to him, then without a word, he turned his head away from her. She sighed then knelt next to him, asking tentatively, "What exactly happened to you?"

"Happened to me?" Rune asked with confusion as he turned back toward her. He hoped she didn't notice his wordless spell, as he had no answers for her.

"Yes." She clarified, "You wouldn't defend yourself with your magik against those boys at your home town, and now you have been in a constant stupor over killing those men to defend yourself. Something must have happened in the past with magik for you to react this way. Maybe if you talk about it, it will help?"

Rune frowned. He wasn't in the mood to make something up to cover his story right now, and it only reminded him more of Feagan and how lost he would be without him. "I killed my best friend with magik," he said, his eyes now filling with tears.

Milla remained silent a few moments, then spoke softly, "I see. It was an accident?" Rune simply nodded. She took in a long breath. "Magik can be a great gift, and a terrible burden. My omi..." she paused and thought a moment, then continued, "She has powers. Because of it, she lost almost everything. Her life mate, her home... but she found happiness eventually. You will too."

Rune turned his eyes to his hands. He forced a small smile before speaking, "I know. Thank you."

Milla smiled faintly, then stood and made her way back to Ethan's side. Rune turned his attention to her as she knelt down and wiped her hands clean before attending to Ethan's shoulder as he ate. Rune frowned again as he watched her fawn over him. 'Who can blame her?" he mumbled to himself. Ethan sat there, confident, and shirtless. A fine example of manhood. A handsome and charming man just like in all the stories Milla had spoken of. Rune looked down at his own thin arms and took in a long breath before forcing it out. He decided it best to sleep, as his stomach didn't desire food at that moment. He rested his head back onto the boulder and closed his eyes.

"It is far too quiet," Ethan spoke resonantly, grinning at Milla as he placed his stripped bone down next to him, "I'm used to army encampments. The constant hum of movement and talking and music."

"Maybe you should start singing then," Rune grumbled back, keeping his eyes closed.

"I could do that," he said after a chuckle, "Or perhaps you could tell us a story. I have a strong feeling you have at least one to tell." Rune furrowed his brows as his eyes opened, and he turned to look at Ethan.

Milla watched the exchange for a moment then piped in, "Rune has been to the Seer Ruins. I'd like to hear about that I think."

"The Seer Ruins?" Ethan repeated, "I had heard of your parents going there."

Rune frowned further, "Yes, I'm sure you heard that. It's where they apparently found the knowledge that gave the North cause to kill them."

Milla quickly spoke again, "I haven't heard anything. Why don't you just tell me what you saw. Let's forget past wrongs for the night." She then began to rewrap Ethan's wounded shoulder carefully and he smiled gratefully at her.

Rune sighed and shifted, before turning to look back toward the other two. "You've both heard the stories I'm sure. How when you enter, the hair on your skin raises and shivers run through your body. How a feeling of dread and sadness gets stronger the further you move inside? How that feeling gets so strong that most need to turn back or they end up taking their own life?" Milla stopped all she had been doing as she listened to Rune. She nodded, confirming each point that she had in fact heard in tales. "It's not only true, it's far worse than that," Rune said, grinning lightly as he watched Milla's face soften with worry. "The further you go on, the more bones you see. Not just, as you'd expect, adults. But also, the bones of children and animals. No one is safe from the dark powers there."

"Children?" Milla said with sadness.

"Oh yes, many children. Babies even." Rune answered quickly, "There is a room near the center where the floor is covered with the bones of small children and infants."

"The center?" Ethan piped in, his expression that of amused disbelief, "You made it to the throne room?"

Rune nodded quickly, "I did. We did. It wasn't the first time my parents had been there."

"Couldn't that be where your parents found whatever it is that they were thought to have found? A source of the... the ancient seer's powers?" Ethan asked quickly.

Rune shrugged, "Maybe. I was too young to remember anything like that. I was too interested in what I was seeing and feeling."

"Why would any parent take a child into that place?" Milla said accusingly, "Weren't you afraid? Sad?"

"They knew how to protect me from the effects," Rune explained. "That is one thing I know. I don't know how, but they were able to..." he stopped as he thought over the words, "It's as if they were able to push it away from us. We had to stay close together for it to work."

Ethan narrowed his eyes as he listened, "But you don't know how? You don't even have a guess?"

"Why?" Rune blurted out, "Do you plan on killing me if I don't tell you?"

"Rune," Milla said softly.

"It's alright," Ethan said as he shifted, "He has every right to be angry. I am from the North after all."

"Well, he can't blame everyone from the North," Milla corrected then looked to Rune, "It wasn't him or his family that killed your parents. He's just another citizen under the Northern rule and he's been nothing but helpful."

Rune and Ethan locked eyes a moment, before Ethan turned his eyes down to the ground. "I know," Rune finally said. He then continued, "Anyway, after we left, my parents told me to never return there again. They made me promise. I don't see why I would ever want to, to be honest."

"Probably because they didn't want you wandering in there without their protection," Milla explained.

Rune thought about that a moment then nodded, "That's probably it."

"I'm sorry," Ethan then said as he looked back to Rune, "About your parents."

After a shrug, Rune said, "It's not your fault. It happened a long time ago. You were probably just a kid then too."

Ethan nodded slowly, "I was quite young yes."

"Thank you for telling us," Milla then said, unsure of what else to say. Rune nodded in response.

The sound of the fire snapped and crackled as a silence grew over the three. They all drifted off into their own thoughts until Milla finally returned to the task of applying the bandages. In the silence, a warbling whistle could easily be heard in the distance. Rune's eyes opened wide as he heard the familiar sound. He stood abruptly and frantically looked around. Seeing a familiar twinkle in the trees, he took only a moment to look back at the two by the fire who both seemed completely oblivious to the sound or his sudden movement. "I need to clear my head," he said to them as calmly as he could, "I'll be back soon." Milla and Ethan offered him an understanding nod and he moved away, trying not to appear too excited. Once he was out of sight, he ran into the nearby woods toward the sound and the light. He slowed as he yelled in a whisper, "Feagan! Is that you?" Hearing the signal again, he ran toward it until he reached a small clearing. His eyes beamed bright as he smiled ear to ear, seeing Feagan sitting happily perched on a horse with Rune's backpack secured to it. "Feagan! You're alive!" Rune called out, a little too loud as he ran to him, "I thought I killed you for sure!"

Feagan smiled and flew up from the horse and toward Rune, landing on his outstretched hand, "Eh, ye only knocked me silly. Ye knaw Ah am toogher than 'at."

Rune pulled him close into a make-shift hug despite Feagan's protesting. He then looked to the horse, "And the horse survived too?"

"Eh," Feagan said then looked sheepish, "Nah, it ran a ways 'en died. It took me some time tae fin' a passable replacement. 'at speel ay yoors packed a wallop. A wee warnin' next time woods be nice."

Rune's expression quickly turned to worry, "Feagan, that wasn't a spell. I don't know what that was, but I didn't cast anything."

Feagan shifted uncomfortably, then flew back to the horse as he said, " Dinnae be silly Rune. Ye did cest, ye jist dinnae remember."

"No, I didn't. I-"

"Ah heard ye!" Feagan said forcefully, examining the straps of the saddle, "Ah hink it was a wind speel. Mebbe th' shock made ye forgit. Vinda. That's whit ye said. Vinda."

Rune furrowed his brows, now questioning his own memory, "Are you sure? But if that's true, it means that I actually do have magik."

"Aye," Feagan said simply, "Noo, Ah was thinkin' Rune. 'at lassie has a new escort an' it's obvioos 'at th' chance ay onie great payment it ay thes has dwindled tae near naethin'. Hoo abit we lit them hae each other an' dump th' thankless wench an' 'er toy. Ye cannae say she's nae safe noo."

"Thankless wench," Rune repeated with a chuckle then sighed, "He's only escorting her to the eastern border though. So yes, she's safe now but if I leave her she'll be alone in the east." He then jumped as he heard Ethan's voice behind him.

"Thankless wench?" Ethan said with a laugh, "That's a little unkind. She's a sweet girl I think."

Feagan's eyes grew wide. He had grown complacent and not been listening for approaching strangers and now he was out in the open and easily seen, " Curse mah lugs!" he yelled, "Th' toy is a sneaky spoon!"

Ethan laughed, "I won't tell a soul, I swear." He examined Feagan as he continued forward, "You are an odd-looking faerie. You're so... brown and... disheveled. My mother keeps faeries and they tend to be bright, colourful, and well… clean."

" Ah will shaw ye disheveled," Feagan growled as he flew toward Ethan angrily.

"Feagan, no! Stop," Rune said with a sigh as he looked to Ethan, who now wore a loose light blue cloth tunic. His left arm was held inside with a sling, "How much did you hear?"

"Enough," Ethan stated plainly, watching Feagan zip around him angrily, "But you are a magi, all magi seem to have odd secrets. Don't worry, I'm not fool enough to reveal them and get on your bad side. Especially with your powers. I value my life. I have never seen a spell hit so hard." Rune swallowed but said nothing in response. "That spell," Ethan continued, "What is the origin?"

"Jist a wind speel Northerner," Feagan piped in, "Naethin' special. Sam effect ye hae when ye tak' yer sark aff nae doobt."

Ethan raised a brow at Feagan, "Take my sark off? Meaning my shirt? Forgive me, but I'm not sure if you're insulting me or flirting with me." He then let out a short uneasy laugh as Feagan made no attempt to clarify as he continued to buzz around him. His eyes then turned to the horse and he made a face as he looked it over. As he moved closer he reported, "This isn't your horse."

Rune cleared his throat, "Yeah, well..."

A silence passed as Ethan gently brushed his hand along the horse's neck. He finally said, "At first I was very surprised to hear Milla say that you were, in fact, a magi." He stopped attending to the horse and turned to Rune, idly resting his hand on his belt, "You see, we are quite knowledgeable about magik in the North. It's well known that it takes a great deal of time to master even the simplest incantations. It seemed to me she was claiming that you had enough power to actually be useful. At your age."

"Ah suppose ye dinnae ken everythin' 'en," Feagan piped in, then landed on the horse's saddle as he eyed Ethan. "Ah can teach ye a hin' ur tois I'm sure."

Turning curious eyes to Feagan for a moment, Ethan responded, "I'm not sure I'd be interested in learning what you could teach me." After Feagan shrugged he continued, "At first I thought that perhaps you were a charlatan. Tricking a young girl with promises of magik to gain payment from her, for your protective guidance on her travels." His eyes turned back to Rune, "How fitting, I thought, that this would come from the son of Weiland." Feagan moved threateningly toward Ethan as he continued, "But then I see it for myself. The most powerful spell I have ever witnessed, coming from this young magi. Not only that, but able to focus and cast your spell while being manhandled." Rune frowned but remained silent. "Rune," Ethan continued cautiously, "I am not your enemy. I have no intention to cause you harm, but you must see how my curiosity is greatly peaked right now."

"Why?" Rune asked angrily.

"My homeland is in the middle of a war, Rune. We are losing. I am not one to believe in the Fates, but Rune..." he stepped closer as he said earnestly, "I could- We, could use you."

Rune let out a laugh, "Use me? You are suggesting that I help the North?"

"And why not?" Ethan retorted, "Surely you know what will happen if the South wins. They see themselves as conquerors. The West will soon follow."

Rune shook his head, "Impossible. They would have to get their armies past the great river or take to the ocean and fight the most powerful ships on the continent."

Ethan nodded then turned back to the horse. He began to gently glide his hand along the horse's neck again as he spoke softly, "Indeed. Much like they must defeat the most powerful army in the realms. The army thought to be undefeatable. The army that proved itself undefeatable not long ago."

Rune let out a long breath, "How are they beating you anyway?"

Ethan shook his head, "I'm not sure. They have somehow boosted their numbers greatly and they have equaled our magikal strength, despite their revulsion for magik. They are also using odd tactics. They use the night and shadows to their advantage. They make a point to destroy morale and spread fear before they attack. It's..." He sighed sharply, "We don't know what to do. I don't know what to do."

Rune let out another puff of air and moved beside Ethan. He began to pet the horse's head as he said, "If I could help, I would. But," he paused and turned to look at Ethan, "Can I tell you something? You can't tell Milla."

Ethan turned to face Rune. He looked at him with a serious expression and said, "You have my word. I won't tell her."

Feagan let out a slow sigh and sat back down on the horse, simply listening to the conversation. "I can't control it," Rune said simply. "I've been trying really hard since I was young, but no matter how hard I try I can't cast. I need to be frustrated or angry or scared and then I don't even remember doing it."

Ethan watched Rune a few moments, his expression unreadable. He finally looked away as he took in a slow breath, then rubbed his head as he spoke, "No matter. I am sure we will find a way. We always do." He forced a smile then began to walk off, but stopped at Rune's side and place his hand on his shoulder, "We should get back to camp. Milla was worried about you."

Rune frowned and looked away, "I'm sure she was."

Ethan grinned down at him, "Rune, you're still young, give it time. You will fill out and grow and she will see you as a man and not a boy. It also doesn't hurt being powerful, trust me. You will find one day you will have your pick of anyone you desire and that will cause you to lose all hope of finding someone who wants you for anything but your power."

Rune frowned then turned an annoyed glare to Ethan, "I think her eyes are elsewhere anyway. You don't have any real powers. You're just a Captain but you have everything else going for you. Look at me. I have nothing."

Ethan frowned, "Well, that will change in time." He then let out a breath and removed his hand from Rune's shoulder, "She might appear to be a 'thankless wench' right now Rune but I get the sense that she is very afraid of something. It's not uncommon for the strong willed to lash out at those trying to help them when they are afraid. Much like if someone is drowning, it's hard to calm them enough so that they do not drown the one trying to rescue them. She is secretly panicking. Give her time. She is an amazing girl Rune; I can see that. It is a rare thing to find one like her. Someone with her spirit, her drive, it…," he paused and looked into the trees then back to Rune and said seriously, "She needs you, whether she knows it or not."

"So, you're saying you like her too?" Rune quickly asked, "If she likes you and you like her why not do something about it?"

Ethan let out a long breath, "Things are not always that simple Rune. Her and I could never be, no matter the feelings."

"She won't take that well," Rune said with a grin.

"As much as thes gab ay kissy-smoochy is entertainin', mair sae if it involves me, aam tired an' woods loch tae rest. Unlike ye lazy bums, I've hud a lang day." Feagan said with annoyance, "If ye need me I'll be in me pooch." He then zipped over to Rune's pack.

Rune let out a small laugh, "I'm glad you're back old friend. Sorry for causing you so much hardship."

"Eh," Feagan grouched as he found his pocket and made himself cozy.

"Is he always like that?" Ethan asked as he smiled with amusement. "All of the faeries I know don't even talk at all."

"Well, he does. All the time," Rune said, mimicking the smile.

"Ah can still hear ye!" Feagan's muffled voice croaked from inside the pouch.

"Well then," Ethan said after he and Rune laughed. He took the reins of the horse and starting toward the trees, "We should get back."
***

As they approached the camp both of their eyes turned to worry at the same time. Ethan dropped the reins and ran ahead, "Milla! Where are you?"

Rune looked around in a panic then shut his eyes tight and listened. He heard a strange humming then turned in that direction. He saw Milla off in the distance, barely noticeable in the dark as she slowly walked away, "Over there!" He yelled then ran toward her.

They ran together, and Ethan asked through pants, "How did you see her? You have amazing eyes."

"I didn't," Rune said and swallowed as he ran, "I heard her."

Ethan narrowed his eyes with confusion. As they slowed and approached her they both noticed her hair bindings had been removed and her long locks flowed in golden waves down her back. Ethan grabbed her shoulder to stop her, but she pulled away as she continued to move forward. "Milla, where are you going?" he asked then moved in front of her and faced her. He then walked backwards as she continued onward, as if he wasn't there. Her eyes were closed, and she smiled lightly as she continued to hum softly to herself. "Something's wrong," Ethan said then knelt down and forced her over his good shoulder. He held her there securely as he stood and winced at the pain it caused the wound on the opposite side. He and Rune then began to walk back to the camp.

"What's wrong with her?" Rune asked as she hummed and struggled, causing Ethan further pain.

"I don't know," Ethan said with apprehension, "Maybe an enchantment. Do you know how to break one?"

Rune shook his head vigorously, "What sort of spell is that?"

Ethan frowned, "It's not magik."

Rune tilted his head curiously then widened his eyes, "A seer?"

"Even worse, a weaver." They rushed to the camp and Ethan placed her down. He battled to keep her there as she continuously attempted to get up and his trepidation grew, "I don't know what to do, should we tie her down?

Rune swallowed hard then asked, "Maybe. What's a weaver?" He rushed to his backpack to search for the bandages he packed.

"It's what we call a seer that has gained powers beyond the sight," Ethan said, "Sort of like the Seer from the stories of the Seer Ruins."

Rune turned worried eyes to Ethan then continued to look around the camp, "I was so sure I packed long strips of bandages," he grumbled, then looked around for a rope of some sort. He noticed Milla's hair bindings on the ground and grabbed them, but they were too short and thin to do any good. He then saw her necklace laying next to where her bindings had been. He picked it up, then examined the curious black and gold stone tied to the center of the leather string. An odd marking was carved into it. It was a marking that Rune recognized from one of the tomes his father had left him, though he didn't know the meaning of it. He was suddenly struck by an odd sensation emanating from the stone. It felt soothing and protective. Soon after, the sound of a calming lullaby played in his head and a familiar feeling came over him, as if he were with his mother as she sang him to sleep in his warm bed. He shook off the feeling and furrowed his brows at the stone. Though he didn't know what it was, he decided to try one of only two options. Either assume this stone was behind the enchantment on Milla and destroy it or... "Here, let me put this back on her," he said as he rushed over. Ethan watched Rune with a curious expression but continued to hold Milla still as best he could while Rune slipped it over her head.

It took only a moment for her eyes to open and peer up at the two with bewilderment. "What are you both doing on top of me?" she asked suspiciously.

"You were enchanted," Rune said quickly, "we were saving you."

"Enchanted?" Milla asked, then quickly sat up while Ethan backed away from her marginally, "What do you mean?"

"You were walking, even though you were sleeping, and you were humming. I've heard of it before, but I've never seen it." Ethan explained.

Rune looked around with worry, "Does that mean there's a weaver nearby?"

"Not necessarily," Ethan answered, "A powerful weaver can reach a great distance."

Rune looked at Milla with concern and their eyes locked "A weaver is a seer," he said accusingly to her.

She shook her head in a clear attempt to quiet him, and quickly spoke up, "How did you stop the enchantment?"

Rune pointed to her necklace, "We put this back on you," his voice still thick with accusation.

Milla's eyes widened as she grabbed hold of the stone on her necklace and swallowed. "Well, I'm better now but we should be careful. Where did you go anyway?" she asked Rune.

Rune thought fast then answered, "To summon my pack and horse." His eyes turned to Ethan, hoping he wouldn't reveal his lie.

Milla smiled happily, "And it worked?"

Rune nodded, still looking to Ethan, who remained silent. "I'll take first watch," Rune piped in, wanting time to talk more with Feagan as soon as possible. "We shouldn't let Milla have a watch tonight, just in case," he added.

"Agreed," Ethan said, still examining Milla and her necklace. Her eyes met his as she was clearly trying to translate his expression. He furrowed his brows at her, then looked to Rune, as he moved off to fetch the horse.

As his eyes turned back to Milla and her necklace she attempted to explain, "It's just a… "

He stopped her with a finger to her mouth. "No more lies tonight," he said softly, then moved to his bed without another word.

Milla frowned and slowly moved herself to rest in her own tent.

CHAPTER 22

Queen Adva jolted awake as she was ripped from her meditation. She breathed heavily, and her eyes tore around the room as confusion gripped her. After taking a few calming breaths, she closed her eyes again, trying to return her mind to where it was, but was unable. Her eyes opened again, and she let out several furious breaths as she frowned. "Otho!" she called out.

Her massive bedroom door soon opened and Otho entered with a look of expectation, "My Queen?"

She tossed her covers off and threw her legs over the side of the bed, then stood and put her hand to her forehead as she walked to the window, "Tell me, how many seers of potential live beneath my heel?"

Otho shook his head, "Only three, and you know of them all."

"Have you heard word of others, in the neighboring lands?" she continued.

Otho shook his head, "No, none come to mind. Other than the rumors of Thane Od. The east and west have banned them, the west being harsher than all others in their execution of the bans, understandably so. News from the south is limited, especially now. With the war," He said as if reminding her, "Why do you ask my Queen? Do you sense a seer amongst our enemy's forces? Should we be worried?"

"Enemy forces?" the Queen then asked, looking confused.

"The war... my queen." Otho rebuked, the annoyance in his voice apparent.

Adva shook her head and said as she waved it off with her hand, "No, I do not feel as if it is coming from the distant south."

"The war is not distant," Otho growled, "It draws closer by the day. If you could only-"

"No," she interrupted, "the war is of little concern to me right now."

Otho frowned deeply, "Adva, this war of little concern, is a war we are currently losing."

She glowered as she responded sharply, "Do you doubt me, Otho? Do you doubt my ability to rule this land? Do you doubt my ability to protect it? I have defended this land through far worse than this petty squabble. I know we will not lose and I will not have my work interrupted by a skirmish that will end in my favor whether I involve myself or not. Do you quite understand?"

Otho grimaced and looked to the floor, "I understand, my Queen."

Adva smiled then sighed as she turned a calmed gaze out the window, "Good. Now tell me, how many more come to my home to bare the fruit of my teachings?"

"There have been no others my queen. We are all but full now as it is," Otho answered.

Adva frowned, "I fear there may be more needed. Amongst them, the one I seek. Perhaps they are being protected... warded. I must not be disturbed until I find out who and where. Do you understand?"

"Yes, my queen," Otho said in a monotone voice with a bow of his head.

The queen moved back to her chair, "When I say no one, I mean it. Not for food, not for drink, not to seek advise for the war. All duties I place in the hands of my husband the king. Is this understood?"

Otho nodded and bowed fully, "Yes, Lucretia- forgive me, Queen Adva," he said, his voice thick with criticism as he turned his eyes up to meet hers.

"You dare," she snarled as she turned toward him threateningly.

"Forgive me," Otho said, lacking the apologetic tone, "A slip of the tongue."

Their eyes remained locked as her fury rose, "Get out of my sight," she snapped and promptly turned away.

Otho raised from his bow, still eyeing her critically. He then turned and left the room.

CHAPTER 23

The day began with a warm, pleasant breeze from the east. It caressed the faces of the young travelers and lifted the spirits of their horses, who now insisted on moving forward in a steady canter while whipping their manes and tails to catch the breeze. The journey continued with few words as was becoming the norm, while the three remained in deep thought regarding the night before. Much to their relief, the night had passed with no further excitement or interruption. Rune and Feagan found a good amount of time for idle talk and silly antics while the other two slept.

By mid-day, they approached a very large and jagged black boulder at the side of the road. Its texture was rough and had embedded flecks that twinkled in the sunlight. As they approached, the large dragon symbol on it became clearer, marking this as the border to the East.

"Already?" Ethan said as he slowed his horse and stopped short of crossing the boulder's path. His horse seemed unhappy about stopping and protested by stomping its foot and bobbing its head. Ethan attempted to sooth the beast by stroking the neck. "They are oddly spirited today," he said as the other two trotted up next to him.

"Are we taking a break so soon?" Milla asked after she moved along his left side and stopped, also stroking the neck of her energetic horse. Rune said nothing as he endeavored to keep control of his own horse that struggled against the reigns to keep moving forward, forcing Rune to walk it in a few circles as the other two spoke.

"I'm afraid this is where I have to leave you," Ethan said with a sigh as he kept his eyes on the road ahead, "I cannot go into the East."

"What?" Milla said, anxiously, "But..."

Ethan pulled his reigns gently, maneuvering his horse to face west. He reached over and touched Milla's hand as he looked to her with a sad smile, "My home and my duty remains in the north. The horses are yours to keep.

I hope they continue to speed your journey."

"But," Milla said again appearing highly distraught, "If you could come this far, why not a little further? At least until we reach a town. Surly there is one not far from here. We can stop for a proper meal and say proper goodbyes. We hardly even had a chance to speak."

Ethan frowned and shook his head, "I'm sorry, I can't." He turned to look toward the west and eyed Rune as his arms were holding the reins wide while his horse walked sideways. He then instructed, "Thankfully, there are no bridges from here to the next town. Be sure to avoid-"

"Is there a law forbidding Northerners to pass into the east?" Milla interrupted.

"No," Ethan said turning grieved eyes to her, "My circumstances are different though. Now if you just follow this road, keep to your-"

"Different how?" Milla persisted.

Rune piped in, finally gaining control of his horse, "Milla, he was kind enough to lead us this far and has given us more help than we could have dared expect of him, or anyone for that matter. We shouldn't intrude on his time more." He then added, "Thank you Ethan, it's been a pleasure riding with you and thank you for everything you've done for us. I hope we can repay you some day."

Before Ethan could respond, Milla held his hand tightly with both of hers as she stubbornly insisted, "Please, just tell me why you can't cross, so I can understand."

Ethan looked into Milla's pleading eyes and let out a hard breath. He then pulled her hands toward his lips and kissed them gently, "Fare well Milla. Be safe." He then pulled away and turned to Rune saying, "You owe me nothing. It's been an honour knowing you. I am confident we will meet again."

Rune nodded, and Ethan rode off without another word. Rune then turned to look at Milla as tears filled her eyes, "Are you alright?" he asked cautiously.

She sniffed and wiped her eyes then growled, "Let's just go," and she kicked her horse gently to start again eastward.

"Look Milla," Rune said as he kicked his own horse, wobbling in his saddle as it lurched forward and caught up, "It was nice having him around to protect us, but we can do this without him. You're tough and good with a bow and with my magik no one can touch us. I think we've proved that by now."

"Let's just not talk for a bit," Milla said as she continued ahead, urging her horse to move faster.

Rune attempted to catch up as he continued, "Milla, we're friends, right? If you need to-"

"We're not friends Rune," she barked back, "We're just traveling together.

I'm paying you remember? Let's just get this over with." she said and urged her horse into a canter.

Rune frowned as his heart visibly sank and he reined in his horse. At that moment, he wanted nothing more than to turn around and head home. He forced angry breaths through his nose then pulled the reins to turn, but something inside him forced him to stop. A strong feeling rose inside him, telling him that he needed to follow her despite his anger. He clenched his jaw and let out another angry breath as he readjusted himself and urged his horse eastward, following a good distance behind.

***

Ethan continued his way west, back towards Silvius. He had stopped several times and looked back to the east, a look of concern set deep in his features, but he resisted the urge to turn back. As he expected, he eventually met up with a company of his own men, his black mount in tow. Once they were at speaking distance, Ethan nodded a greeting, "Captain Argus, I didn't realize you would be with the others."

"All clear," Captain Argus said in response after a salute of armoured hand to chest.

"You found none?" Ethan asked, clearly disheartened as he dismounted his horse and moved his belongings to his usual steed, first checking the site of the injury it had taken days before. "You heal far quicker than I, Kenget."

"It looks like there are either no remaining traitors, or they are staying well hidden for now." Argus answered as he casually turned his horse back toward the west, and the other men followed suit. "We have a camp nearby. It's all ready for you." Ethan gently caressed the neck of the kir'og as he drifted off in thought and the beast sniffed at his wounded shoulder. "Your highness?" Argus asked after a few moments passed.

Ethan came out of his thoughts and looked to him, then tapped the beast on the side. As it lowered itself down he spoke, "So this was for nothing then."

"Better to be cautious. We should head out. The sun will set soon."

Ethan nodded lightly then threw his leg over the lowered beast to mount it. It took the loose reins into its mouth and handed them to Ethan and he smiled, "I missed you, boy." He took the reins then rubbed the beast's neck before tapping it on the side again. It raised itself back to standing and Ethan winced lightly as the jolt pained his shoulder. He pulled the reins to the side to urge the beast to turn, but it pulled back and shook its head. Ethan laughed, "Is this how we're starting the day?"

"Perhaps you should ride the horse for now," Argus suggested. "He's been like this all day."

115

Ethan smiled, "He's just upset I rode out on another." He patted the beast then looked off to the east again. "Tell me Argus, if you were heading into the east and unknowingly came to the Myrkwood fork, what would be your choice, knowing nothing of the area?"

Argus thought a moment then answered, "I would take the south road. It is the high road."

Ethan nodded slowly, "That's the soldier in you talking. What if you were not a soldier?"

Argus sighed quietly, clearly tired of the question, "It would depend where I was going I suppose. With the war in the south encroaching I might take the north path thinking it safer." Ethan cursed under his breath at this answer and Argus raised a brow at him, "Should we not head to camp now, your Majesty?"

Ethan turned an annoyed glance to him, "It's Captain. How many times must I insist?"

"My apologies, Captain Ethan." Argus returned with a hint of insolence, "Your speedy assent into the ranks does make the title slow to the lips."

Ethan furrowed his brows lightly, then ordered. "You and the men make your way to the camp. I will join you later. Wait for me there." And he began to urge his beast toward the east.

"Captain, I cannot just-," Argus started.

"That's an order!" Ethan called back as he urged his mount into a gallop.

Argus clenched his jaw as he watched Ethan speed off, then looked around to the other men, "It seems Captain Ethan has given us an order. Our task will be delayed."

***

Time passed slowly as they continued. Their surroundings eventually changed from the soft greenery and rolling hills that they had seen from Silvius until the border. The grass changed from the long, bright green, wavy strands - to thicker, darker green blades. The land changed from rolling hills to jagged mounds, and a thick evergreen forest slowly encompassed the area. It hadn't taken long for Milla to slow to a walk and allow Rune to close the distance between them, though he remained a good distance back still. The sun was now ready to complete its regular decent into the horizon and Rune was beginning to think it was time to set up camp but dreaded the thought of trying to speak to Milla about it. To his relief, he didn't have to initiate anything, as he saw her slow and then stop at a fork in the road. The road split around a rocky ridge, inclining to the southeast and declining the northeast. There was no sign indicating where the roads lead and she seemed to be stuck pondering as she looked up one way, and then down the other while Rune approached.

"Which way?" she asked as he moved up next to her.

"How would I know?" he snapped, "I don't even know where we're going other than 'east' and both of those roads go east."

"You're the one with magik," Milla growled, "Make it guide us."

"Where?!" Rune barked with a fury.

Milla seemed shocked by his outburst as she turned sharply to look at him. She scowled and seemed ready to say something, but sneered instead and urged her horse forward, taking the northeastern road.

Rune frowned deeply as he followed, now even more upset, as it appeared that they wouldn't be making camp any time soon. The sun continued to set, and the haze of dusk crept over the land as they entered the opening of the evergreen forest. The forest itself would have been quite difficult to travel through without a road or pathway, as the land amongst the trees was riddled with bushes and ferns of all sorts, as well as plenty of large boulders and fallen trees, young and old. Thick moss, ivy and fungus grew plentifully, and emitted a fragrant earthy aroma.

A fog then slowly began to roll in from all around, thickening at the base of the earthen ridge to their left. Rune sped up his horse to move closer to Milla, partly from the need to keep her in sight, and partly from fear, as their surroundings began to gain an eerie appearance. They continued until the fog thickened so much that they could only see a few steps ahead of them. Rune finally spoke up, "Look, I can barely see the road, maybe we should stop for the night."

Milla turned to him with a frown, seeming ready to argue but sighed, "Maybe you're right, I-"

"Look!" Rune interrupted and pointed ahead.

Milla quickly turned to see what appeared to be lights in the distance ahead, "Do you think it's a town?" she asked with high hopes.

"Maybe," Rune said as he began to ride toward it, "There's only one way to find out." Milla urged her horse into a trot and they followed the road toward the lights. After riding for several moments, they both reigned in and stopped as they didn't seem to be getting any closer. "Odd," Rune muttered as he peered at the lights thoughtfully, "What do you think it is then?" Milla shook her head, then jumped slightly as the lights instantly disappeared. "I don't like this," Rune said as the hairs on his arms stood and a feeling of impending doom took over, "Maybe we should turn around."

"Agreed," Milla piped in anxiously then began to turn her horse. As she did she let out a yelp and looked to her arm to see what it was that caused her pain. A tiny spear stuck out of her skin and dangled lightly. She reached to pull it out but cried out as she was struck again further up her arm.

Rune hollered as he was then struck and flailed as he was pierced several times quickly after. "What in the-!" he yelled out and both horses began to shriek and rear, forcing both riders to hold on for dear life. Milla regained control through the pain and kicked her horse into a gallop, back in the direction they came from. Rune couldn't regain control and fell from his horse. It quickly bucked and ran to follow Milla but passed her swiftly. He huddled and howled as he covered his face and head while being struck several more times.

Milla screamed as her horse skid to a stop due to a wall of faeries that quickly formed in front of her. They buzzed and taunted as they threw their tiny spears with a sea of high pitched laughs. She then fell from her horse as it reared and shrieked, and she hit the ground hard but quickly huddled to protect her eyes from the onslaught of spears that followed.

"Milla!" Rune yelled out as he heard her scream then tried to run toward her, but the spiking pain from all directions became too much. He let out a growl and yelled out as a force burst out of him, creating an ear numbing boom. Trees and branches nearby splintered and cracked from the force, that also propelled all faeries and spears close by away from him. Although Milla was now a distance away, the force even reached her and hurled her backward, skidding her along the dirt road a short distance. The faeries surrounding her were scattered like leaves in a gust of wind and they all quickly disappeared out of sight. Rune's eyes widened as awareness of what he just did settled in, but he thought fast and ran for Milla. As he reached her she pushed herself up and began gasping harshly. He grabbed hold of her and forced her to stand and run with him, but she continued desperately gasping for air as they scurried away.

"Rune!" Milla heaved, "I can't!" she gasped again and forced him to stop as she dropped to her knees wheezing heavily. They were quickly surrounded by a swarm of faeries, so Rune dropped down and wrapped his arms around Milla to guard her as best he could, then buried his head as he tensed and awaited the spikes of pain. Not a single spear had been thrown though, as the sound of a man yelling distracted them. A torch flame burst through the fog followed by Ethan's blaring war cry, and the faeries scattered and zipped off in random directions, disappearing into the fog.

"Take it!" Ethan yelled to Rune as he forced the torch into Rune's hand. Rune grabbed hold of it and Ethan quickly removed his sling and used both arms to lift Milla and throw her over his right shoulder, growling through the pain. He then grabbed Rune tightly by the arm and dragged him into a run. "Wave it at any that get near!" he ordered as they ran.

Rune looked around waving the torch at every shadow before he heard a familiar voice crying out, "Rune help!" His eyes widened as he turned to see Feagan buzzing his wings fiercely as he was being pulled away by several of the savage faeries.

Rune pulled back trying to get Ethan to let go of him, but the grasp was too strong. "Let me go!" he demanded, but the hold remained unshakable as Ethan continued his charge.

They finally made it out of the forest and the fog began dissipating. Ethan began to slow marginally and move towards the black mount that he had abandoned there. It happily and obliviously sniffed at the grass by the side of the road, as if following the scent of a small creature, taking little notice to their approach. By the time they neared the beast, the fog had almost completely dispersed. Ethan released Rune as he stopped and panted heavily. He then placed Milla down who continued her gasping as she put her hand to her chest. Ethan swallowed and began plucking the remaining tiny spears from Milla's body as he asked through his heavy breathing, "What's wrong? Why are you gasping?"

"Rune," she wheezed and coughed, "His spell. It hit me."

Ethan turned wide eyes to Rune who returned a fearful and apologetic look. After a quick moment of thought, Ethan swiftly and carefully moved her to the side of the road and laid her down, "Try to be calm," he said soothingly, "Slow, steady breaths." He began demonstrating how he wanted her to breathe as he moved his hands over her ribs. She tried her best to comply as her cheeks flushed. He completed his check of her back and front ribs then sighed in relief. "You've just had the wind knocked from you I think. Just keep breathing steady, you'll be fine." Milla nodded and complied as she rested her head back into the grass. "I heard a voice," she said in an outward breath, "Calling for Rune's help."

Rune's turned back toward the fog with a look of distress, "I have to go back," he said as he held up the torch in an attempt to see through the deepening darkness.

"No!" Ethan roared, "Whatever you left or dropped isn't worth it. They'll tear you apart. Faeries are far stronger than they appear."

Rune hesitated, "I have to! I'll use my magik again to get rid of them!"

Ethan stood and stormed to Rune, grabbing him by the shoulder, "You go back in there then you better damn well hope you can rely on that magik or you're not coming back out!"

Rune shifted unsteadily as he spoke quietly, "They have him."

Ethan's eyes widened, and he lurched toward the valley himself, then stopped. He paced a moment as he placed his right hand on his forehead while he thought.

"You're bleeding, "Rune piped in suddenly as he looked to the large wet blood stain on Ethan's left shoulder.

Ethan looked to the blood and cursed quietly. He then let out a sharp breath and placed his hand back on Rune's shoulder, squeezing it lightly and speaking softly, "He wouldn't want you to throw your life away. We'd have no way of finding him. He's so small and Myrkwood is so big."

"That was the dark forest?" Rune asked with despair, then dropped to his knees and covered his face with his free hand as he continued to hold the torch up, "No..."

Ethan nodded solemnly, "The outskirts." He then moved back to Milla who was now beginning to regain her breath. As he knelt down to check on her, she quickly jumped up and wrapped her arms around him. He winced in pain, then widened his eyes as he was unsure how to react.

She squeezed tight as she exclaimed, "Thank you so much for coming back for us!"

Rune looked to them, then back toward the valley. Anger rose up in him and he stood and growled loud, "Why didn't you come sooner? What took you so long? You could have stopped us from even going in there! Why didn't you warn us?"

"Rune!" Milla barked, "He just saved our lives and that's how you thank him?"

Rune let out another frustrated growl and looked back toward the declining road. He paced back and forth in front of it as he continued, "Just a few moments sooner, why not a few moments? Why did you even come back?"

"Rune!" Milla barked again.

"It's alright," Ethan said to her, "He's right. This is my fault. I meant to warn you about the northeast path. I didn't realize that I hadn't until I was well on my way. I turned around and returned to you as soon as I could. I am deeply sorry."

"What matters is that you arrived in time to save us. You were under no obligation to tell us anything or return, so thank you," Milla said then hugged him tight. He awkwardly returned her embrace then turned an apologetic look toward Rune.

"You're right," Rune then growled, "This isn't his fault. It's your fault! You distracted him. You're the one that chose the path. This is your bloody journey and you don't even know where in the bloody void you're going!" At that he threw the torch to the ground and turned to look down the path.

Milla and Ethan both turned wide eyes to Rune's outburst. Milla's eyes began to tear, but she quickly shook it off and pushed herself to stand.

Rune fought back tears of his own as he then shook his head, "Let's just get back to the fork before the faeries get brave and leave the fog. You need to have your shoulder looked at quickly anyway I think," he said as he roughly picked up the torch and moved down the path, kicking a rock out of the way.

Milla took a quick look at Ethan's shoulder and her brows furrowed with worry, "Your stitches broke."

Ethan turned up half his lips in a forced smile, "I think it was the skin that broke."

Milla scrambled to help him stand. "We need to fix it as soon as possible. Let's go."

Ethan took the reins of his horse as he passed it, and the three trudged back towards the fork, saying nothing else.

CHAPTER 24

A deep darkness engulfed the land as the moonless night set in. Major Peleg sat casually on his horse as he watched over the massive, distant campsite to the south from the high ridge. Hundreds of campfire flames lit the horizon into a haze of orange that seemed to darken the land outside the light's reach. A cool breeze danced in from the south, carrying with it the smell of burning wood and mud. "There is a foul wind tonight," he gnarled toward the man next to him.

"With all due respect, Major, keep those thoughts to yourself," Commander Ronen said with a grin as he adjusted in his saddle, "We can't have the men sharing your feeling of doom. The south has never been able to take the ridge. If we do our duty well, that will not change on this day."

Major Peleg frowned deeply, "Thirty men, Commander. Thirty traitors in our midst. Men I have known and trusted for years, turning on their own realm with such vigor and fire. Willing to lay down their own lives to avoid capture. What could have turned their hearts from our good and honourable realm? What could have turned their will so profoundly? Not dreg or power. What good is that in the afterlife?"

Commander Ronen adjusted in his saddle again, saying nothing at first. Finally speaking he shook his head, "Turning on the realm is a story as old as war itself. Their reasons will come to light in time. What I can not fathom was their turning on the Captain. Seeking not just his defeat but his death. Prince Ethan is a popular man and he treated the soldiers well, even better than thought acceptable by most. Did they forget all the victories he had lead them through time and time again? Maybe his brother was more political and had the grander title, but Ethan had something far more precious; the admiration and trust of his men. But now..."

Major Peleg allowed the thought to hang. After exhaling slowly, his gravelly voice rippled through the silence, "The Captain was confident that there were even more traitors amongst us and was set to weed them out after I left. I worry for his safety now."

"Weed them out how?" Ronen asked as he turned curious eyes to Peleg.

The Major remained silent a moment as his eyes narrowed. He then answered, "When he asked for volunteers to stay behind with him to deal with a threat in the North, that was his first move. What traitor would not want a chance to remain near him and gain an opportunity to strike?"

"A dangerous move," Ronen grunted, "How will he know which are traitors, and which are loyal men only seeking to help their realm?"

"He also kept some of his most trusted men behind with him. Captain Argus among them." Peleg continued. "He was fortunate enough to find two travelers caught in a hard position. Their timing could not have been better. It seems he intends to use them as bait."

Commander Ronen nodded his head slowly as he looked back toward the distant camp, "A dark time indeed when such tactics are necessary."

Peleg nodded at that, "Even now, sleep does not come easy for any of the men. They fear a blade from the bed next to them. For many nights to come, we dine on confusion and mistrust."

"And so, we are weak, which is what the South wants, I suppose," Ronen said with a sigh.

"And so, the foul wind blows, Commander. They look to strike soon, before our morale is recovered."

"Perhaps," Ronen said, then narrowed his eyes as they both looked out to the vast encampment.

"I have not seen any movement," Peleg then muttered, "None at all."

Ronen's eyes narrowed further, "Nor have I."

"No sign of torches carried, no shadows walking across flame and fire. Nothing." Peleg shifted uneasily in his saddle then turned his eyes away from the glow of the encampment. He attempted to focus into the surrounding darkness.

Ronen's eyes turned to Peleg, "It's nearly unheard of to attack at night."

"Isn't that what we thought the last time they attacked?" Peleg growled, "Not only did they attack at night, but it was during a storm."

"They don't have the noise of the storm and the distraction of a misleading forward assault from another direction this time," Ronen continued.

"Missing the point entirely Commander, they used trickery to overwhelm us." His eyes continued to drift over the darkness. "There have been no signs of large scale troop movement and our scouts have reported nothing. How would they gain ground on us on such a quiet night?" Peleg asked.

"They couldn't. It would be impossible."

There was a short silence between the two as they gazed out into the night. It was instantly broken by a crackling thunk followed by a sputtering gurgle. Peleg's eyes turned to the sound, only to see a reddened arrow pierced through Ronen's neck as blood erupted from his mouth and nose. Peleg reared his horse from shock then heard and felt the clang of an arrow on his armour. Quickly turning and leaning forward to protect his own neck, he spurred his horse toward his own encampment. "The enemy! The enemy is here!" He yelled out as arrows sped by him. His horse shrieked as it was struck in the rear causing it to gallop even faster.

Soldiers rushed from their tents and armed themselves as the night watch hurriedly moved to defensive positions with spear and sword ready. Archers promptly prepared themselves and aimed into the shadows beyond the encampment as Peleg leaped from his horse and unsheathed his blade as he turned, ready to take on whatever enemy lay in the blackness.

A long, resounding silence soon enveloped the encampment as they all waited in prepared anticipation. Time seemed to slow and drag on, but the silence remained.

"Where's Commander Ronen?" A nearby soldier asked Peleg.

Peleg turned his view to the soldier then shook his head once as an answer before he returned his eyes to the darkness.

"What should we do?" Another soldier then asked. It was clear he was not the only one becoming anxious with the long silent wait as a hum of murmurs and shifting began to get louder and louder.

Peleg cleared his thoughts and called out, "Hold your ground! The enemy is out there; they wait for us to show weakness!" The men seemed to regain focus as they quieted down.

The silence was broken with the whistle of many arrows that swiftly showered the camp. Shields quickly moved to cover and only a few men were hit, but the cries of those struck echoed and unnerved the other men still taking cover.

"Steady!" Peleg cried out as he too awaited the end of the hailing onslaught while sharing a neighboring shield. As soon as the arrows stopped, the encampment was rushed by mounted soldiers, howling a beastly war cry. "Attack!" Peleg roared as he pushed out of shield cover and swung out at the first enemy that approached him.

The familiar sound of battle then ensued as blade clashed against blade, armour, and flesh. Cries of war, pain and terror echoed through the air as the battle erupted amidst the camp. Confusion and disorganization set Peleg and his men at a significant disadvantage as the enemy surrounded and herded them into a massive, tight crowd. Major Peleg saw the battle turning against them and cried out, "On me!" as he charged north in an attempt to break the enemy line. He and the soldiers successfully burst through and Peleg promptly called out, "Second with me! The rest retreat to the North! Back to Silvius!"

He and the Second Sons turned and protected the rear and flank as the rest retreated north. The clash continued until the bulk of the army finally passed, allowing Peleg and the Second to begin their slow retreat as well. They took heavy losses, but eventually were able to break safely from the battle and retreat. The south army didn't pursue, and instead turned back to the ridge encampment to reap their rewards of the supplies, horses and survivors left behind. The retreating army continued their way north unhindered, in the silent walk of defeat.

CHAPTER 25

Rune yawned as he held the torch above Milla to give her enough light to finish her stitching of Ethan's reopened wound. She had already completed the entry wound on his back and was now finishing up the exit wound. Ethan hissed as needle punctured skin one last time then firmly rubbed the sweat from his brow. Milla spoke softly as she finished, turning concerned eyes to Ethan, "Helping us just seems to make your injury worse. You should be resting and healing."

"It will be fine," he said with a reassuring smile. "How did you learn to stitch wounds anyway?"

"My omi taught me," she answered then removed the wet cloth from her shoulder to wipe the area around the wound.

"She taught you well," Ethan smiled faintly at her, clearly near exhaustion.

"We could use more bandages," Milla then said as she re-examined her work.

"I thought I packed a bunch, but I couldn't find them the last time I looked," Rune said with a sigh. "I'd look again if I didn't lose my pack again."

"And you'll get it back again," Milla said softly. "I doubt the faeries took it at least."

"We should figure out a way to set a trap for those pests and kill them all, so they don't do that to anyone else," Rune grumbled, "Shouldn't there be a marker, warning travelers?"

"From what I've heard, they've tried," Ethan answered as he watched Milla dab the wound lightly to clean it. "The faeries always remove it or turn it in the other direction." As he watched her stand and move to the fire he continued, "And I don't think killing them is the answer, it would just make their kind hate us even more."

"Is that even possible?" Rune griped, "They hate us enough to attack random travelers and even lure them away from a safe path right into their tiny spears. They want war. I say we eradicate them. Then they won't be able to harm anyone else."

Ethan turned chastising eyes up at Rune, "They're not all bad Rune. You should know that better than anyone. They have reason to hate us."

"Do you think the stories are true then?" Milla asked as she carefully cleaned the needle in a small bowl of water. "They used thousands of faeries to suppress the Great Seer's powers?"

"Likely," Ethan answered, as he adjusted himself into a more comfortable position. "It's common practice in the north to keep faeries as a ward against seers. It's still widely thought that they can block seer power or influence. How true that is, I couldn't tell you."

"They keep them as pets?" Rune asked with a frown.

Ethan nodded a few times in answer as his tired eyes drifted to the fire.

Rune frowned deeply then moved to sit by the fire, "Well, you are now the only one with a horse or supplies. What are we supposed to do now?"

Milla looked to Ethan with sadness in her eyes, "Will you be leaving us again?"

Ethan turned his eyes to hers as he took in a slow breath. His mouth opened as if to answer, but instead he just let out a noise, shook his head, and looked off into the darkness. After a moment of quiet he looked up to the sky, "It's an especially dark night. I will at least make camp with you until dayspring."

Milla turned her glum expression to the ground as she stood, "I'll set up what I can, then."

"I'm sorry," Ethan said as he painfully pushed himself to stand, "May I suggest that you both return to Silvius with me. If for nothing else than to resupply. I would happily make sure you both have all you need for your journey."

Milla nodded, "We really have little choice than to turn back now. We have nothing to survive on." She moved to the calm black mount and began to unstrap Ethan's pack from the saddle.

"I truly did intend to warn you," he continued, "If I would have..."

Rune shook his head as he placed the torch next to the fire. "What's done is done. Milla was right, at least you came back."

Ethan shook his head and rubbed his tired eyes. Rune moved closer to him and whispered, "He's one of them. I can still have hope that they haven't harmed him. I just know he didn't leave them on the best terms... he said he could never go back."

Ethan lowered his hand and looked to Rune. He then offered a reassuring nod and smile as he whispered back, "I have heard they're not known to harm one of their own. Even for the worst crimes they often just banish-,"

"Do either of you hear that?" Milla spoke up as she stopped all movement and listened. The other two stopped their whispering and listened. The sound of stomping and heavy breathing faintly resonated from a distance unseen. "What is that?" Milla said with fear.

Ethan grinned, then let aloud clicks of his tongue, followed by a sharp whistle. Moments later, both Milla and Rune's horses calmly walked into site, snorting and bobbing their heads. Rune ran over to his horse with high hopes, swiftly checking his pack. The pocket that Feagan had prepared as a temporary home for himself was ripped open and all the soft contents had been pulled out. His shoulders dropped as he frowned, "Well, at least we have our supplies. No need to turn back."

"Bandages?" Milla quickly asked as she moved to place Ethan's pack closer to the fire while he stood and moved to gather her horse.

Rune checked the pack and frowned as he realized Feagan's oversized flask was taking up the spot that he had put the bandages. He quietly laughed before a sad expression took over. "No bandages," he finally answered. "But I have this."

Milla narrowed her eyes as she moved closer and tried to make out what he held out. She then raised a brow. "Well I suppose that's useful too. We can clean the wound with it. My herbs should suffice for now though."

"Let's get to setting up camp then," Ethan suggested as he moved to Milla with her horse in tow. He placed his hand on her shoulder before she could step past to her horse's saddle, "If I knew where you plan on going, I might be able to give you safe directions."

Milla swallowed as she turned to face him, "I don't know. East."

Ethan's eyes narrowed, and he tilted his head, "That's an odd answer. What exactly is your business in the east?"

"You can tell us both," Rune added as he moved next to Ethan, "I think at this point we both deserve to know."

Milla thought a moment then placed a hand on her head as she sighed, "I'm looking for my little sister Lorelei. She was stolen."

"She was taken east?" Ethan asked, with a puzzled expression, as he removed his hand.

Milla shrugged then moved off towards her horse, "I don't know. I don't know much really. I just..." She struggled to remove her pack from the saddle as she continued, "I was out picking herbs when it happened, so I don't know anything for sure. I just know that when I returned I found my mother crying. When I finally got her to tell me what was wrong she told me Leilei's real father took her. I didn't even know that my father wasn't Leilei's real father until then."

"And this man who is her father, he lives in the east?" Ethan prodded, still trying to make sense of the situation.

Milla looked to him sheepishly and shrugged, "I don't know. I don't know who he is, I just know I need to go east."

"Tell him how you know that," Rune scoffed.

Milla turned her head violently toward Rune, frowning deeply at him. She then closed her eyes and let out a sharp breath. Giving up on her pack for now, she turned to face them both and crossed her arms, "I knew an old woman, a seer, nearby... my omi. So, I went to her to find out where my sister was taken." Her eyes turned to Ethan expectantly, but he only seemed ready to listen, so she continued. "She told me her sight was blocked by a darkness in the east and that all paths to my sister would be blocked until I cleared it. She told me to head east, find Rune, and continue east until we cleared the darkness. Once we do, I go back to her and she will be able to direct me to my sister. I hope. So, I go east."

Ethan frowned and nodded, "Your mother wouldn't tell you the identity of Lorelei's father?"

Milla shook her head, "She's... she hasn't been quite normal for a long time. Something broke her mind not long before she had Lorelei. It was hard enough getting what I did from her."

"My condolences," Ethan offered with an understanding frown. "So, let me be sure that I have this straight. Someone, most likely her father, took your sister. Then your omi, who is the seer you spoke with, told you specifically to find Rune?"

Milla stopped and thought, "Well, she didn't say his name, but she directed me to his town and told me to accept the magi offered."

Ethan turned his next question to Rune, "How many other magi are in your town?"

Rune shook his head, "None."

Ethan took a moment to mull over the information as he looked at Rune with great curiosity. "So, despite her not using a name, she did, in fact, direct you to Rune. A boy who just happens to be the son of Weiland. A man that, if the stories are correct, discovered the secret to the power of the Great Seer. It also, just so happened, that you yourself were enchanted by a seer, and directed off to- well, we're not sure where you would have ended up. All that saved you was that necklace."

Milla grasped at the necklace and spoke softly, "She told me to never remove it. She made me promise."

"Clearly it is intended to protect you from something then. I would be curious to see where it leads you," Ethan added as he eyed the hand enveloping the stone.

"Nowhere good," Milla said as she continued to hold tight to it. "She made it very clear that any other path I took that was not Rune's would lead to my death."

"So, it is Rune who leads us after all," Ethan said as his eyes turned distant.

"Why do we call him the Great Seer?" Milla quickly asked, "Didn't he have a name?"

"Superstition," Ethan explained as he returned from his thoughts. "Many fear that saying the name might summon him back to us. So, the name is not spoken. For those that aren't superstitious, it is simply impolite to say the name. Regardless, I need to put this together in my head."

"I see where this is going," Rune barked, "You're somehow pointing the blame at me for this. You think this is some sort of evil plan of my father's."

"You have to admit the coincidences are adding up Rune," Ethan piped in, "Whether you are aware of it or not, Milla finding you was not a coincidence and it is your path, wrought with continuous danger, that we follow."

"We walked right in between a war!" Rune retorted.

"Exactly," Ethan returned, "A darkness that needs to be cleared, as Milla's seer said. She thinks you can stop this war. Maybe she sees the danger of this war to her land and somehow, she knew of you. Maybe she thought your parents left you with whatever it was that they found. Something of great power that can end this war."

Rune folded his arms and turned away, "This is ridiculous. They didn't leave me anything but a few tomes and my clothes."

Milla then piped in, "This has nothing to do with Rune. My omi only cared about saving Leilei and making sure I survived to be able to find her. I admit I'm impressed by Rune's power too but how can a young boy stop a war? We've been barely getting through it as it is, and not once were we given any opportunity to end it or even get involved other than getting captured. Whatever the darkness she was referring to is, it must be further east. Unless you can tell me that, despite now being in the east, we hold the fate of your war in our hands."

Ethan furrowed his brows as he looked back and forth between the two. His expression then turned to a deep-set worry and he turned to his horse, "We'll worry about it at dayspring. Let's set up camp."

Milla and Rune gave each other a confused look as Ethan easily dropped the subject and moved to unbuckle the bedroll from his pack. He struggled with it as the pain in his shoulder still resonated down his arm. Milla quickly moved to him and placed her hand on his arm to stop him. His eyes turned to hers with a face of clear frustration. She smiled kindly at him then completed the unbuckling and removed the bedroll. "I'll get some herbs to help with the pain after I lay this out." She said as she unrolled the bed near the fire.

Ethan rubbed his forehead then stood and moved to the bed, smiling down at Milla as she passed to move to her pack. "Thank you," he said then moved to the bed and laid down.

Milla returned the smile then moved to retrieve the herbs as Rune set out his own bed and said, "Imagine where Ethan would be if he ended up helping travelers with no herbs at all."

"In a lot of pain," Milla answered as she turned with what she needed and looked to Ethan. Her lips turned to a faint smile as she noticed he was clearly fast asleep. "He suffers so much because of us," she spoke softly to Rune and quietly moved to Ethan's side and knelt down next to him.

"You should let him sleep," Rune said after a sigh. "He clearly needs it."

"Yes, he does, and I don't want him waking in pain," she returned as she opened the satchel that contained the remains of the poultice she had made during their last night at camp. Ethan remained still and sleeping as she gently smeared it onto the wound.

CHAPTER 26

Lorelei giggled as she watched the group of girls play in the soft grass as she happily munched on her fluffy sweet bread. The tallest of the group had wrapped a white sheet around herself in a makeshift gown as she pretended to be the queen. She walked around the others with her nose held high, issuing ridiculous commands to those that were pretending to be ladies of the court. "And you there! You must wash all the fish in the bay! I will not have dirty fish in my realm!" She ordered haughtily, and Lorelei laughed again as her legs dangled beneath the bench.

Her head turned as she took notice of someone sitting down next to her, but the bright morning sun blazing through the large garden gate made it difficult to see who it was at first. She guarded her eyes from the sunlight to see a slender, elegant woman gracefully adjusting herself into a comfortable position. The woman's white brocade gown caught Lorelei's eye the most, as the gold embroidery and lace sparkled in the sunlight. The cuffs and collar stood rigid and long and were lined with a soft and lustrous golden fabric. Lorelei's widened gaze then drifted up to the woman's golden hair, done up in many large braids and wrapped into a high bun. Weaved within the braids sat a golden crown, decorated with clear sparkling crystals.

"Why do you not join them?" her womanly voice asked as she turned a warm smile down at Lorelei. Lorelei did not speak at first, still in awe of the woman who waited patiently for a reply. When none was given, the woman looked to the girls playing and said with a small amount of humor, "The sweet bread is that good, is it?"

Lorelei broke from her enchantment and looked down at her snack. She spoke softly, "It is very good. I'm Lorelei. Who are you?"

"I am Adva," she said turning a warm smile to Lorelei, "The head mistress told me of you. She said you do not remember coming here."

Lorelei shook her head and corrected, "I do remember. I remember some of it. I remember being in the forest alone. I couldn't find momma and Mimi. Then I was in a dark cart with other girls." She began to tear up at the memory.

"Are you sure it wasn't a dream?" Adva said with a whimsical smile.

Lorelei looked down at her feet that were now covered with soft white slippers and shook her head, "I don't think it was."

"Many girls are sent here because they are vivid dreamers, Lorelei. Sometimes, when dreams seem so real that you feel they are real, it is a sign of something else. Do you dream often?"

Lorelei didn't answer. Instead she looked back to the other girls.

"You do not have to fear answering me, dear child," Adva continued with light annoyance, "We do not fear dreams here. We do not fear magik or those with any special gifts. In fact, we encourage it here. We help you understand it, control it, and make it stronger. So, I will ask you again, do you dream often?"

Lorelei remained quiet for some time. She finally spoke, "Can I go home now?"

Adva forced a smile then folded her hands delicately onto her lap. Looking down to them she said softly, "Perhaps soon. We will have to talk to your family." She then paused before adding, "The head mistress told me something else about you, Lorelei. She said your eyes are the most beautiful golden yellow she had ever seen. May I see them?" Lorelei looked shy at first then turned her eyes to Adva, who then examined them closely. "Were you aware, Lorelei, that it is said; you can see where a person's power lies, by looking into their eyes? Have you heard this?" Lorelei shook her head very slightly. Adva smiled warmly and continued, "I have heard tales that claim that those with yellow eyes have a strong connection with the strands of fate, and that they are destined to have great power. It is said, yellow eyes are a sign that you will become a great seer."

"My sister has green eyes," Lorelei said with a frown, "Momma said she will never make children because green eyes are a curse."

Adva chuckled, "Western superstition."

"But the story about yellow eyes isn't?"

"Well," Adva said as she placed her hand on Lorelei's, "I suppose we shall find out."

"My village says that seers always go mad and they're dangerous and evil," Lorelei said with a frown. "I don't want to be a seer."

"That-" Adva said, then hesitated, "They are not evil, and it is rare for them to be dangerous. A seer simply sees. They can see things that most people can't. The past, the future, even things happening right now, far, far away. Does seeing sound dangerous to you?"

Lorelei shook her head. She then asked, "Why are there only girls here?"

Adva hesitated then smiled as she squeezed Lorelei's little hand, "That is a story for another day."

"Are you a seer?" Lorelei then asked bluntly, turning her eyes up at Adva.

Adva offered her a confused smile, "That is an odd question. Why do you ask?"

"Because you can see," Lorelei said bluntly.

Adva giggled, "Well, I have eyes. Of course, I can see."

Lorelei nodded, then looked back to the other girls as they all sat together in the grass, "Yes, you have very pretty eyes. I have never seen orange eyes before."

"Indeed," Adva said with a smile, "I hear it is quite rare. It is even more rare than yellow, so I am told."

"And they can see like a seer," Lorelei stated simply.

The smile dropped from Adva's face as she asked, "And how would you know that?"

Lorelei looked back up with a frown and said softly, "I can see it."

Adva narrowed her eyes curiously at Lorelei while she asked, "You can see that I am a seer?"

"I see lots of things. I saw a creature once, in the woods, when I was playing with Mimi. Mimi said it was hunting us, and I was very scared. Mimi protected us though and killed it."

Adva laughed lightly, "What does this have to do with anything?"

Lorelei looked down at her own hands, "It got very close to us, and I looked into its eyes. Just like I looked into yours. I was so afraid because all I saw was death and hunger. All it wanted was for us to die so it could eat. But it also liked killing. It wanted to kill us, because it liked killing."

"Yes?" Adva said, now looking concerned and a little annoyed.

Lorelei looked back up at Adva with a frown, "That's what I see in your eyes too."

Adva's scowled, "How dare you. I have never killed for the sake of killing." She stood abruptly with a rage and stormed off.

Lorelei watched her leave and swallowed hard as she put down her treat and slowly rested back into the bench.

CHAPTER 27

Frothy gray clouds darkened the morning sky as the three adventurers packed up their camp and secured their belongings to their horses. As Ethan struggled to secure the final belt with his good arm, he turned his eyes towards the rising sun, now only a hazy glow behind the clouds. "The closest town isn't far from here," he explained, "Cubilios is the name, I believe."

Milla moved to him and helped him with the belt, "Is there any wrong forks or turn offs we should know about?" she asked with a grin.

Ethan turned a smile to her, "Just keep straight. The road breaks off twice, but you'd miss them if you weren't looking."

Rune turned abruptly toward the others, his face twisted in confusion, "Ethan, the horse that you left with wasn't black." Ethan turned his head swiftly towards Rune but didn't offer an explanation. Rune continued, "It was a sort of bluish gray, darker on the tips. How were you able to switch horses in such a short time?"

"I ran into some of my men on the way back," Ethan explained as he looked back toward his black steed, "I was only borrowing the blue roan. This is the breed I am used to riding. It is also far better trained."

"They just happened to have it with them?" Rune asked as he crossed his arms.

Ethan turned a smile to Rune, "You didn't think they would allow their Captain to ride off alone without a rear guard, did you?"

Milla eyed Ethan oddly as Rune narrowed his eyes, "So when we ran into the trolls at the bridge, we could have just waited for your men to help us?"

"No," Ethan answered then dropped his head, "It's-" He remained silent as he thought over his words. He then restarted, "I didn't know how far behind they would be or if they had even left Silvius yet. Their orders left the time frame quite large."

"What orders?" Milla asked cautiously.

Ethan shook his head and looked to her, "That, I can't tell you."

Rune let out a humorless laugh, "Secrets everywhere."

"Yes Rune," Ethan turned his head sharply toward him, "There are. Many are necessary, are they not?"

Rune shrunk a little then nodded. He moved to his horse and began the task of mounting it as he said, "So, if the next town isn't far," he grunted as he lifted himself and threw his leg over the saddle, "and you're already in the East now, would it really be such a bother riding with us the rest of the way?"

A long breath shot out from Ethan's mouth as he dropped his head again. After a thought, he turned to look at Milla who pleaded with her eyes, then looked west down the road. Finally, turning his eyes east, he let out another sharp breath and thought deeply.

"You don't have to," Milla said softly, her voice betraying the sorrow in saying it, "With your injury it might be best to head back to your men anyway. We have really been taking advantage of your kindness more than we should have."

After a shake of his head Ethan looked to Milla again, "It is the other way around, my dear lady," he said softly to her.

Milla tilted her head with a look of confusion, "What do you mean? You've fed us, given us supplies, helped us on our journey and saved us from the dark forest."

A silence fell again. Ethan shot out another breath as he looked away then placed his arm against the saddle, resting his head on his forearm soon after, "You have no idea the danger I had put you two in. The danger is now passed, or so my men have informed me. You must understand it was for the good of the realm."

"The good of your realm. But you can't tell us what the danger was, right?" Rune said as he glowered down at him.

There was no response to that as Ethan finally stood straight again, "I will ride with you to Cubilios, but you must promise me that you will not offer my name or rank to any we might come across."

"Ethan, you don't-" Milla started.

But he interrupted, "I do, Milla. I have made up my mind, that is the end of it." He then tapped his mount on the ribs. Milla backed off as it quickly lowered itself to the ground and waited patiently as Ethan threw his leg over and sat in the saddle. He tapped the horse again and it lifted back up, pushing up on its front legs first then back. Ethan winced lightly at the jarring motions. The steed then took the loose reigns into its mouth and handed them to Ethan. Milla's eyes widened as she watched, "It has fangs," she pointed out.

Ethan let out a small laugh, "And claws if you look past the excessive hair around the ankles. As I said, this is the breed I'm used to riding. It has kir'og blood. It's not a full blooded kir'og but carries much of the intelligence."

Milla raised her brows high as she moved to pet the mount's neck and examine the face closer, "I didn't even think they existed. I thought they were only in stories."

Ethan nodded a few times, "There are none in our lands save for those carried here over the sea from the lands beyond."

"Deotus," she said with a look of awe and excitement. "I've always dreamed of traveling there. The birthplace of magik, and dragons and faeries."

"And giants, and dwarves and the Droathe," Rune added.

"And many dangers," Ethan continued. "From what I have heard, it is a perilous land full of monsters and horrors beyond imagining. Besides the fact that dragons still rule there."

"But people travel there all the time," Milla cut in.

"And few return," Ethan countered, "Even the Easterners, who claim it as their homeland, rarely travel there."

"Who would want to return to this boring land?" she said with a taunting smile as she moved to mount her own horse.

"Indeed," Ethan laughed, "All we have is Great Seers, magik, higher learning and, what else?" He quickly added, "Ah yes. War."

Milla made a face at that and Rune piped in, "I'll avoid the land with dragons and take the warring land, thank you."

Ethan nodded in agreement then returned to their previous discussion, "Do I have your promises then? My name and rank will not be given?" Milla and Rune both agreed in unison, and Ethan bowed his head in thanks, "Then let us be off," he said and they all started eastward.

***

The sun had not yet reached its peak when Ethan slowed and turned his body as he heard horses trotting at a distance behind them. He frowned as the other two walked their horses to either side of him, both turning as well to see what he was looking at. "Black and blue surcoats. South soldiers. What are they doing in the East?" he murmured quietly. "There are only three of them. Continue as if we are travelers. If they ask, we are returning to our home in the east, you are brother and sister and I am your hired guard." Ethan then started forward again, moving to the left side of the road to allow the soldiers room to pass on the right as he casually set the reins down and placed his right hand on the hilt of his sword. Rune and Milla moved to follow behind, trying their best to not look worried.

The lead soldier yelled out as he approached the three, "It's him! Halt!

Stay where you are!"

Ethan veered off to the right as he darted distressed eyes back to the soldiers. He turned his horse to face them, then barked a quiet order to Rune and Milla as he passed by, "Run. Get to Cubilios. No questions, just go." He leaned over and slapped Rune's horse on the rear as he continued past, startling it into a gallop and shocking Milla's horse to do the same. Though both heeded his command, Milla turned distraught eyes back as Ethan drew his sword and moved his horse sideways to block the road.

The soldiers slowed their horses as they approached Ethan, then drew their swords as well. "Drop your sword and get off your horse and we might not kill you," the lead soldier ordered.

Ethan remained steady a moment, then gave a quick look toward Rune and Milla, to check their distance. Seeing that they had a good head start he grinned at the soldiers and bowed his head. He then sheathed his blade calmly, followed by a swift move to grab the reins and kicked his mount into a gallop, following Milla and Rune eastward. The movement caught the soldiers off guard, and they fumbled to sheath their own blades and urged their horses to follow in a gallop. Ethan's horse covered the distance to Rune and Milla with remarkable speed, leaving the soldiers a good distance behind as he slowed to match the speed of Rune and Milla's horses. He then bellowed out at their horses to urge them to move faster and his mount nipped at their back-ends to assist. It didn't take long for them to near the thick stone gate of Cubilios and they slowed as the gate guards raised a hand each, signaling them to stop. "Please, let us pass," Ethan started through heavy breaths as he moved closer, "We're being pursued by South soldiers."

The guard on the left asked suspiciously, "Why would South soldiers be pursuing you?"

"I don't know," Ethan said with frustration, "Does it matter? They think us enemies and are pursuing us on Eastern territory." The south soldiers could now be heard nearing from the distance and Ethan sighed with frustration, "Please let us pass and shield us! There are only three, we can take them together!"

The guard laughed then neared Ethan and pointed his spear towards him, "The enemy of our ally, is also our enemy." The other guard moved to the opposite side, mimicking the first guard's actions and Ethan's eyes widened. He reached for his sword, but both guards stepped forward aggressively as the one on the left commanded, "Draw it and you die."

Ethan stopped and raised his hand in surrender, "Run!" He then hollered to Rune and Milla, "Save yourselves!"

"Do that and we kill him where he stands!" The right guard instantly bellowed afterwards as he moved his spear closer to Ethan.

Rune and Milla turned their eyes to each other, both expressing deep distress. Milla then sighed and raised her hands, then Rune did so as well. "No!" Ethan growled, "Let them kill me! Run!" But they both stayed put. Ethan eyed them with a desperate fury then turned to the gate guards, "How can the East be allied with the South? That's impossible! You have hated each other for generations!"

The south soldiers caught up in full gallop and the closest rammed into Ethan, battering him off his mount. The other two reined in, then roughly hauled Rune and Milla off their horses. Ethan groaned and tensed as he recovered from the fall.

"You're going to regret running like that!" the soldier yelled to Ethan then jumped down from his horse and bent over to grab him by the hair.

Ethan's mount turned violently on the attacker and kicked its front claws out at him, causing him to lose balance, then bit down on the back of his neck as he fell forward. The soldier let out a scream while the two guards set their spears toward the beast. A loud crack was heard as it bit down harder, then released. It quickly dropped the now convulsing soldier on top of Ethan as it spun around, smashing its thick neck into both attacking guards and sending them flying off their feet. Ethan pushed off the jostling body, as blood gushed outward from the gaping neck wound. He then yelled out to the horse after rolling to his right, "Retu Kenget! Sagje treba!" The horse turned fierce eyes towards Ethan. It snorted loud then took off westward in a gallop, before any of the enemies recovered enough to stop it.

Both guards recovered and scrambled to stand as they grasped their dropped spears. They then charged at Ethan with obvious intent to skewer him. "No!" Milla shrieked, "Leave him alone!"

She was swiftly shaken by the soldier holding her, "Quiet!" Though her plea did stop the two guards in their tracks. They simply stood over top of Ethan, pointing their spears down at him as he collapsed onto his back and breathed heavily.

Anger built up inside Rune as he watched. He immediately closed his eyes and calmed himself, worried about what might happen to Milla and Ethan if he lost control again.

"Why are you pursuing these ones?" the vocal Eastern guard asked angrily, "Two children and a guard hardly seem worth the effort and the life lost."

The soldier holding Milla scoffed as he forced her forward while nodding down at Ethan, "It's this one here. We were sent to capture and kill him."

"And who is he?" the guard asked, suddenly curious as he placed the spear tip on Ethan's neck.

"Prince Ethan. Son off the Northern High Queen Adva. First in line to become King, now that his brother is dead," the south soldier answered with a laugh, "Traveling with two kids and without his guards no less."

Milla and Rune's eyes both opened wide as they looked to Ethan. He continued to lay still and breath heavily as he slowly turned his eyes towards them. His face remained without expression as he then looked away.

"Take them to the cells," the guard laughed, "I think we're all going to get a good reward for this one."

"Our orders are to kill him!" the southern soldier barked.

"Your orders mean nothing more than faerie spit here black-born," the guard growled back, "We take them alive and wait for orders from our superiors."

The guards and soldiers stared each other down, before the soldier finally relented, "As you wish. To the cells then." The guards forced Ethan to stand, insisting the soldiers walk ahead of them before making their way towards the city, leaving the dead soldier behind.

CHAPTER 28

"Lieutenant Doron, you must retreat now. There is no-" Major Peleg started as he stormed into the war chamber, his brow drenched in sweat and his voice hoarser than usual.

"Major Peleg," Lieutenant Doron interrupted sedately. His wide, armoured frame stood tall and still beyond the table in the center of the room. He faced the large golden sun that hung proudly in the center of the stone wall as he drank down the last of his mug's contents then turned to Peleg as he asked, "They broke through the inner wall then?"

"They will at any moment. Silvius is lost. General Remus has already retreated north with the First and the bulk of the men. I will be remaining with the Second to see you and your men get out safely," Peleg explained as he shifted anxiously. Doron stared down at the floor and offered no response. "You must go now Lieutenant. Your loss would be a great blow to the morale of the men. Especially after the loss of Prince Arik."

"Lieutenant Arik," Doron corrected, "He was a great man. We will lose many more great men before this war is over. Just as we will lose the North." His legs seemed to weaken, and he collapsed into the chair next to him.

"Lieutenant?" Major Peleg asked with concern as he moved toward him.

"What of Captain Ethan? What news of him?" Doron asked as his eye lids became heavy.

"No news as of yet," Peleg said as he moved to Doron's side examining him, "What have you done, Lieutenant?"

"Lieutenant," Doron echoed as if correcting him. He then dropped his mug as his head fell forward and he fell silent.

"No," Peleg said in a pained voice as he rushed to check on the Lieutenant. Discovering that Doron no longer drew breath and his heart was no longer beating, Peleg snarled, "You damned coward." Lifting the mug, he took a quick whiff of the remaining contents then swiftly stood and threw it across the room. Turning back to the door, he charged out and almost collided with a scout that rushed towards the room. "Report," Peleg ordered as he continued out of the keep.

"Still no word," the scout answered as he followed a step behind.

"And you are sure none of the men took the bait of his trap? Not one man sought to follow Prince Ethan as he left alone with the westerners?" Peleg asked as he stopped just outside the keep's door and turned his eyes up to the gray mid-day sky.

"None. Commander Argus watched for any traitors leaving himself from Kremm's rock, as ordered."

A loud explosion at the gate of the inner wall sent a pillar of flame several stories high, interrupting the conversation and engulfing the area in an orange glow. Major Peleg recovered from the shock as he cursed, "That damned magi!" He then ordered over the clamoring noise that followed, "There's nothing that can be done now. Get a message to Commander Argus to lead Lieutenant Doron's men out. Lieutenant Doron is dead and-"

"Forgive me," the scout interrupted, "But the Commander is still out searching for Prince Ethan."

"What?" Peleg barked, "His orders were to remain behind and watch for traitorous pursuit! If he found none he was to await Captain Ethan's return on the road at the marked location. He was strictly ordered not to pursue under any circumstances! Why would he-" he closed his eyes as he stopped himself then cursed under his breath. Gathering his thoughts, he then instructed, "Tell Commander Asher to lead Lieutenant Doron's men out of Silvius, then get yourself a horse and ride as fast as you can to find General Remus. Tell him," he paused and reached behind his chest armour, pulling out a palm sized golden sun marked with the crossed swords that symbolized a Major's rank, "Give this to him. Tell him Major Peleg has sent you with this message. Commander Argus is the traitor." He slapped the golden emblem into the scout's hand then ordered, "Go!" The scout rushed off as commanded and Peleg made his way down the keep's steps towards the gate. The remains of the Second waited behind barricades as they watched the high flames envelope the massive gate. As the Major approached, all eyes turned to him. He unsheathed his blade, stretched his arms then neck, then turned a smile over the men. He called out, "What say you men? A square of land rewarded for every black-born boot-licker you take out!"

The Second erupted in cheers and laughter as they prepared themselves for the fall of the gate.

CHAPTER 29

Dawn approached and stretched its light through the small cell windows. Several empty cells separated Milla and Rune from each other in the dark cellar, and the jail guard had been strict, not allowing them to speak at all through their detainment. Both sat in silence and worry, not only with concern for their own fates, but for Ethan's. Neither had seen him since they were dragged into the dark dungeon below the garrison and all questions had been left unanswered. Even as they heard movement from the stairwell, neither moved from their stone bench.

A group of five flooded the small area in front of the cells. Their yellow tabards branded with the red dragon logo marked them as eastern soldiers. The leading soldier's armour was far more elaborate and bulky than the others, distinguishing him as one with greater importance. He turned to speak with the guard as the others moved to Rune and Milla's cell doors, "Open their cells," he ordered.

"Yes Commander," The guard responded then quickly complied. Rune moved to the door, ready to be taken, but Milla remained sitting. The two soldiers at her door were forced to move into her cell and drag her from her spot. Both prisoners were taken to a small cell wagon outside of the garrison and thrown inside. Within, they found Ethan laying lifelessly on the cage floor. He had been stripped of all his armour and weapons, leaving him with only his muddied pants and boots. His body and face bore several new bruises and his shoulder wound was red, blistered and raw, clearly having been sealed with fire, as was the way of the Eastern people. After the two were thrown inside with him, Milla rushed towards him to see if he still lived.

"What did they do to you?" she asked as she teared up slightly and put her ear on his chest to listen for his heart. To her relief, not only did she hear it beat, but he let out a rumbling groan as he woke.

He tiredly rolled to his side, then with Milla and Rune's help, he pushed himself into a more comfortable sitting position against the side bars. He fought to keep his eyes open as he looked to her and mumbled with a small smile, "You're alive."

Moving next to him, Milla sat close, then cradled his head onto her chest as she looked to Rune, who returned a look of worry. Ethan immediately fell back into a deep sleep, and the wagon jarred forward as it began its journey. Rune looked to the road ahead and sighed as he whispered to her, "This one will be much harder to get out of."

Milla nodded as she brushed Ethan's hair off his forehead and away from his eyes. "Even if we escaped," she whispered, "Where would we go? I don't think Ethan would be strong enough to run for long in any case." She sighed then asked, "Is there no spell that can take us from here to somewhere else? Like a summoning spell, but in another direction?"

Rune shook his head, "Not that I know of."

Milla nodded and laid her head back on the bars, then closed her eyes, "I don't understand. Is all this what was supposed to happen?"

Rune turned to watch her a moment, "You're talking about your Seer's vision?"

Milla nodded lightly, "She said take you east, and I took you east. Now we all might very well be killed." She opened her eyes and looked sorrowfully to Rune, "It might be my fault that a Northern prince is killed. If he didn't take the time to help us..." she stopped then turned to look over Ethan's face. "Maybe he was right. Maybe the darkness was the war and we were supposed to stay and help him stop it?" She let a silent thought hang then continued, "Why didn't you tell us, Ethan?"

Rune remained quiet as he watched her speak, his eyes then drifting to Ethan. Without a further word, he looked back to the road, his eyes filled with apprehension and dread.

CHAPTER 30

The thick smell of burning wood barely covered the stench of gore that wafted through the streets. The dark night was lit up by several fires that still blazed throughout Silvius. A hooded messenger darted down the main street to reach her target, and as she approached the large man, she said hastily, "General Oddr, all gates are claimed and secured. Silvius is ours."

General Oddr nodded his thanks and the messenger darted off. He continued to move his massive frame to the city square where two awaited his arrival. He lifted his hefty, spiked hammer from his shoulder and allowed it to crash to the ground on its flat end as he stopped in front of the two Easterners.

Zal's crystal blue eyes, that contrasted heavily with his ebony skin, turned up at the giant of a man before him. General Oddr looked him over and shifted his weight to one side as he crossed his arms. The blazing fire behind Zal formed an aura of light around his long white hair, inducing an odd illusion of him being there, and yet not. "In this light, I see why they call you the Phantom," General Oddr said with a hearty chuckle.

"I had thought it obvious in any light," Zal returned with a taunting grin. "Much like it can be seen, in any light, why they call you the Titan."

Meretat piped in as she looked back and forth between the two men, "And one can also see why it is never claimed that the peasants are clever. They should leave the pet names to the Dro bards."

Zal turned his crystal gaze to Meretat as he joked, "Are you envious my love? The peasants have not seen fit to bless you with a name of equal significance."

Her light brown eyes rested on him, maintaining a look of irritation. She finally spoke, "Let us get to the business of war, shall we?"

"It seems our new alliance is proving useful, General Zal," Oddr piped in as he stroked his braided beard, "We should be upon the capital in no time at all, at this rate."

Zal allowed a teasing expression to remain on Meretat a moment longer before he nodded and looked to Oddr, "As you have reminded us time and time again, General; our alliance has little to do with our victories. Your king's new... friend, has empowered this fight in such a way to make us unstoppable. I must say, I fear what our world will become once his ends are achieved. But, I suppose that is what he desires, is it not?"

Oddr bobbed his head slowly, "Just be grateful you are here and not near Regintun."

"I think if we were," Meretat chimed in with annoyance, "I would have been consumed by now." As if sealing the point, she looked away abruptly and pulled her long raven hair over one shoulder.

"He does not take all magi, Lady Meretat. Only those amongst the enemy," Oddr explained.

"How comforting," Meretat said, thick with sarcasm as she looked up at Oddr, "Who is to say that we would not become his enemy once our ward is removed, as he has so impatiently demanded."

"King Brandr is to say," Oddr barked, "He has made a promise and he is a man of honour. Nevertheless, this is an argument for another time and a higher rank. We must see to our current victory. I hear Lieutenant Doron was killed?"

Zal scowled as he nodded, "It seems he took his own life. It was a Major that led the final defense. Major Peleg, I believe was his name. He and his men created a large dent in my forces, and I intend to see him pay for that."

Oddr chuckled, "A feat that demands honour, not revenge. Where is he now?"

Zal's frown deepened. "I do not make light of losing my own men as you Blackborn do," he growled then looked off toward the soldiers awaiting his orders. He snapped his fingers, "Bring the Major."

"As I will never piss on honour as readily as you mud bathers do," Oddr sneered in return. General Zal offered no response as he waited. Two of his men soon dragged the bruised and bloody Major Peleg over, then dropped him at Zal's feet. Peleg struggled very little but was able to force himself to his knees. "Where is Prince Ethan?" Oddr asked calmly. Peleg only spit at the ground in response. General Zal, without warning, raised his short staff and struck Peleg across the cheek, driving him back to the ground. Oddr's eyes drifted to Zal and he snarled, "I prefer he remain conscious until my answers are had."

"What does it matter where this prince is?" Zal growled, "His mother's realm will soon be lost. There is nothing he can do about that, is there?"

"It matters because Eilifatli has deemed that it matters!" General Oddr barked. Peleg pushed himself to his knees again, breathing heavily and turning defeated eyes to the ground ahead of him. "I ask you again," Oddr spoke patiently, "where is your Prince Ethan?" Peleg offered no answer and Zal raised his staff again. Oddr stepped forward and grabbed it before Zal could strike down. "I do not know, or care, how you do things in the east, but in the south, we deal with honourable men honourably."

Zal growled in return, but he was interrupted before he could respond as a messenger rushed toward them. "General Oddr, we just received word. Prince Ethan has been captured. He had attempted to escape into the east. They will be taking him south to Regintun."

Meretat snickered, "Ah, it seems he had bypassed the honour of the south and allowed the east to do the job for you."

Oddr growled and released Zal's staff forcefully, saying to them both, "Do not make it seem to be any more than fortunate coincidence." He turned to the messenger to speak, "Their orders were to kill him. Why is he being taken south?"

"The easterners wouldn't allow it," the messenger said as she eyed Zal and Meretat accusingly, "They wanted to show Eilifatli that it was they who captured his target."

Zal snorted a laugh then pulled a long dagger from his belt as Oddr's back was turned. "Honour and glory," he scoffed then swiftly and smoothly flicked his dagger under Peleg's chin, opening his throat. "There are only allies and enemies." Oddr turned quickly as he heard Peleg sputter and fall, then turned enraged eyes to Zal while he cleaned his dagger and continued, "And that, is how we deal with our enemies."

General Oddr stormed toward Zal who promptly snapped the dagger up towards him. Oddr stopped, though his nose flared with angry breaths, "You forget, General Zal, that those who are your enemies today may be allies tomorrow. Honour dictates how you are treated by your future allies. You would do well to remember this in the future." Zal only sneered in response. Oddr's eyes remained fixed on him for several breaths, before he turned, lifted his heavy hammer, and stormed away.

CHAPTER 31

The cell wagon bumped and swayed as it continued down the well grooved road through the light, grassy plains. As one of the large wheels hit a small crater, the wagon jostled violently, forcing Ethan awake with a start. Milla woke immediately after, grumbling in annoyance at the pain that had developed in her rear end. Ethan raised his head and upon noticing that Milla had been allowing him to use her as a pillow, he turned a thankful smile to her. She returned a warm smile of her own and he then forced himself up to sit. After she gently assisted him, she adjusted herself, thankful that she could finally change positions again. As he shifted, he winced and held his chest. "How long have we been traveling?" he asked through a dry throat.

Rune, who had been awake for some time, looked to the clear, mid-day sky and shrugged, "More than a day now. They've only stopped twice so far and only long enough to eat, drink, shit, switch drivers and change horses. They must really want to get you somewhere," he said with an edge of bitterness. Ethan nodded lightly and glanced around, trying not to move overmuch but wincing again as the wagon swayed. The rushing of a nearby river could be heard while the three passengers remained silent for a time. Finally, Rune spoke up. "A prince," he said sharply.

Ethan turned half-awake eyes to Rune and took in a slow, pained breath. "I thought telling you might put you in danger," his voice scratched, and he let out a dry cough.

"Not telling us put us in danger," Rune corrected, still with a biting tone. "I would like to know why, before we all die. Why did you travel with us? Why put us and yourself in danger like that?"

Ethan closed his eyes, "I'm sorry, I-" he stiffened painfully as the wagon jostled heavily again while making its way onto a large, curved bridge. The sudden slight incline forced them all to shift and hold the bars so as not to slide to the back.

"You what?" Rune asked after adjusting himself, looking hurt. "You lied to us? We already know that much. I just want to know why." Ethan turned sorry eyes to Rune but didn't offer an answer. Rune continued, "Well, if they wanted us dead they would have killed us already. They must have some purpose for us if they are taking all this effort to get us somewhere."

Milla piped in quietly, asking, "Do you think they plan on torturing us?" Ethan turned saddened, unsure eyes to her. Taking in a slow quivering breath, she turned her eyes to the tree line. "Poor Leilei," she then said as her eyes filled with tears and she turned away, "I failed her. I hope she's not suffering."

Rune frowned at her, though she couldn't see it. "I hope none of us suffer," he added, his dry tone continuing.

Milla closed her eyes and covered her mouth as she fought back tears. Ethan grunted as the incline changed and all three were forced to stop themselves from sliding toward the front. The movement forced Ethan to shift towards Milla, so he used the opportunity to place his hand on her back comfortingly, "There's still hope, you two have gotten out of this before, you can do it again."

She wiped her eyes and turned to Ethan, "Do you really think so?" Ethan nodded quickly, trying to look as believable as possible.

Rune wasn't fooled by Ethan's acting. He could see the hopelessness that remained in his eyes. Turning his gaze down the road, his thoughts turned to Feagan, who had constantly lectured him to drop his obsession with magik. In the end, after too many close calls, that obsession likely had gotten Feagan killed or worse. Now, without a friend by his side, Rune felt at a complete loss as he rode towards a likely painful death of his own. Unless, of course, he could figure out and control the odd power that had made itself known on this perilous journey.

The wagon wobbled violently again as it left the bridge. "Hey," Ethan grunted as he shifted and rested his back against the bars. Rune regarded him curiously. "Look on the bright side," he continued with a grin, "We get a free ride, and we can sleep on the way." Rune furrowed his brows, wondering how anyone could possibly make light of such a dark situation. His eyes then widened as a faint glowing aura began to emit from Ethan. After closing his eyes and shaking his head, Rune returned his gaze, relieved that all had returned to normal. Ethan tilted his head curiously and asked, "What? What's wrong?"

"Nothing," Rune answered and looked away.

"Really, Rune," Ethan said again, in a persistent tone, "What were you thinking just now?"

"Nothing, my eyes were just playing tricks on me," Rune explained, "It must be the lack of sleep and food or something."

Ethan sighed then rested his head against the bars, "It's just that my mother has looked at me like that several times before. I could never figure out why and she would never tell me."

"Your mother the High Queen?" Rune asked, in a taunting voice as he looked back to Ethan.

Ethan nodded, ignoring the tone.

"The same High Queen that put my parents to death?" Rune continued, shaking lightly with his anger. Ethan slowly lifted his head and turned his eyes to Rune. His mouth opened as if to speak but he said nothing. Instead he let out a frustrated sigh and allowed his head to fall back against the bars again. "If we get out of this alive I won't drop the subject so easily," Rune grumbled, then looked back toward the road.

Milla raised her head and looked to Ethan, "Why is a Prince out here fighting wars instead of in a castle somewhere?"

Ethan stared at the cell's ceiling as he answered, "It is customary for the queen's sons to take up a political skill of some sort. My elder brother Arik and I chose to be soldiers like our father, who leads the Northern armies," Ethan explained then coughed dryly, "It seems like we will share the same fate as well."

Milla spoke as she slowly sat up, "I'm sorry about your brother," He turned a saddened smile to her and dipped his head in thanks. After allowing a long silence to pass, she finally asked, "So, you are next in line to be King?"

Ethan shot out a breath and shook his head as he swallowed, "In a sense. It's complicated, but I was banished from Albusinia, as was Arik when he came of age. After me, Idan, the next youngest, and just recently Ori were also banished. The twins, Udom and Yavius, are still too young."

"You're all banished?" Rune said with great curiosity, "She can do that? Why would she?"

"She can do anything she likes," Ethan explained with a frown, "The people adore her and wouldn't dare question her. As it should be. She has guided our land through some very tough times and they trust her implicitly."

"But why would she banish you? Doesn't she want her sons to become King?" Rune asked in a persistent tone.

Ethan shook his head and shrugged very lightly, "At first I believed her explanation; that she wanted the King to be strong and worthy of their position. Therefore, he must be sent away to prove himself. I could see the sense in it." He coughed again before he continued, "As King, we would take on a majority of the responsibility of the realm, only answering to her if she decided to step in. The position requires a great deal of strength, knowledge, and respect. But..." he stopped and sighed, "After my brother Arik died, all the banished brothers were allowed into the castle grounds for a day to view his funeral pyre. My mother, she-" he stopped and shook his head.

"She?" Milla prodded.

Ethan sighed and winced as he adjusted lightly, "She was not the same person I remembered. She told me, in the strangest tone, that if my brothers and I sought to be worthy of her approval, we must follow the steps of my eldest brother." He sighed and looked to his boots, "I pushed her for meaning but she refused to answer me. Since then, I have wondered if she meant that we should reach the heights of success that he did, or if she hoped that we all die, as he did. I haven't spoken with her since."

"What sort of mother would want her own children dead?" Milla grumbled.

Rune answered sharply, "The same type that would order the death of my father for having power he wouldn't share." Ethan drifted his eyes to Rune but still said nothing. Rune persisted, "It was her, wasn't it? She made the order."

"I was very young when that happened," Ethan finally answered, looking to the road behind the wagon.

"Old enough to remember," Rune pressed.

Ethan shot angry eyes towards Rune, "It was her, yes. I think you should take a moment to look at this through other eyes though, Rune. Your parents were thought to have likely uncovered power that the ancient tales explain as having caused more hardship and destruction than we could even fathom, despite our constant wars. An ancient power that even to this day kills any who dare brave the Seer Ruins. All but you and your parents, that is. Attaining that power was, and should be, something everyone would fear - with good cause."

"Fear?" Rune returned frowning, "Or want for herself?"

Ethan calmed as he let out a relenting sigh, "I don't know, Rune." He searched his thoughts before speaking again, "She is a seer. A powerful one at that. I fear the seer's madness may slowly be taking her."

"Then it's a good thing she didn't get that power," Milla interjected, "A High Queen with the Seer's madness is already dangerous enough. Even to her own sons if she's demanding they die to gain her approval."

"It doesn't matter," Ethan continued, closing his eyes and resting his head back on the bars again, "It looks like I may gain her approval now anyway. I will be following my brother soon enough."

"Don't talk like that," Milla growled, her fire now returning in her voice, "We'll get out of this. Rune will find a way. He always does." Rune's lips turned up in a smile, though his eyes filled with worry at her blind confidence in him.

Ethan nodded and grinned, "Of that, I have no doubt. But when you do escape, you must leave me behind."

"What? No!" Milla protested emphatically.

Ethan carefully moved his hand to hers and looked her in the eyes, "Milla, listen to me. I am injured and will only slow you down. I also am the only one they wish to keep, and they will do whatever it takes to find me if I escape. If it is only you two, they will give up the search."

Milla shook her head fiercely and enveloped his hand with both of hers, "No, we won't leave you."

"And your sister? Would you condemn her too to save me?" Ethan barked. Milla frowned and fell silent, unsure of what to say.

Rune's eyes drifted between the two. He didn't know what to say as he knew logically, Ethan was right. But despite everything, he didn't want to leave him behind either. He closed his eyes to think and struggled to conjure up a plan in the darkness of his mind. Thoughts swarmed around recklessly, but without Feagan's help, he couldn't conceive one to fit their needs. As his mind wandered, he had the odd sensation that he might be dreaming. His thoughts sped through many light-filled strands, and as he approached one that was brighter than the rest, he grasped onto it. After a flash of light overwhelmed him, he was consumed by darkness. Within the darkness, he saw the outline of a castle. A blue light then glowed behind the castle, revealing a giant dragon, as dark and blue as the evening sky. It raised its wings and roared towards the stars. Shortly after, it let out a shrieking scream and fell dead, disappearing behind the castle. Sunlight then took over, and there stood Ethan, in full black armour and a crown, smiling triumphantly. The image then disappeared, replaced by a burst of light. As it dimmed, a beautiful, flower filled garden appeared. Within it, there was a small girl draped in white, huddled in a corner and crying. As he moved to her, she looked up to him, her golden-yellow eyes wide with fear. She then smiled, and he reached out to her.

"Rune! Rune!" his name was called, and his eyes opened. He was on the floor of the jail cart with Milla and Ethan above him looking concerned. Rune quickly scrambled to his knees as his eyes darted around and he desperately tried to make sense of the images he just saw. "What happened?" Milla asked with great concern as she searched his eyes.

Rune shook his head and swallowed, still trying to figure out that answer for himself. He looked to Milla, then Ethan, "I think I must have passed out. Maybe I need to eat."

Milla helped him to sit against the bars and Ethan eyed him skeptically while he painfully sat back, "Did the thought of leaving me cause you such stress?" he asked with a suspicious grin.

Rune didn't answer at first. His mind was still consumed by the vivid images. He looked at Ethan seriously and stated, "We're not leaving you." Milla and Ethan looked at each other, then back to Rune. "We should all rest," Rune then said as he laid his head back, "We'll need our strength for when we escape."

Milla and Ethan looked at each other again but decided not to question him further. They both heeded his advice and made themselves comfortable to rest.

CHAPTER 32

Queen Adva launched up with a gasp as she broke from her deep slumber. Her widened eyes glanced around the dark room and her breath heaved heavily in the silent night. As the shock wore off, she swiftly threw her legs over the side of the bed and rushed to the door. After she opened it, she turned to the nearest guard, "Fetch me a servant and a light," she commanded, then turned and closed the door.

The servant arrived promptly with a light and hustled about to help Adva dress. Once finished, the Queen swiftly made her way down the grand and long hallways and staircases of the castle. Servants and guards followed her obediently as she exited the castle and started for the academy. "My Queen," the head guard trumpeted hastily, "Should we not fetch your carriage?" She declined with a shake of her head as she continued down the well-lit street at a rushed pace.

Once inside the academy, she turned to her entourage. "Stay here," she commanded, and the group hesitantly complied.

She made her way towards the dormitory. After she entered, she stood motionless in the dark, silent hallway. She closed her eyes and listened intently, then began taking slow, soft steps forward. Her elegant frame moved haltingly down the thin corridor. Each time she passed a door, she placed her hand on it, attempting to sense the one she hunted. Finally, she stopped, as her hand touched the door she sought. Quietly unlocking it, she moved inside.

There she found young Lorelei laying in her bed. Her opened eyes were white as they remained rolled back, her mind immersed in a deep trance. Adva charged to her, then shook her roughly to break the trance. Lorelei slowly awoke, then took a moment to take in her surroundings. Seeing Adva above her, she scurried to the corner of the bed, as far away from the queen as she could. "Why do you fear me child? I have been nothing but kind." Lorelei didn't respond, and simply eyed her with caution. Now deeply frustrated, Adva continued with a frown, "So, you truly are a Seer then. How is it that you have so much focus while so young? What was it you were looking for? I felt you reaching out a great distance." Still, Lorelei remained silent. "Were you seeking out your mother? Your sister?" As Lorelei again offered no response, the Queen growled with anger, "Dear girl, I am trying to help you. Just tell me who you seek, and I will send out for them. Tell me where your sister is, and I will bring her to you. I promise you this."

"You're the tower blocking the sun. You let the shadow in," Lorelei said with wide sad eyes.

Adva scolded, "My dear, you are speaking nonsense. Tell me what it is you seek."

"The one that can help me stop you," Lorelei answered with fear and indignation.

The queen remained silent for several breaths. She then stood, "Stop me?"

"You're the tower blocking the sun. You let the shadow in," Lorelei repeated, "Now darkness is coming, and no one can stop it. The tower has to fall for the darkness to end. If it stands, we all fall. When it falls, this world will end." Lorelei said, her lips beginning to quiver as tears filled her eyes.

The queen blinked her wide eyes several times before letting out a slow breath, "My dear child, has the madness taken you already?"

Lorelei cried out as her hair began to raise up on its own, "No! You have looked into the sun so long that you are blind. My back is turned to the light and I can see the storm." The tapestries on the wall began to lift lightly and the small chair below the desk shifted.

Adva fretfully looked around the room, before her eyes returned to Lorelei, "How are you doing this? What power is this?"

"I won't let you kill Mimi!" Lorelei screamed out and the room began to rumble lightly.

Without another word Adva rushed out of the room. She trembled as she locked the door behind her, then rushed down the hallway. Otho had just cautiously entered the dormitory hall with several guards. His eyes turned to worry as he saw Adva tearing down the corridor, her face ghostly white and filled with terror. "What was that?" Otho asked with a thick foreboding tone, "We heard a scream, things were floating, and the ground rumbled."

The queen rushed past them and they followed a step behind as she answered, "It was Lorelei. The one I spoke to you about. She has a great deal of power. We should separate her from the other girls. She may be dangerous. Fetch as many faeries as you can get a hold of."

Otho nodded slowly, "I will have her removed in the morning and assessed." He hesitated then asked, "My queen, if what we just saw was a result of her actions; perhaps we should deal with her before she becomes a danger to the city, and perhaps more? I can think of only one other with such power. You know of whom I speak."

The queen quickly shook her head, her fear now being replaced by hopeful anticipation, "No. Absolutely not. She may be exactly who I am looking for. I will not throw away what might be my only chance."

"Only chance for what, my queen?" Otho asked with suspicion, "What of the safety of the realm?"

Adva's voice raised in annoyance, "Am I not the High Queen, Otho? How dare you question my intent to keep my realm safe. I have given you an order now follow it!" She then stormed off, toward the academy's exit. Otho's eyes turned back toward the dormitory, stricken with worry. Turning back, before exiting, Adva added, "One more thing. Find out where she came from and do it quickly."

Otho bowed deeply, his face stricken with distress, "As you command, my Queen."

CHAPTER 33

A frigid wind swept over the rich, mossy green grasslands beyond the walls of Steinnborg. Rippling white clouds evenly divided themselves across the rich blue sky above, allowing plenty of sunlight through, though it seemed to do little to warm the land. The famed clifftop city bustled with activity as the citizens within the city walls went about their daily routines. Loud and inharmonious sea birds circled above their heads for their morning scavenge as the day seemed to start like any other for the inhabitants.

Just over two days had passed as the wagon holding Ethan, Rune and Milla proceeded through the black gate of the timeworn city. The bordering wall was larger than any in the wagon had ever seen, and their eyes remained locked on it as they passed underneath the archway.

The three prisoners had been given little to eat or drink on their journey; just enough to keep them alive. Despite this, as the wagon now steered its way down the cobblestone lane, all three mustered the energy to rise and view the grand buildings that lined the overwide streets. The residents they passed by, would often stop and turn to stare at the eastern led wagon and gaze upon its unwilling passengers. It soon came to a stop as the road became clogged by a crowd of locals, purposefully blocking the way forward. The driver stood from his seat and barked, "Let us pass! We are on the King's business!"

A large man covered in layers of furs, emerged from the crowd. As he moved, the clack of his elaborate staff echoed as it collided with stone on every other step. The thick, wiry animal furs enveloping his shoulders were adorned by a large black bird, perched on the same side as the leather patch that covered his blind eye. Children amongst the crowd took this time to gather around the wheeled cage, to get a better look at the prisoners within. Passing by the eastern soldiers without word, the large man slowly made his way to the side of the cage amongst the children. The three inside studied him warily as his eye drifted amongst them, landing on Rune, and then Ethan. Without a word, he turned a nod to the crowd and they separated to allow the wagon through. After a hasty snap of the reigns and a command, they started forward again. The observant crowd kept their vigilant watch on the strangers while the children followed behind with exuberant excitement. The three prisoners kept their eyes on the mysterious man as he leaned on his staff, returning their interested stare.

"Damn black-born," The driver crowed angrily after they bypassed the bulk of the crowd.

"That was very strange," Milla said quietly as she eased herself back down to sit.

"If I'm not mistaken, I believe that was Thane Od," Ethan said with a hint of enthusiasm. "He is the subject of many great tales that reach us in the North. He is a great Southern Warlord and the father of the infamous General Oddr. He rules Steinnborg like a King and is rumored to have strange and mystical powers. Some say he is a powerful seer. No one has dared question his ownership of the land, not even the South King, King Brandr. Steinnborg is home of the Black Mines and it is believed to be the greatest power in the South."

"Why doesn't he take the throne and become King then, if he's so powerful? And why is he walking amongst the people? Isn't that dangerous?" Rune said as he continued to watch the Thane.

Ethan eased his way down to sit, grimacing at the pain it caused, "From what I hear, he doesn't want to be King. As for danger, well, did you notice that our drivers stopped their barking once the Thane showed himself? No one would dare turn on him, and I've heard his people adore him. The tales claim he is descended from the Dragon Lord Mayon. If you know the history and lore of the Dro, they are both said to be descendants of their Mother Goddess; the mother of all life and spirits."

"Do you think any of it is true?" Milla asked with the doe eyed look of a child listening to a bedtime story.

Ethan chuckled and turned whimsical eyes to her, "I doubt it. The stories also say he is taller than a house, creates earth tremors when he walks, and his missing eye has the power to see into the minds of his enemies. They're just stories spread by the peasants to give reasoning to the man's greatness. The truth behind the tales, is that he is widely feared, and his victories are unmatched."

"Peasants like us, you mean?" Rune piped in.

Ethan's face turned sour, "My apologies, I didn't mean..." he let out a frustrated sigh and fell silent. The silence continued as they were driven into the grounds of a grand stone keep. The wagon stopped, and the eastern soldiers stretched, then hopped down to greet the guards of the keep. A quiet conversation was had, then the cage door was opened. All three prisoners were led into a broad side-doorway by pointed swords, then down a wide, torch lit staircase.

Below lay a sizable dungeon that housed a single extensive jail cell. Small, barred windows lay just above ground level, yet at this depth, they were high above the reach of any man. It was dark, damp and had the smell of old boots. The keep's guards urged them down to the large chamber, past the sizable support pillars, towards the far wall. All three were then seated next to another prisoner whose overgrown beard, filthiness and smell suggested he had been there for a while. Bulky metal cuffs, connected to a heavy chain secured to the wall, were then clasped around their wrists and ankles. Leaving them there without a word, the guards locked the hefty jail door, and soon after made their way out.

Rune looked to the man they were chained next to. His face and upper body bore healing wounds and bruises and his pant leg had been ripped open, surrounded by a large, dried blood stain and revealing a neglected wound. Rune asked him, "How long have you been here?" but the man ignored him. The silence hung in the air for some time before Rune asked the man, "How often do they feed you here? I'm starving," He was still ignored as the man stared ahead with uninterested eyes. Continuing, Rune explained, "We were brought here from the east. All the way from Cubilios. They captured us there. We had just traveled through the north but we're actually from the west. I guess we've been to every land now. Lucky us." Rune laughed lightly but the man still said nothing, the deadpan stare remaining on his features.

"Rune," Ethan then said, with an uneasy grin, as he attempted to shift and get more comfortable, "I don't think he wants to talk."

"I don't blame him," Rune said then sighed as he twisted the metal cuffs around his wrists, "This place must just drain the life and hope right out of you." He turned to look at the prisoner again, "How did you get injured?"

"Does he ever shut up?" the man finally said, his voice hoarse and gritty, but spoke to Milla and Ethan.

"I'll let you know," Milla responded dryly and Rune frowned at her response.

The man let out a grating laugh then spoke again to Milla, "The name's Wulf. I'm a messenger from the Western Capital Gottswai."

Milla perked up and smiled, "Gottswai? My town is only a day's travel from there. I've never been there myself, but I hear it's impressive."

Wulf nodded, "It is indeed. You've never seen so much life and color in one place. The High Queen's palace gardens are unmatched by any of the pretender ruler's castles in the lands east. The message I brought was from the High Queen herself."

Milla turned her eyes to Ethan to see if he'd react, but he showed no intention of doing so as he looked to the chains connecting his ankles and listened. She returned her gaze to Wulf, "Why would they capture a messenger of the High Queen?"

Wulf shrugged, his raspy voice grunting before he spoke, "The way I hear it, the South king has gone mad. He's demanding all realms bow to his rule and combine to form a single realm under one crown. His own. The High Queen Erma found his demands humorous, so she rejected them, sending me and two others to relay the message. Unfortunately for us, any who don't submit are rebels and traitors in his eyes, and no honour is to be shown them as they are crushed under his heel."

Milla's confusion continued, "So he captures messengers?"

"I wonder why the East agreed to ally with him," Ethan interjected, "The South and East have always hated each other."

Wulf shook his head, seeming uncomfortable, "Don't know. It also seems to me that if he was as mad as people say, he would have been removed from power. I hear rumors that he's gained some wicked power. I don't know from what for sure, but there's rumors he's working with a High Dragon."

"That can't be possible," Milla said fearfully, "If there was a dragon, people would have seen it. Right?"

Rune's thoughts raced over the vision that he had in the jail cart. The dark dragon over the castle, roaring over the land. He squeezed his eyes shut, as he remembered. It had seemed so real, despite how surreal the images were. His mind drifted a moment and he abruptly felt that same odd shift. He opened his eyes and he was somewhere else. Looking around frantically, he saw a castle of ebony stone before him. The sky beyond was dark and cloudy. Silent lightning struck nearby. The same colossal dragon then emerged from behind the castle. It stretched its long neck high as it released an ear-piercing scream to the sky. Rune dropped and covered his ears, horror filling him as he watched frightful, red-eyed specters pour from the beast's mouth and rush around him. He felt the words "No magik can destroy me" rumble through the air. A blaze of heat then passed him as the specters turned to a blue flame speeding across the land. The flame destroyed everything in its path, laying waste to castle, home, and forest. He turned to look out towards the path of destruction, and his expression turned to dismay as he was able to see his own town consumed by the blaze. He closed his eyes, not wanting to see any more, and suddenly felt calm. Carefully opening them again, he discovered that he was now somewhere else. Light stone walls encasing a magnificent courtyard garden surrounded him. A single barred door lay in each direction and above he could see the bright sun blazing in the sky. Then, hearing a little girl crying, he moved to find the source. There, huddled behind a bush, the same young girl in a white dress sobbed. She turned to look at him. Her bright, golden-yellow eyes filled with tears. "Can you save me?" she asked.

Rune knelt and reached out to her, "Save you from what?"

"Rune," her lips formed the words, but it was no longer her voice. "Rune!" the voice yelled again, and he woke, realizing the voice was Ethan's. He sat up with a start and looked around to see he was still in the cell with the others. "Are you alright?" Ethan asked.

Rune blinked and thought, trying to regain his senses, "I... uh," he stuttered.

Milla watched him with an uneasy expression, "What happened?"

Rune shrugged and shook his head, "I- I'm not sure."

"I can tell you what it looked like," Ethan started as he watched Rune, his expression grim. "I've seen-" he was interrupted by a clash of footsteps rushing down the stairs, and the cell door being opened soon after.

The guards made their way straight to Ethan, the lead guard grabbed him by the arm as the others swiftly unlocked his cuffs. Milla immediately moved to grab hold of Ethan as she cried out, "Leave him alone! Let him go!" Once he was unlocked the lead guard tried to force him to stand but Milla continued to pull him down. Ethan winced as the struggle tugged on his injuries. The other guards roughly ripped Milla away and Ethan was swiftly yanked up and moved out of the cell.

Milla began to sob quietly, "What are they going to do to him? Oh, poor Ethan." Rune remained silent as he settled back against the wall, a look of dread overcoming his features. He placed his hand on Milla's and she turned saddened eyes to him. After placing her other hand on top of his, she leaned against him. "Oh Rune, I am so sorry I got us all into this. I'm sorry for everything. I want you to know that. We are friends, I'm sorry I was so unkind to you."

Rune turned a slightly gladdened smile to her, "We'll get out of this," he said then leaned up against her as well, "We all will." And he placed the side of his head against hers.

Wulf huffed at them both and shook his head before turning to rest against the wall.

CHAPTER 34

Otho caught the bold scent of the bonfire as he rode his horse down the forest path. Thin, winding and riddled with low branches, the path forced anyone riding down it to keep to a slow pace. The small cottage finally came into view, lit up in the bright orange glow of the large nearby fire. Otho could make out the two figures seated near the fire, idly conversing. He waited until he was close enough to dismount to declare his greeting. "Ho there Valdr. Argus, I thought you would still be near Silvius handling the prince?"

Argus shrugged after taking a long drink of his mead, "Slipped through our fingers. Valdr here assures me the outcome is under control though."

Otho looked to Valdr as he flipped his reins over the branch of a nearby tree, "Oh?"

Valdr nodded a few times as he idly stroked his thin beard. "The East has him now. They are taking him south."

"And this is good?" Otho asked as he moved to the fire, adjusting his large fur coat before seating himself on a stump.

"It is," Valdr said in his typical bored tone. He pushed his lean frame up to stand as he watched the fire. "He and his traveling companions live. They will not make it to the king."

Otho nodded and turned his eyes to the fire as well, "He is alive and not in the North then. Just as your prophecy required."

"Indeed," Valdr answered, offering no more explanation.

Otho cleared his throat after a long silence, "What is it that will stop his journey to the southern king? Will his traveling companions save him?"

Argus piped in, "They're just a couple of kids. Not much they can do."

Valdr watched Argus a few moments as one might watch a village idiot, then responded, "Fate has seen fit to interject."

"Good, good," Otho said with a sigh. "I have no choice but to trust your word on this."

"I hear doubt in your words," Valdr returned as his grey eyes turned to Otho.

"You are from the south," Otho said simply. "It could be just as likely that you say what will make me happy, so your brethren win this war."

"I have long since lost interest in your invisible borders, puppet. There was a time when only vast stretches of water claimed border in this land."

"That was ages ago," Argus put in. "Like it or not, these borders have been fought over long before any of us fine folk were birthed, and they'll remain for ages more. Mark my words."

Valdr turned contemptuous eyes to Argus and spoke in a cynical tone, "Of course. We shall bow to your wisdom."

Argus frowned, but before he could defend himself, Otho interjected, "The High Queen has actually sent me to you as an order." Valdr said nothing as he looked to Otho to continue, so he did. "Of the young enchanted girls, you gathered for her, there is one she would like to know more of." After again receiving no response, Otho added, "She is a young blonde thing. Eyes of gold. She wore no shoes."

"She wishes to know her origin so that the ties to home can be broken," Valdr said plainly.

"I say this," Otho continued, "I do not think it wise that we help the queen use this creature. The child has abnormal powers. We should do away with her, not her kin."

"That is not your order," Valdr argued.

"Did we not agree to work against the queen fulfilling this mad prophecy? This child is exactly who she was looking for."

Valdr started to laugh as if he had just heard a joke, "She should more fear the fulfilment of the prophecy she has fought so hard to stop. Was she not afraid that the only one who could overthrow her is a daughter of the throne?"

Otho eyed Valdr a few moments, clearly not finding humor, "This is not a subject to joke on. The infant daughters she killed, to stop that prophecy from coming about, still haunts me."

Valdr laughed again, "All in vain."

"What do you mean?" Otho pressed, "Is this young girl somehow her blood?"

Valdr shook his head. "Indeed, she is not. Her mother also has no relation to the High Queen at all."

"And where is her mother?" Otho asked.

"Her mother is a broken thing. Her body lives but her mind left her a long time ago. She lives in a cottage a half a day's travel from Alauno," he explained.

"You just happen to know this without a second thought?" Otho asked.

"Is that not what I do?" Valdr said with a grin.

Otho narrowed her eyes, "Has she any other family in the west?"

Valdr nodded with a grin, "Just one more. Her mother's mother. A seer as well in fact. She lives in a cave by Alauno falls. She knows you are coming and is aware of your intentions. A good woman. I have met her more than once. I ask that you make her death quick."

"You think well of her and yet you tell me her location freely?" Otho asked, his voice thick with confusion.

Valdr returned a questioning look, "I do. Is that not what you wanted?"

Otho shook his head in disbelief, "Why is it so many seers can be so heartless?"

"A soldier takes another soldier's life in war. Both are innocent, and the surviving soldier is not thought heartless. He is thought to have done his duty. You ask me to reveal a truth that will surely mean the death of one who stands in the way of our greater good, and I offered it. Have I not simply done a duty? The young enchantress' rescue must be delayed."

Otho shook his head and looked away, "I will not argue. I have asked, and I have received an answer. Thank you Seer Valdr. I do still fear the queen's intentions with this creature she has found."

"You have nothing to fear from the young enchantress, puppet. Now do your duty." Valdr said as he pulled his long grey-blonde braid over his shoulder and pulled up his hood. "Destiny awaits." And he made his way off into the forest without another word.

"Seers," Otho grumbled once he was out of hearing range.

"They make my skin crawl," Argus agreed.

CHAPTER 35

A sense of dread took over the remaining prisoners as the familiar sound of footsteps resonated from the stairwell. Five guards made their way into the cell and marched toward the fearful group. Milla and Rune held tightly to each other while Wulf simply watched with wide eyes. To his relief, the guards turned their attention to Milla and Rune, unlocking their bindings. The nearest guard idly looked over Wulf then asked, "Ready to have that leg looked at?" Wulf spit at the ground in response. The guard shrugged and continued with unlocking Milla.

"What are you going to do to us?" Milla asked, but the guards said nothing as they attended to their duty. Once their bindings were removed, each arm was grabbed by a guard and they were easily lifted and guided out of the cell by the large men.

After being lifted up the stairs and into the keep's large black-stone courtyard, a pleasant smell of roasting meats and spices surged into their noses and their empty stomachs churned. They were directed to the massive main doors of the keep, then taken inside and down a wide hallway towards the huge, wooden double doors, with a guard on each side. The delicious scents strengthened with every step towards the entry. Just before approaching, the guards tapped their heavy spears on the doors, which opened soon after, revealing a great hall. At the end of the hall, Thane Od could be seen at the center of a table that had been raised up on a platform. A feast of savory food and drink was laid out before him, and he ate and spoke with those sitting on either side of him. He took no notice of the opening doors, or the two prisoners being led in afterward. Milla and Rune eyed him fearfully, then turned to look at the tables on the left and right of them. They were not on platforms, but they were also covered in a great deal of delicious, generous helpings of food. Milla and Rune both swallowed hard as their mouths watered, and they were finally shoved to the center of the room. The guards backed away and allowed them to stand freely, without bindings, as they waited for the Thane to take notice of them.

Thane Od's eye finally turned to them and he raised his hands to hush those around him. He offered a welcoming smile beneath his thick beard and asked, "What are your names?"

"I'm-" Rune started but was interrupted by Milla.

"What did you do with Ethan?" She demanded.

A deep quiet fell over the hall as the guests turned tense expressions to the Thane. He replied in an even tone, "You will first answer my questions. What are your names?"

"Rune and Milla," Rune said quickly, then gave Milla a cautioning look.

"Rune," Thane Od repeated, "How fitting. Tell me Rune, what were you and Milla doing with the young prince? Why did you travel together?"

"He was helping us," Rune answered swiftly, "We were travel-"

"The truth," Thane Od interrupted, "Now. I am not interested in tales."

Rune hesitated as he looked to Milla, unsure of what to say. She answered for him, "We are from the West, we were traveling through the North and-"

The Thane slammed his fist on the table, silencing her as she jumped from the sudden noise, "I am aware you are from the West. That is not what I asked. I asked you why you traveled with the young prince."

"We didn't know he was a prince until we were captured," Rune blurted, "We thought he was just a Captain, helping us out of kindness."

The Thane remained silent, after Rune spoke, for some time. "You were not led to him? Perhaps by this one?" He motioned to Milla.

"I didn't know he was a prince," Milla argued hastily, "But he-"

"How is Lieve?" He cut her off, "It has been ages since I last saw her."

Milla's eyes widened, "You know my omi?" His eye narrowed in return and she quickly got the message, answering, "She was good, the last time I saw her."

"Indeed," Od said thoughtfully, "She was always good at seeing hidden paths, if I remember correctly. Tell me, how are you at staying on a path laid out for you?"

Milla shook her head indignantly, "I followed all of her instructions."

"Did you?" he asked quickly, "Think hard before you answer." Milla furrowed her brows and looked off in thought. He gave her a few moments to think then started again, "How many times have you faltered from the path?"

"I haven't," Milla said defensively, "I-," she stopped then took hold of her necklace. "Once I suppose."

"Just the once?" he asked, seeming amused now, "Are you quite sure of that?"

Milla now seemed annoyed, "I followed her instructions exactly and found…"

"Found Rune, yes." He leaned forward onto his elbows, "And then?"

She answered sharply, "And I took him east, like I was told to. Just as she told me."

"Is that what she told you? Take a moment to remember."

Milla shook her head again and let out a frustrated noise, "Yes. She told me to take him east. She told me the path was his from there on."

The Thane smiled as he pushed himself up to sit against his backrest, "The path is his? If that path is his, have you followed his guidance?"

"Well, he couldn't exactly guide me. He didn't know where we were going," Milla answered.

"I didn't," Rune confirmed.

The Thane let out a sigh, "At no point did this young man suggest a direction that you did not take?" Milla's look of confusion deepened and she thought it over silently, clearly wracking her brain for an answer. Another silence fell. Thane Od then stood and motioned to the lower table on his right, "Sit. Eat," he ordered.

Rune lurched in that direction, not needing to be invited twice but Milla grabbed him as she asked the Thane, "Where is Ethan?"

The Thane eyed her, then lowered himself to sit. He looked down to his plate as he decided on which morsel he would eat next, "King Brandr has ordered his death."

"No, please," Milla begged as she released Rune and moved towards him, "There must be something-"

"You ask me to defy the King of the South?" He barked as his single eye turned up to view her.

Milla frowned deeply then dropped to her knees, "Please."

Yet another long silence fell, this one lingering longer than the others. Thane Od then began to laugh. Others around began to join in as he laughed louder. He finally calmed himself then urged the others to do the same. Milla turned confused eyes around then back to the Thane as he turned to look behind him. He motioned to a guard who promptly rushed off, "Why is it you care so much for a man you claim to have just met?"

"I-" Milla stuttered, "We're friends now."

The Thane laughed again, "Indeed." Looking Rune in the eyes he offered a small nod and again, motioned him toward the table. Rune looked to Milla, then rushed off to sit at the table. Milla remained where she was, unwilling to move without her question answered. The Thane seemed to ignore her for some time. He ate a few bites of food, then gulped down a large amount of his mead.

Rune quickly did so as well, stuffing his mouth full of the food now in front of him. Despite the silence, he looked to the fur covered man to his right and said through an overstuffed mouth, "Is'th goo'." The man turned a raised brow to Rune and grinned.

Wiping his mouth, Thane Od then spoke, though still examining his plate, "There was a time, before your omi was young, that our land was overrun by wars and chaos. All four realms warred, and the palace of the Great Seer stood tall and separate from these wars. Have you heard tales of the Great Seer?"

Milla hesitated then nodded lightly as she spoke softly, "A few."

"Do you believe them?" He asked, looking up to her.

Milla hesitated again as she glanced around at the faces watching her around the room, "I'm not sure what to believe."

The Thane grunted a laugh, "Smart girl." He then rested back into his chair as he spoke, "Whether this Seer was a villain, or a hero has been lost in tale, as the truth often is. There is one, undeniable fact that remains." He leaned forward as he placed his elbows on the table again and crossed his fingers together, "The Seer, was greatly powerful, and used that power to change the world amidst the chaos."

Milla slowly turned her eyes up to him as she spoke, "What does this have to do with us? What does this have to do with Ethan?"

Thane Od chuckled, "Everything, dear girl. Everything." He stopped and reached for his drink. Finishing it, he held it out for a servant to fill as he continued, "Do you believe your meeting of this young boy, Rune, is a coincidence? I think you know otherwise," he pulled his drink forward and continued without giving her time to speak, "Taking that to mind, do you think meeting the Prince of the North, the heir to the Throne of Light, was a coincidence? Think carefully before you answer." He took a long drink as he awaited her reply.

Milla looked around the room again as she thought. After taking a slow breath she answered, "What would the purpose be? To get him caught?"

Thane Od finished drinking and placed his mug down. He gave a nod, "It is possible."

Milla barked in return, "My omi would never use me like that. She would never-"

"Oh, but there are greater powers at work here," the Thane interrupted, "Greater than the queens and kings. Greater than the power that holds the South. Even greater than your dear omi."

Milla snorted a sarcastic laugh, "What? You?"

The Thane raised his brows at her. Leaning back as he grinned, he answered, "Fate." A clamor sounded at the back of the room as a barred door opened. From it, a guard led Ethan. He was now cleaned up and given new clothes, though metal cuffs remained on his wrists and ankles. Milla's eyes widened and she froze as Ethan was led to her. He smiled at her, seeming relieved. "I have no intentions of releasing you to the South King.

It is by my will that you were brought here." Thane Od said, then motioned to the guard and ordered, "Remove his bindings."

As the guard removed Ethan's cuffs Milla asked, "But why?"

"Because I am a servant of Fate, and I am its master," Thane Od answered as he stood. Milla wrapped her arms around Ethan as he was made free and he held her close in return. The Thane continued, "Fate has seen fit to bring you three together for a purpose. Three will become five, and together, you will set in motion the first step to your world's destruction."

Milla released Ethan as she turned puzzled eyes to the Thane, "What do you mean? What could we possibly do? How do we not do it?"

"There are times," the Thane said as he moved away from his chair, "That a corrupted forest must burn down to make way for new, untainted life. It is the way of nature, the way of fate. Sometimes, all that is needed is a spark of flame," he turned his eye to Rune, "And the means to carry it to the destination." He moved behind his chair, as if ready to leave, but instead he turned around. "You are all free to eat, drink and travel within my walls. No harm will come to you here. When you are ready to leave, you will make your way to Regintun."

"To do wha'?" Rune asked through a full mouth.

"To bring light to the consuming darkness," the Thane answered.

Ethan narrowed his eyes, "And if we refuse?"

Thane Od chuckled, "You won't. I have seen it. I have guided it. I captured the wolf to lure in the beast and his master. I have reflected the light and brought his muse and I have brought before me, the Dragon Lord's apprentice. The path is set." A short silence set in as the Thane was eyed curiously by all three.

Rune piped in, though his mouth was still half full of food, "I think I might refuse. I don't want to destroy the world."

The Thane turned his eye to Rune and he smiled wide, "If you do, fate will return a lost friend to you." Rune's eyes widened. "If you do not, you may never see him again. It will also lead you on a path to discovering the secrets of your parents, as well as the secrets they sought." Dropping his shoulders, Rune stopped chewing and looked down in thought.

"With all due respect, there is nothing you could say to me to make me go," Ethan chimed in indignantly. "Kill me if you must, but my only concern is for the safety of realm. I will not be a part of its destruction."

"No?" The Thane chuckled, "If you do not, the war that your people are losing will end, and the South will win. I wonder, what fate will befall your youngest brothers when the South storms the White Castle?"

Ethan snarled and crossed his arms, "How could going to Regintun end the war in our favor?"

"It will not. But it will end the war," the Thane answered. "And it will end the war before the armies take Albusinia. Your family will be spared." Ethan's upper lip quivered as he continued to snarl, but he also looked down and ended his protesting.

Milla looked to the Thane expectantly and his eye turned to her, "You already know what you will do. You know what fate brought you here. You know why the darkness must be lifted. This will be your first step in doing so," Milla nodded lightly then looked to the floor. The Thane then smiled triumphantly as he moved off, "Enjoy the feast." With that he made his way out the back door.

Milla promptly turned her attention to Ethan, "Did they hurt you? Are you alright?"

Ethan smiled brightly at her then guided her to the table next to Rune. As he did so, he replied, "I am fine. I had put up a fight, but in the end, they only wished to help heal my wounds. They have strange magiks here that I have never heard of." He pulled down the neck of his tunic and revealed his shoulder wound. It was no longer red and inflamed. All that remained was an unsightly scar.

Milla quickly checked it and turned widened eyes to his, "That's impossible."

"Apparently not," Ethan chuckled then motioned for her to sit on the bench as he did, "Let's eat. I'm starving."

CHAPTER 36

Rune, Milla and Ethan were provided room and board in a well-furnished home, temporarily vacated by the owner to allow them a comfortable stay. In addition, they were provided food, supplies, weapons, arms, and the means to wash up and ready themselves for their journey. The three woke early that cloudy morning, their minds consumed with unease about the near future. After finishing their morning meal, they sat around the table silently, all anticipating a mutual agreement but none eager to initiate the conversation.

Ethan finally spoke up, "If, we go," he started, "and Thane Od is correct in saying we will destroy the world by doing so, wouldn't the purpose be in vain?"

"I still don't see how we could possibly do something that horrible by simply going somewhere," Milla added, "In the stories I've heard, some seers twist words and speak in riddles. I don't think it means what it sounds like it means. Maybe he means we will end an era."

Rune stared intently at the pattern on the table, "Or it really means we're going to pull the wrong thread that unravels the tapestry."

Milla looked to Rune, "That sounds like something my Omi would say."

"Have you changed your mind then?" Ethan asked as he crossed his arms and slid back into his chair.

"No," Rune answered, "If our world can end so easily, then someone is going to pull that thread anyway. It might as well be me if it means..." he stopped and allowed the sentence to end without finishing it.

Ethan offered a hesitant nod in agreement, "I will not see my brothers suffer if I can have any hand at stopping it. Especially when the cost of doing so is so vague. After we do what must be done, I will head home and gather all the Seers in our land. Collectively, they may be able to see what our act has done and perhaps see a way to turn it around."

Rune shrugged, "From what I hear, dabbling in the future rarely has the results you intend. Isn't that usually what speeds the Seer Madness? Trying to interfere with or guide future events? For all we know," Rune added, "our actions here, are what cause you to seek out Seer guidance, which causes another event like the Great Seer's desolation but worse. That's the thing. Anything we do could be the thread."

"Then, if the future is so unsure, even the Thane's premonitions could be wrong," Milla said.

Another silence fell. The three remained in their own thoughts for some time before Ethan spoke up again, "So it's settled then? We travel to Regintun?" The other two nodded solemnly. Ethan took in a slow breath then stood. "Then we will leave in the morning. In the meantime, I intend to see as much of this city as I can. I wish to see the places here mentioned in the stories I've heard. You're both free to join me if you'd like."

Rune made a scoffing noise, "I have the biggest, softest bed I have ever known in the next room. There's a good chance I won't have anything like that again any time soon after this, if we even survive. I plan to make the best of it. Not spend my last day before we go in cold, wet weather."

Ethan smirked at Rune, "As you wish," then turned a look to Milla.

Milla then jumped up. "I'll go! But I haven't heard many stories of Steinnborg."

Ethan motioned to the door with one hand and offered the other to her with a smile, "I can relay them to you as the landmarks arise."

Milla quickly took his hand, moved to the door that was then opened for her and slipped outside with Ethan close behind.

Rune frowned as he watched the door close, "I can relay them to you as the landmarks arise," he repeated in a mocking tone. He then stood and looked around the large room that housed the kitchen, eating area, and sitting room. He let out a bored breath then started moving around, at first just touching and playing with random furniture pieces and ornaments. Seeing a large floppy hat, he decided to try it on, though it was far too big. He turned his head around the room a few times to find out the hat impaired his vision quite a bit. He looked back to the end table where he found the hat, lifting the rim slightly to see better. On the table, he saw an old gnarled wand. He picked it up and looked it over idly then sighed sadly, remembering how Feagan used to mock his attempts at using his own wand at home. Moving to the closest chair, he plopped down onto it, looking silly with the large hat hiding his face and shoulders while he rested both arms on the oversized armrests. He pointed the wand up with his hand then whisked it around with small wrist movements.

"If I commissioned a picture of how the world should remember you," Rune quickly removed the hat as he heard Thane Od's voice, "That would have been it." He put his hand out to gesture Rune to remain sitting as he clearly was ready to stand, then sat down in the chair across from him.

"I didn't hear you come in," Rune said as his face reddened, and he settled back in the chair.

"Nor did you see me," the Thane added, "And yet, here I am."

Rune nodded slowly then raised a brow as he removed the hat and placed it to the side with the wand, "What brings you here?"

"Curiosity," the Thane answered simply.

"What are you curious about?" Rune asked as he idly played with the brim of the hat.

"You," Od answered as he examined Rune.

"I'm nothing special," Rune said then slouched back into the chair. "Just a magi that can't use magik on purpose and a guide that gets people lost."

"That sounds like a good start to a tale," Od laughed, "Tell me, how do you see the tale ending?"

Rune licked his bottom lip then shrugged, "If it's like every other story, the hero prince wins and lives forever happy with his huntress, while the magi, with accidental magik trips over his own feet trying to help and blows himself away." Rune answered as he continued playing with the hat.

The Thane let out a laugh, "You should remember you said that in the future. It will bring you a good laugh."

"You can see the future," Rune put in, not seeing the humour, "What do you see happening?"

Od watched Rune a moment then leaned back comfortably in the chair as he pushed his fingertips together. "I see many things. I see you accepting a gift. I see you touching the sky while walls are built up around you. I see your hand guided by an ancient monster in disguise to tear down a tower of shadow. I see you destroying your enemies with an unborn child, which will in turn give rise to the world turning on end. A Servant will become king. The land will be split in two and dragons will reign half as the servant king rules the other half. A great darkness will return within the chaos. I see a profound betrayal leading to the rise of the greatest evil in our lifetime. Our only hope will lay within the golden bird. Whether the golden bird succeeds or not, the world will be ripped asunder in the wake of these events. The servant king will raise up as a god and he will reign as King and God to a world ruled by Princes."

Rune gave Od an odd look, "That story makes no sense. No one fights off enemies with a baby."

"I offered more than that but," Thane Od said then sighed heavily, "if that is the image you wish to latch on to..."

"Really," Rune added, "Who hits people with a baby? That's just wrong."

Od sniffed and watched Rune with a stern expression, "You miss the point."

"No, a baby is missing a point," Rune added, "That's what I'm saying. It's not a weapon at all. Even the bones are soft if you want to get deep down to it. It's just wrong and gross."

Od sniffed again, "Well, don't look at me. It's a vision of you."

Rune frowned at that, "I'm not sure I like myself very much if I hit people with babies when I'm older."

Od let out another sigh, "We are off topic entirely. Let us get back to what you see."

"Nothing to do with hitting people with babies. I can tell you that." Rune said with a frown. Od continued to stare at Rune with a dry expression. After a few moments of the two watching each other, Rune answered, "I don't see anything. I'm not a seer."

"Humor me," Thane Od continued, "What is it you see when you close your eyes? When you are in that place between wake and sleep?"

Rune frowned lightly, then looked to the floor, "Dreams are just silly nonsense."

"They are never that. Even without sight." Od insisted.

Rune shrugged, "We heard some guards talking about a dragon a while ago. So, I've been having these nightmares about a dark dragon behind a black castle destroying the world." He then thought a moment, "Well, in one of my dreams he destroys the world. In the other, Ethan saves us."

The Thane nodded a few times, "Interesting."

"I'm pretty sure he uses a sword though. Not babies." Rune finally added.

Od gave him an unimpressed look. "Food. We should find food," he then said as he stood and moved toward the kitchen. Rune jumped up to follow enthusiastically.

***

Ethan and Milla wandered down the broad cobblestone street for some time, taking in their surroundings. Tall stone buildings surrounded them on every side, wetted by a light misting rain that chilled the air. Despite the chill, the two continued through the damp weather. The walk, so far, had yielded no sightings of famous landmarks, so instead they leisurely spoke of the architecture, pointing out differences in comparison to what they had seen in their homelands. "Even in my home, Albusinia, they use more wood than they do here," Ethan started as he eyed the tops of the buildings. "I wonder how the structures can handle the weight of all that stone? I'm fairly confident that the techniques we use in the building of our castle and walls would be ill-suited for the average building here."

Milla followed his gaze and agreed, "I can only speak from very little experience, but from what I've seen in the towns surrounding Gottswai, there are no buildings that are all stone."

They stopped briefly as they spotted the bodies of their eastern escort hanging in a nearby thoroughfare. They turned astonished eyes to each other, "I wonder what prompted that," Ethan said, then looked back to the hanging bodies.

"I can't imagine they took the news well that the Thane intended to let us go," Milla answered, choosing not to look back to the bodies.

Ethan nodded a few times in agreement. They continued to make their way through the crowd of the main roadway. Statues of two large, black dragons facing each other could be seen not far away, marking the entrance of a massive square building constructed with black bricks. Ethan began to speed up as he said, "There it is!"

"What?" Milla said as she kept up and looked to the statues.

"The Dragon Lord's Temple," Ethan added with excitement as they continued. "According to the stories, this used to be a tower so high you couldn't see the top from below. Even now, the base is told to be so wide that it takes half a day to get from one side to the other." He eyed the base a moment before continuing, "No doubt a slight exaggeration. But also, according to the tales, there were openings large enough for a high dragon to land. The Dragon Lord would gather the greatest of dragons, and the greatest powers and minds of the land here when discussing terms of the Dragon Alliances."

Milla's eyes widened with interest as she gazed toward the structure. They eventually made their way in between the towering dragon statues, heads turned up as they both examined the colossal effigies. Milla's gaze slowly moved to the immense structure's entrance while Ethan's eyes moved around the whole of the base with keen interest. "What happened to the tower?" Milla finally asked.

"Toppled in the dragon wars," Ethan quickly explained, though his eyes continued to examine the area, "Apparently, it was a devastating fall. Many were killed. But they used the bricks to build up the town and walls around us."

"The dragons knocked it down?"

"No," Ethan said then looked to her, "The Dragon Lord did. Something happened, no one knows what, but it caused him to go mad and turn on his own kind and dragon alike. He destroyed this tower and everyone in it… many around it as well. He then rebuilt a new tower further north. That is now the Great Seer Ruins."

"Wait," Milla said, looking to him with confusion, "He built the Great Seer's tower?"

"Well yes. They are the same man."

"The Great Seer is the Dragon Lord Mayon?" Milla asked with deep shock in her tone. Ethan nodded quickly, seeming pleased to relay the story. Milla shook her head, her eyes wide, "All the stories I've heard of the Dragon Lord are about how he was a great hero that lived for generations, never aging. He helped us live in peace with dragons. How is it even possible that he's the Great Seer as well?"

Ethan shrugged, "I suppose it just took him longer than other seers for the madness to take him. Very few know of their connection, as most are not willing to share that part of the story, out of fear. If it's even true, that is." Milla's eyes turned to the large building as she drifted off into her thoughts. Ethan continued watching her process the information, a smile faintly touching his lips. Her eyes turned back to him as her mouth opened to ask a question, but she stopped as she saw his expression and instead smiled shyly. Ethan quickly looked to the ground and cleared his throat, "Some believe the Great Seer still lives," he added as if trying to fill the silence.

Milla nodded as she bit her lips together and looked back to the building, "I've heard that. It's impossible though, isn't it?"

Ethan gave a light shrug then smirked, "I suppose if we see another excessively tall tower built somewhere, we'll know for sure."

Milla let out a small laugh, "You shouldn't joke about that. Not with the way things are going."

Ethan's smile grew as he watched her fondly, "You're probably right." A few moments passed as both searched for words. Ethan soon blinked several times as he regained his thoughts and turned to look again at the building. "It's too bad we can't go inside. I'd be interested to see what it looks like in there." His attention was turned as a flash of distant lightening lit up the sky.

Milla looked to the flash as well, then turned to see the crowds in the street slowly dispersing and heading into buildings. "That's probably a sign that we should head back," she said, turning a grin to him.

"You're not afraid of a little storm, are you?" Ethan joked as he smiled down at her.

Milla crossed her arms as she playfully smiled back, "I can handle it if you can."

Ethan's smile grew as he raised his brows. "Then we will see how tough they make you Westerners," he taunted, crossing his arms as well. Large drops of rain began to fall as they continued to stare with playful, taunting smiles, but the rain quickly turned into a thick downpour. Milla scrunched her nose and blinked away the rain as best she could, then began to shiver slightly, still making no complaint. "Alright," Ethan spoke loud through the loud downpour as he uncrossed his arms, still smiling, "I give up. We better head inside." Milla nodded with a laugh as she hugged herself tighter for warmth. He wrapped an arm around her and they turned to head back down the way they came. She let out a shriek as lightening cracked with a deafening sound above their heads. She grabbed tight to Ethan as her shoulders raised up in a cower and she looked up to the sky. He held her tighter and urged her forward faster down the streets. They kept close to buildings and under cover whenever possible, thankful for the excessive number of covered walkways.

They finally reached their borrowed home, stopping under the veranda, and turning to view the deluge they had just escaped from. "Just so we're clear," Milla said as she continued looking to the rain, "I won."

"You did not," Ethan scoffed as he looked down at her, "We left at the same time."

Milla turned an impish grin up at him, "Only because you gave up."

His eyes narrowed as his smile grew, "You were shivering."

Milla tilted her head, "Maybe, but I didn't give up. We Westerners are made of tougher stuff."

Ethan let out a laugh, "That's not tough. That's stubborn."

"Different word. Same outcome," Milla said and bit back a laugh.

Ethan didn't argue as he continued to beam a smile at her. His smile slowly faded as he watched her and took in a slow breath as he wiped the wetness from her brow. "We should head inside," he said softly, then released her and forced the door open before she could respond.

They closed the door behind them, then laughed as they looked at each other, dripping wet by the entrance. Ethan stroked the wet hair from her forehead as he smiled and took a step toward her. His mouth opened to speak, but he was interrupted as he heard loud voices of an argument in the kitchen. Half of the argument was clearly Rune with a full mouth. "No, because if they did, then what would happen to the rest of them? You can't just shrink like that. The rest of you must go somewhere. Are you sure that part doesn't just turn invisible?"

"You miss the point entirely my boy," Thane Od returned, also with a full mouth, "They are not like us. They are of a different world entirely. So, when they shrink to our size and take on our features, it is not a matter of size but more what they are made of. It's the same with faeries."

Ethan and Milla looked to each other with confused smiles as they turned and made their way to the kitchen, "You can't tell me faeries and dragons are related. Faeries don't even have scales."

"Again, you miss the point," Thane Od returned, "Their bodies do not work like ours. How else do you think a faerie can carry things that are so much bigger and heavier than themselves."

"Magik obviously," Rune answered then looked to Milla and Ethan as they entered. "Wow, you two are soaked." He said, then swallowed his mouthful before taking another bite, "Is it raining?"

Ethan smiled and nodded, "A little bit. We're just going to find something dry to wear," he said then guided Milla out of the room by her shoulders then up the stairs.

Rune frowned lightly as he watched them. Od watched his expression then said, "She is not your golden bird."

"Don't start with that or I'll start with the unborn baby weapons again, old man." Rune grumbled.

"You do that, and I'll start back on the concept of pinching time again," Od retorted with a frown. They stared each other down angrily for a few moments, then both let out laughs.

Milla and Ethan both quickly made their way into her room and he promptly grabbed a blanket and wrapped it around her. "Rune seems to have made a friend," Milla said with a laugh.

Ethan turned smiling eyes to her, "I'm not sure if I should be happy for him or worried." They both laughed, and he continued, "Find something dry to wear. I'll do the same and make sure the fire is burning hot. I'll meet you downstairs."

Milla nodded as he turned to make his way out, but stopped as she held tight to his hand, "Ethan," she said sheepishly, "I've been meaning to ask you something."

Ethan looked to her hand then to her eyes. His own eyes betrayed a hint of fear of what she might ask. Milla studied his expression a few moments, then stuttered before asking, "I only-" she sighed and looked down, "I suppose I was wondering what you said to your horse."

"My horse?" Ethan asked with deep confusion.

Milla shook her head at herself. It was clearly not her intended question. She released his hand and pulled the blanket around her tight, "Before we were captured. You said something to him and he ran away."

Ethan watched her a moment before murmuring, "I spoke to him in the few words of his homeland that I had learned. His name is Kenget. It means warrior in their tongue. I told him to run home."

"I see," Milla said, now seemingly having a hard time returning eye contact.

"Thank you for coming with me," he said softly with a smile. Milla nodded and let out an agreeable noise as he turned and left. She then pulled the blanket tighter and flopped down to sit at the edge of the bed.

Ethan made his way down the hall hurriedly, entered his room, and closed the door behind him. He leaned his back against the door as he let out a frustrated noise and hit the back of his head against the door once. After taking in a slow breath, he pushed himself off the door and moved to find dry clothes.

.

CHAPTER 37

A cold wind plagued the group as they made their way down the steep, stone-walled road towards Regintun. The large blackstone city could be seen in the far distance lining the seashore cliffs, that were being assaulted by strong waves. Just across a sturdy stone bridge, the towering black castle covered the entirety of a rocky coastal island.

Despite the furs and wool clothing provided them by the people of Steinnborg, the chill still broke through. All three enveloped themselves as best they could as they held the reins of their sturdy mountain horses that eased their way down the rough brick-laid path. Dark gray clouds formed overhead and sped through the sky, casting a shadow over their journey and withholding any warmth the sun might have offered. The steep decline finally began to ease as they neared sea level and the protective wall ended, revealing a jagged lush terrain of short thick trees, massive boulders and steep crags splitting the mossy, green landscape. Rune scratched an itch caused by his new wool pants then adjusted his newly acquired sword as he looked back to see how far down they had traveled. He let out a grunt of awe as he beheld the tremendous black cliffs on either side of the road. Steinnborg was all but a memory now as it could no longer be seen. Milla and Ethan turned at Rune's grunt, then followed his gaze, the same look of awe taking over their features.

"I had-" Ethan started but was cut off as an explosion of fire erupted nearby. All the horses reared and shrieked but were calmed quickly by the three riders as they turned toward the rising blaze that soon after lowered and smoldered. Their eyes and bodies turned and twisted as they sought out the source of the explosion.

Soon after, a large, armed group of people emerged from behind the crags and boulders, surrounding them. Two men stepped ahead of the group. One tall and lean with flaxen hair, wearing hardened leather armour. The other, a giant of a man with cropped brown hair, bearing leather armour plated in a dark gray metal. He held a large hammer over his shoulder as he quietly examined the travelers.

"You don't want to be traveling this way friends," the flaxen haired man called out with a smile. "Best if you turn back."

"Want and need are two very different things," Ethan answered, being sure not to make any threatening moves, "We do not want to go to Regintun, and yet, that is our destination."

The flaxen haired man took another step forward and eyed the three, "What is your purpose then?"

"We were sent by Thane Od," Ethan replied.

"Thane Od," the blonde repeated then turned to the group that followed him and motioned them to disperse. The large man stayed. "Thane Od has ignored all of our messages and refuses to allow us passage through Steinnborg. Yet now he sends three to pass us by to the cursed city. Why is that?"

"Damned if we know," Rune piped in, "He's not the type of man that allows many other options than to do as he asks."

The blonde chuckled, "So I hear. The name is Alberic, this here is Milo. We have been trying to guide these people out of danger for some time now. A foulness has taken over the city of Regintun. All who try to escape, the guards attempt to chase down and put to the sword. The ones you saw here are some of those we have rescued. If you are acquainted with the Thane, perhaps you can see fit to ask him to allow these good people through to safety?"

"Perhaps," Ethan answered, he then concluded the introductions, "I am Ethan. This is Milla and Rune. We may be able to speak to the Thane on your behalf, but only after we complete our task."

"And your task is?" Alberic prodded.

"To make sense of pointless riddles," Rune grumbled.

Alberic chuckled, "I am good at riddles. Try me."

Ethan grinned at Rune then answered, "We are to bring light to whatever darkness has consumed the city of Regintun it seems."

Milo shifted and frowned as he looked down to Alberic. Taking note of Milo's uneasiness, Alberic offered him a nod then replied to Ethan, "It seems we can help each other after all then."

"Oh?" Ethan asked with great interest.

"Follow us," Alberic said as he turned, "We have a warm fire and information you will need." He then made his way behind the jutting crag with Milo in tow. The three hesitated, but Ethan urged his horse to follow. Milla and Rune quickly followed him.

***

Amongst the trees and natural rock walls, a large encampment housed many refugees from the city and surrounding area of Regintun. In a spacious central spot, a sizable bonfire blazed and emanated its warmth a good distance around. Alberic and Milo walked to warm themselves by it as Ethan, Rune and Milla secured their horses nearby. They moved eagerly to the fire near the two refugee leaders.

"Quite the camp you have here," Ethan started as he held out his hands to draw in the warmth, "How long did it take you to build such numbers?"

"Mere days, if you'd believe it," Alberic answered with a grin as he watched Rune and Milla approach closer. "We had been following whisper and rumour to locate a friend of ours, Wulf. Everywhere we went there were people in need. Not to say I'm one to help every desperate soul I cross. My friend Milo on the other hand..." he said looking to Milo.

"We couldn't just leave them," Milo said simply.

Alberic shrugged as he smiled, "At any rate, our numbers grew until we finally... came upon... a rumor that our friend was taken to Steinnborg. We've been stuck here since."

Ethan nodded, "We met a man named Wulf in the prison we were kept in briefly."

Alberic raised both brows as Milo let out a relieved sigh, "It's good to hear he lives. Is he well?"

Rune then piped in, "He looked like he had been beat up but other than that he was fine. Grumpy and dirty and refusing help to have his leg healed but fine."

Alberic smiled at that, "Well, grumpy and dirty is his natural state, and it does seem very like him to be too stubborn to accept help as well."

"You are from the West as well then?" Milla asked. "Rune and I have come from the West."

"Indeed, we are," he answered with a smile to her then turned a saddened gaze to the fire, "Though I think perhaps we've seen the last of it." He then cleared his throat as he changed the subject, "Do you three know very much about dragons?" he asked them, keeping his eyes on the flames.

"Dragons." Ethan repeated, "I have to say I do not like where this is going."

Alberic chuckled, "But I'm sure by now you have had your suspicions."

After a sharp sigh, Ethan responded, "Dragons have not been around for generations. Anything we would know of them would come from ancient tale and legend. We cannot make claims to the accuracy of them."

"Yet, it is all we have," Alberic returned, turning his teal blue eyes to Ethan. "We must assume that there is some truth in them."

Ethan frowned, "If we are to assume that, then we would also assume that no blade or spear can kill them. We would need to somehow gather enough magi, whom, as you know, are quite rare in our day and even more-so in this land, or..."

At that point, Milla perked up and asked with a smile, "Or the Wardens of Light? You speak of the stories of the Wardens of Light, right? They are my favorite of all stories."

Alberic smiled at her, "That is exactly what I thought to mention. An ancient order of Light Wardens and Seers who had discovered the secrets to a dragon's destruction that did not require a herd of magi to sacrifice themselves."

Ethan turned a grin to Milla before he responded, "Yes, shining heroes in all the tales. The problem with this being obvious; They no longer exist, if they ever had."

"I think they did," Alberic said, then sighed, "Or perhaps I hope they did, if killing a dragon proves impossible. We do not need the order; we only need their secrets."

Rune then asked, "Have you seen the dragon?"

"No," Milo finally piped in, "But we spoke to him."

Alberic confirmed this with a nod and continued Milo's thought, "We were prisoners, sent to the creature as a sacrifice. It was too dark to see him, but I am confident, after hearing the rumors and putting together the scattered information, that he is in fact a dragon. He calls himself Eilifatli. The fact that he keeps himself cooped up in a cave avoiding moving and being seen, tells me that he is weak. Dragons in the tales are said to make a grand effort to show themselves. Especially his type."

"His type?" Ethan repeated.

After a nod, Alberic explained, "In my possession, back in my home land, I have an ancient Book of Dragons. It explains the appearance and purpose of all the known dragons at the time. It explained that observers found a pattern of behavior in dragons. Each seemed to embody an emotion. The more powerful the dragon, the more powerful the emotion. They were also said to be able to emanate the means to cause this emotion and seemed to feed off those in the area feeling said emotion. I had thought this book to be spreading myth and lies, but now that I have come close to Eilifatli, I believe it to be true. He is a dragon of horror. His type enjoys showing themselves to spread horror."

Milla frowned deeply as she spoke, "Well, that sounds lovely. Are you saying it can make us all feel horrified just by being near it?"

Alberic nodded, "Milo and I can confirm this to be so. It is difficult to even explain the feeling. I should also add the unfortunate truth, that a Horror Dragon is one of the class of High Dragon. They are massive in size and very powerful."

Rune's thoughts turned to his vision as Alberic spoke and he frowned, "How is it you even live then?"

"Quite simply," Alberic explained, "I was able to ward us both from the dragon's powers and escape. As I said, I believe the dragon to be weak, as it did not pursue us. It also made no attempt to get to us. It instead attempted to lure us to him. It almost worked."

"What do you think is causing it to be so weak?" Milla asked as she moved in a little closer.

"I had the same question," Alberic began, "I had thought maybe the dragon ward in the south still had power, but then he would soon be destroyed which would seem a pointless sacrifice. As far as I've heard dragons do not get sick, so barring any lacking information I concluded that he is simply dying of old age. He speaks as though he has been around for a long time. It is not unheard of for a dragon to die of age when they lack what sustains them."

"So why not just wait for it to die?" Milla continued, "Wouldn't that be safer than attacking it head on?"

Alberic shook his head, "Even in his state, he could still have generations of our lives left in him. It is not worth that risk, especially if we have secrets that could ease our hands to his destruction."

Ethan looked to Rune and Milla who shared the same troubled expression. "I assume then, that you know something of these secrets that the Wardens kept?"

Alberic nodded and explained, "Before my journey to Regintun, I had been plagued by a strange whispering in my thoughts. I had thought I was going mad of course, but I could make out words from the whispers. They were in another tongue, but I felt meaning in them. When we had finally confronted Eilifatli, these words saved us. They are a form of incantation, much like those used by magi, but strangely different."

Rune moved in closer as he asked, "Different how?"

Alberic thought this over then answered, "I myself am a practiced magi. I am, in fact, quite good if I do say so myself. The blaze you saw, was my doing." Instead of continuing, he waited for a reaction.

Rune moved closer, even more interested now, as Ethan spoke, "That could be quite useful, but I am as curious as Rune clearly is, as to how these incantations differ."

"Well," Alberic started, seeming disappointed by the lack of reaction at his unveiling, "When a magi is successful in casting, it is a feat of raw focus. It is a demand on the elements that surround us. If the words are not believed and understood to mean only what you demand, you will fail in casting or the strength of it will be weaker. The amount of focus required to cast a spell of any use is quite significant and, as you can imagine, quite draining. But the words offered me for the incantations against the beast, there was no true focus. It was more of a will, a request, if you catch my meaning. It was a clear request made and answered, and the power given was not of the elements. It was of inner strength and..." he paused looking seriously to Ethan, "Light."

Ethan took in a slow breath, "And whispers in your mind offered you these words?"

Alberic nodded, "Not the whispers of madness I think, but the whispers of a seer."

"Thane Od perhaps?" Ethan suggested.

With a shake of his head Alberic answered, "It was a woman. An old woman."

With that, both Ethan and Rune looked to Milla, whose curiosity was also peaked, "Old woman? Did she say anything else? Anything else that could help?"

Alberic looked to Milla as he thought over the whispering, "She did. She said many things, more-so after we had escaped the dragon. She told me that a dragon must be 'revealed' before it can be slain. She told me that a seer must be present once the dragon is revealed, for only a seer can remove the 'heart' of a dragon to destroy it."

"Can you speak with this seer now?" Ethan immediately asked, "Perhaps ask her for clarification?"

Alberic shook his head and lowered his eyes, "I might have been able to, but she is now gone from this world."

"Wait," Milla piped in quickly, "Gone? What do you mean gone from this world?"

"She is dead," Alberic clarified, "Her last words to me were that the shadow had finally reached her. The rest I didn't fully understand. I believe she was dying as she spoke with me. She asked me to 'tell her to let the sun in to find answers'."

Milla's face knotted with confusion as she looked off. Ethan watched her with sad eyes then said to Alberic, "So, in order to kill this dragon, we need a seer. The only one I know of nearby is the Thane."

Alberic nodded then turned his eyes back to Ethan, "Who has refused my many requests." Ethan looked off in thought, then Alberic turned his eyes to Rune, who was staring into the fire in thought. "The seer told me to expect a boy seer to join us. She said he harbors a great deal of power."

Rune turned his eyes to Alberic and shook his head, "I'm no seer. She wasn't talking about me."

Milla and Ethan both looked to Rune, "Who suggested that she was talking about you?" Ethan asked.

"Alberic," Rune said as he motioned to him.

Ethan looked at Alberic who now grinned lightly, then back to Rune, "He said nothing of the sort."

Alberic chuckled then clarified, "Forgive me, I needed to test it before I was sure. I did say something to him. You see, the seer had explained to me that seers have a sort of bond that allows them to speak to the mind of others, as well as receive the thoughts of others. Seers can speak to other seers, if they know how, from a great distance. So, it seems I have cleared up any question of my sanity. She had told me that I held the capability not only to give power to the words she gave me, but also to speak with a seer through thought."

"I'm not a seer," Rune repeated.

"You are," Alberic insisted, "How could you possibly be unaware?"

Rune turned his gaze around at the others as all eyes now rested on him. Their expressions of confusion mirroring his own. "I'm not a seer," he repeated yet again, "I'm learning to be a magi."

"Alright," Alberic said with a grin, "Show me what you have learned so far."

Rune thought quickly over the many spells that he had learned the words for. He thought over which best to try. But, his shoulders dropped, "I haven't been able to cast anything yet."

Milla piped in, "Don't be silly Rune. Your summoning spells and you were able to lift my bag with your mind. You even used your power to throw a group of evil men into a river. I saw it all myself."

Rune turned sad eyes to her then shook his head. Alberic continued to grin as he said, "Summoning spells are a myth, and lifting a bag would require a great deal of wind magik, as would throwing men. That would be a great power indeed. Show me," he said with amusement, "lift something."

Still frowning Rune answered quietly, "The summoning spell and the pack lifting were a trick, Milla."

"A trick?" Milla asked, her voice rich with confusion.

"He had a friend," Ethan explained, "that was helping him fake his powers."

Rune nodded and looked sorrowfully at Milla, "I wanted to tell you but-"

"But you decided to lie instead?" Milla roared, "So, you were the wrong person. This whole time you were the wrong person? No wonder this all happened!"

"Milla," Ethan intruded, "You forget the men flying into the river, and the incident with the faeries. That was no trick."

"A powerful wind spell then?" Alberic asked.

Rune slowly shook his head, "I don't know what it was. I didn't cast anything."

Alberic's face turned grim. "You..." he swallowed, "You're not just a seer, then. You're a Weaver, just like the Great Seer."

Rune turned widened eyes to Alberic, "What? No! I'm not!"

Steadying himself, Alberic shook his head, "Amazing. I would have never thought..."

"I'm not like the Great Seer!" Rune barked again, "I'm not even a seer! I haven't seen anything!"

Ethan and Milla watched the back and forth between the two with wide eyes. Ethan finally spoke, "Rune, do you know what it was your parents took from the Seer Ruins? Did you use it?"

"I didn't use anything!" Rune roared, "I'm not a seer! Just ask Feagan!" He then frowned, remembering his lost friend.

"Feagan is the friend that helped him fake the spells?" Alberic asked.

"Yes," Ethan answered with a nod, "Feagan is a stray faerie."

Alberic's brows furrowed, "When you are not in his presence, do you ever have visions?"

"Visions?" Rune asked as he furrowed his brows as well.

"Visions," Alberic repeated. "It is believed that faeries have the ability to suppress visions of willing seers. Perhaps unknowing seers as well?"

Face now pale, Rune flustered, "And how do you know all this? Did your whispering seer tell you?"

Alberic moved toward Rune with a smile, "Amongst being a magi of no small talent, and prone to the whispering of old women," he chuckled, "I am also a highly learned man. I serve as Clerk of Histories at the palace in Gottswai. I was sent here with my fellows by the High Queen Erma, to not only deliver a message but to look for sources to the dark rumors the Queen had been hearing. Our Queen is often dismissed by the other realms as being naive and unaware of anything beyond the Great River, but they are quite wrong. She does not involve herself in the petty squabbles, but she is quite aware of them." Rune was unable to form words after Alberic spoke. His mind now overburdened with the possibility of what he might be.

"Rune," Ethan said softly after a silence, "Not all seers are evil. Just because you carry those powers, does not mean-"

"No," Rune barked, "No, just... I need to think." He said as he walked away in a daze.

Ethan lurched forward to go after him but Alberic grabbed his arm, "Give him time to let it settle."

Looking to Alberic, then to Rune, Ethan let out a sigh and nodded. Turning back to the fire he spoke quietly, "So we have our Seer I suppose. Do we have a plan?"

"At this point," Alberic said, turning back to the fire, "We have all the information we will be able to get in the short term I think. Milo and I will join you three. We will lead you to Eilifatli's cave and hope that somehow, our young seer will be able to remove the heart."

Milla watched Rune wander off towards the trees with his head down, "What about revealing it? Do we know how to do that?"

"I can only assume the words given me are the key to that," Alberic answered. "When spoken, one brought light to the cave. It 'revealed' the horrors around us, while the other seemed to give the inner strength to face the horrors. All we can do is assume this is what we need."

Milla then turned a small, tentative smile to Alberic as she asked, "Does that mean you're a Warden of Light?"

Alberic laughed lightly, "I am not part of an order that no longer exists, but it does seem that I can make use of their secrets. Take that as you will."

Beaming a smile now, Milla said, "I feel like we're part of an epic tale. Facing a dragon with a Light Warden. Saving the world."

Ethan watched the back and forth between the two as his brows slowly furrowed, "Destroying the world," he promptly reminded.

Alberic's smile dropped as he asked, "Doing what now?"

Ethan sighed, "Thane Od. He told us we were to come here and bring light to the darkness, but in doing so, we would destroy the world."

Alberic let out a humorless laugh, "The amount of damage this dragon has done, and killing it will destroy the world more than he? I think not."

Ethan offered a grim nod, "We can only hope." After a moment, Ethan continued, "We should ready ourselves. The five of us should set out soon."

"Three become five," Milla then said with wide, distant eyes.

Ethan, his expression still grim, frowned lightly at Milla's words. "So, the Thane was correct on that. Let's hope it ends there."

CHAPTER 38

Rune wandered by himself around the large encampment, always being sure to remain in earshot. In his wanderings, he eventually found a crystal-clear pond that reflected the darkening gray sky above. He sat himself in the spongey grass at the edge and huddled inside his furs as his mind strained over the revelation of his powers. Replaying each incident since early childhood, he could see the truth now clear as day. As night enveloped the sky, he buried his head into his knees and tears filled his eyes. All his hopes and dreams of being a magi, like his father were now shattered. Instead, he was to take on the role that ended in madness or villainy in every story he had ever heard. He sniffed as he thought over his most recent dreams that he knew now to be a seer's visions, understanding now that Thane Od must have somehow known all along. Even with that understanding he still could make no sense of them, other than the obvious; that they would defeat the dragon, or they wouldn't. He snorted at how unhelpful it was. His mind then turned to the young girl that stole him from his visions each time. He wondered if she herself was another vision, or if instead she was a seer reaching out to him like the old woman reached out to Alberic. After taking in a slow breath he began his attempts to try to reach her by going to the same place in his mind. Despite many strained tries he was unable to find her, so he gave up and allowed his mind to return to thoughts of self pity.

Time drifted on as he remained still in his own thoughts, fluttering in and out of a restless sleep throughout the night. The sky eventually lightened as sun approached horizon. He turned tired eyes to the sky now that had lost all sign of clouds. Letting out a quivering breath into the cold air, he sadly dropped his head back down to his knees.

"Rune," Milla said softly as she approached. "They are making food. Are you hungry?"

"No," he grumbled loud into his knees. Without word Milla moved to his side and sat next to him. She huddled into her own furs and remained silent for a good amount of time. Rune finally lifted his head and looked to her. "Aren't you hungry?" Milla shrugged and began picking at the mossy grass next to her. After another silence Rune asked, "Do you hate me now?"

Milla jolted a look to him with brows furrowed in confusion, "Hate you? Why would I hate you?"

"I'm a seer," he answered plainly.

Milla's mouth opened as she realized his meaning, "Rune. My omi is... was... a seer. I loved her more than everyone except my sister."

"Was," Rune repeated.

Milla nodded a few times as she fought off tears. "I think she is the one who was speaking to Alberic. In fact, I'm confident it was her."

Rune nodded a few times then looked to the water as they both turned to silence again. He finally spoke, "She was a good person?"

"So good," Milla said with a smile as she looked distant in memory. "She was kind and so funny. She could make the best out of even the worst situation." Milla started to tear up again and Rune put a hand on hers.

"I'm sorry you lost her," Rune said with honest sympathy.

Milla sniffed and turned a smile to him as she spoke through tears, "My point is that, I'm not going to hate you because you are a seer. In fact, I respect you for it. It is one of the hardest paths a person can take. But I already see that you are a good and kind person. Like my omi."

Rune's eyes teared up and he looked away to hide it. After gaining some composure he sniffed, "You don't think I will become an evil villain?"

Milla laughed and wrapped her arm around him, "Of course not silly."

"But the stories-," Rune started but was interrupted quickly by Milla.

"Are just stories," she put in. "They're stories because they are wild and different. Not because they are normal. The reason you don't hear stories about the good seers is because it's not as dangerous and exciting. They, at most, are a side character giving advice on a path taken. The only one that will tell stories of my omi is me and maybe Leilei...if she remembers. It's not exciting to hear stories of how a woman cared for her family and protected them."

"And Thane Od," Rune added. Milla eyed Rune curiously after his addition. He explained. "He knew her. Maybe he tells stories of her."

Milla smiled brightly, "I should ask him about her someday." She squeezed him tight then released him and began to stand, "Besides, you have me to keep you in line." Rune smiled up at her as she offered him a hand. "Now let's go eat," she insisted. He took her hand and rose to make his way back toward the camp with her.

***

Alberic had spent the largest portion of the day going through the camp, looking for volunteers to try the words he had learned. At first, a steady flow of volunteers was had, though none showed a promising gift to adding power to the words. Once rumor had spread that the intent was to get help in fighting the dragon, the volunteers all but stopped.

Despite seeing Rune re-enter the camp with Milla, Alberic had decided to leave him be for the time being, but now with no volunteers remaining he opted to make his way back to the newcomers. He first approached Ethan who knelt by the fire, poking at it with a long stick. "I had a thought," he started as he kneeled down next to him, "We only have one seer, it's true, but any of us might be able to wield the power of the words. We should determine which among us can. That way, if anything were to happen to me, we might still succeed."

Ethan thought this over a moment, then nodded, "Good idea."

Alberic then pointed off to a nearby spot, shadowed by thick trees, "Regin ala lysa," he spoke, and the area became illuminated for a moment. Ethan's brows raised and Alberic continued, "Say it exactly as I did."

Ethan took in a slow breath then pointed to the same spot, "Regin ala lysa," he repeated and to the surprise of him and many nearby, the area lit up very brightly for a moment.

"Well then" Alberic said with a shocked face, "That was something."

Milla and Rune came running over after seeing the light. Milla asked excitedly, "Did you see that? Who did that?"

Ethan continued to look shocked as he answered, "That was me I suppose."

Milla smiled gleefully as she spoke in an excited manner, "You're a Warden of Light too then!" Ethan remained in wide eyed shock which he then blinked away. "I can use the words at least." Alberic then demonstrated for Milla who then made her attempt at speaking the words. The area lit up only very slightly. She remained in between the joy of it succeeding and the sorrow that the light was so dim. After a moment, they all looked to Rune.

"Don't look at me, I'm the seer," he reminded them. Without a word, they continued to look to him expectantly. "Fine," he grumbled, then said the words. There was no effect. "Happy?" he griped then moved closer to the fire.

"We, at least, know each of our potential in that regard," Alberic answered. "It will help with formulating a plan." He then moved himself to Rune's side and stared into the fire with him.

"So," Rune started as he noticed Alberic move in. "Does that make you a seer, magi and a Warden of Light?"

Alberic slid his hands into his pockets and raised both shoulders. "I've never had a vision of any sort. I can't predict the future as far as I'm aware.

If you are referring the seer speaking with me though," his shoulders dropped, "I would assume there is a hint of a seer in me."

Rune looked up to him, "That doesn't scare you?"

Alberic raised a brow, looked around then back to Rune, "Scare me? Why would it scare me?"

"Seer madness and all that," Rune explained.

Alberic made a scoffing noise, "Not at all. Despite my clear lack of any tangible seer powers I've read enough to know the seer madness doesn't come with the powers. It comes with the meddling with them."

"Meaning?" Rune prodded.

"Seer madness only afflicts those who try to control the world around them with it, and really, it is generally harmless. Unless, of course, you fear those who rock in corners and speak to the cracks in the wall."

Rune laughed, "The Great Seer wasn't harmless."

Alberic let in a slow breath then let it out, "I would argue that he didn't have the madness. He was quite in control of his actions. His actions were chosen. I have no intent on looking for a way to destroy the world with my limited seer powers, so no. I am not afraid." Rune nodded thoughtfully a few times. Alberic then asked, "If you ever decide to destroy the world though, a warning would be greatly appreciated." Rune scowled at him and he raised his hands in surrender, "I'm just throwing that out there." Rune frowned sadly and looked back to the fire. "Oh, come now young Rune," Alberic said with a nudge of his elbow, "You know yourself. You know what you want and who you want to be. Do you see yourself murdering hundreds of innocents and locking yourself in a tower while killing babies?"

Rune gave Alberic a disgusted look, "Of course not!" He then thought a moment, "But apparently, I will destroy my enemies with a baby at some point."

"Say what now?" Alberic asked densely.

Rune explained, "Thane Od told me. I will thwart my enemies with an unborn child."

"Unborn is not a baby yet," Alberic pointed out.

"Well it is, just not born yet," Rune returned.

"Hmm, but that's still impossible." Alberic then protested, "What are you going to do, hit them with it? Their bones are far too soft to do any real damage for one thing."

"That's what I said!" Rune agreed loudly.

"You two are ridiculous," Milla grumbled then moved to kneel next to Ethan who grinned quietly at the conversation.

Alberic mumbled quietly to Rune, "It's a completely logical argument."

"You don't have to tell me," Rune said shaking his head.

The two then looked at each other and laughed. Alberic then asked, "Where did you meet Feagan anyway?"

"My home town, Skera Braka," Rune explained. "I was still really little. It was just after my parents died. I was wandering around the town and I saw Bera, the Mayor's wife, hitting something with a broom and cursing. When she was done, I ran over to see what it was. That's when I found Feagan laying there all beat and battered on the ground. I thought he was likely dead, but I had never seen a faerie before and I was curious so, I took him to my shack and made a bed for him." Rune laughed quietly, "When he came too, he just stared at me at first. Eventually, when he could fly again he just followed me around." He paused a long moment, and all remained silent. Finally, he continued. "I was really sad one day, and was crying because I missed my mother. He threw something at me," he laughed. "I think it was a rock. I was so shocked I stopped crying. He then started taunting me, so I got angry and chased him around. At first, I was really mad, but then it started to turn into a game and we both started laughing. That's when he started talking to me. I didn't understand him very well at first, but I learned to. He's my greatest friend in the world now." A tear dropped, and he looked away to wipe his eyes.

"He'll show up," Alberic said with a smile.

"How could you know that?" Rune asked as he looked to him.

"Call it a gut feeling," Alberic said with a smile. "We should probably plan our attack at some point I suppose." The group mumbled their agreements. "Let's go wake up Milo then." He said as he moved off. The others quickly followed.

CHAPTER 39

Night fell and the cold wind that plagued the day calmed to a cool breeze. All cloud cover that trickled in had long since dispersed, leaving the pale moon to glow its bluish haze over the land and all the stars to clearly display their glimmering constellations on the black canvas. With Alberic and Milo's guidance, the small group found the foul-smelling entrance to Eilifatli's cave. An eerie quiet enveloped the area causing each of their quiet steps to seem as loud as that of a careless beast stamping through. All creatures, large and small, had abandoned the area and even the breeze seemed to sneak through in hopes of passing by unnoticed. The five hopeful dragon slayers peered into the small cave opening cautiously as a slow, creeping fog drifted out from inside. Rune then whispered, "How did a large dragon fit into such a small entrance?"

"There must be another entrance," Ethan whispered in return then boldly began to move inside.

"Wait," Milla whispered as she grabbed his arm fearfully, "We should go over how we're going to do this one more time."

"Our first and foremost objective in the plan," Alberic stated in a loud whisper as he still peered inside, "Don't die."

Rune scoffed lightly, "Really?"

"Especially you," Alberic added, turning his eyes to Rune, "You need to live until the end of this or it will all be for nothing."

"You're a seer too," Rune pointed out, "You could take my place the same as you could take Ethan's"

"What little trickle of that I may have is not worth risking our lives if it doesn't work," Alberic stated seriously. "It would be like relying on you to cast a spell."

Rune frowned, "It wouldn't be anything like that. I-"

"Alright," Ethan interjected, "Alberic, Milo and I will go on ahead. I will do my best to make myself a nuisance. Milo, you do the same and Alberic, use your magik to distract him. Milla, guard the exit. If you see anyone coming, come in and let us know."

Milla frowned, "I'm still not happy about being a door guard. I can distract as well as any of you. Maybe even better."

"We need to know if Eilifatli summons help," Ethan ordered quietly, "Covering the rear is just as important as the frontal assault."

"Then let Milo guard," Milla growled.

Milo shook his head as he objected, "I stay with Alberic. Always."

Ethan waited for the two to finish, then continued, "Right. As soon as either I or Alberic have an opening, we will use that incantation and hope it's what we need to reveal this dragon. Rune, you come up behind and wait for your chance. If the worst happens and the two of us fall, get to Milla and have her try. Are we all understood?" The group all agreed silently with nods. "Good then. Alberic and Milo, you're with me." He then started into the cave again, covering his nose with a prepared and scented cloth to block out some of the smell, with the other two in tow doing the same.

"Regin ala megin," Alberic said as they moved and they all hesitated as they were filled with a sense of courage and strength. Ethan grinned at him then continued.

Rune looked to Milla who frowned sadly, obviously still upset with her role. He commented with a small smile, "I bet you didn't think you'd be looking to slay a dragon when you first found me."

Milla smiled lightly, "You better get in there. You don't want to miss your chance to be a hero." His smile brightened, and he did just that.

The forward group took quiet steps as they moved into the dark, foul smelling cave. Seeping fog enshrouded their feet as they crept ahead. The further they moved in, the wider the tunnel became until they found themselves in a massive cavern. They could see a dim, blue toned light coming from the large room ahead and to the left. Slowly, they made their way toward it, despite the intense smell increasing as their scented cloths helped less than anticipated. Peaking around the rock wall and into the large open room, they gazed up to the ceiling and saw pale blue moonlight trickling in from a large hole above. "That's definitely how it got in," Ethan whispered as he drew his blade.

Rune made his way closer to the three, but as he saw Ethan readying his sword, he decided to huddle into a dip in the cave wall until the others were ready. Alberic and Milo had seen this room before, but it had been far too dark to see much of anything on that night. They drew their own weapons and inched their way further inside. Together, the three moved until they came to the end of the thick cave wall, now able to see into the other side of the extensive cave room. Their eyes all widened in fear as they got their first glimpse of the massive sleeping beast. Its body, even laying down, stood taller than each man there could reach if they stood on each other's shoulders. Several grey curved horns of varying lengths lined the beast's jaw and the crest of his head, then followed down his spine. It lay wrapped around a massive stone that had large carved writing on it, its own height reaching almost to the ceiling.

The dragon's deep blue scales gleamed in the moonlight from the ceiling hole. A dark mist seeped from its nostrils and seemed to be the source of not only the fog, but the smell. The three looked at each other, all seeming unsure of the next step. "That's the ward stone that it's wrapped around." Ethan then pointed out in a whisper. "We have one just like it in the North."

Alberic whispered sarcastically, "I get the feeling it's no longer working."

"A small meal you five," a deep rumbling voice emitted from the dragon. The three jumped, then swallowed in near unison as they turned their eyes to each other. None had been expecting a beast of this size, and all questioned their ability to slay such a thing. The dragon let out a rumbling laugh which forced more of the rancid mist from his nostrils. The mist heightened and crept around the group. They all covered their mouth and nose as their eyes watered from the fetid smell. "You fools seek salvation and light, but instead walk into the flame. I am Eilifatli. I am the glorious nightmare. You think you can end me, but my shadows will find you and devour you long before you reach me." The room then appeared to darken greatly, the moon's light seemed to dim and the shadows in all the furthest corners blackened. Shadow phantoms seemed to creep and dart in every dark corner.

"Not again!" Milo complained then dropped his hammer and huddled, covering his head. "The flesh monster will come for us again!"

Alberic swallowed hard as his body began to shake, but he was able to resist the brunt of the fear that struck him. "Regin ala lysa," he called out and pointed his sword into the darkness.

Milo screamed out at a higher pitch than any thought possible from the large man, as the light illuminated horrific red eyed creatures of shadowy sludge, "Why do you keep doing that!" Milo roared at him.

"It's dark!" Alberic defended, "I was trying to give us some light!"

"Well stop it!" Milo roared back and Alberic grunted in return, not being able to argue further.

Ethan, seeing the mass of creatures surrounding them shouted, "We are outnumbered, we must esca-" a man then appeared in front of him that halted his words and made him falter. The grayed body of Major Peleg stood before Ethan. Peleg's dead eyes stared at him fiercely and his severed throat leaked blood continuously. "M-major Peleg? What happened?"

"You abandoned us," the corpse murmured, causing blood to leak over his lip, "Our deaths are on your hands, and now, your death will be on ours.

A great deal of the shadowy creatures then changed form, becoming a horde of soldiers, all of which Ethan recognized from his own company. Their deadened eyes locked on him as they slowly moved closer. He stared back, unable to move or react, "I didn't – I wasn't..." was all that past his lips as his face whitened with fear and regret.

Alberic's nostrils flared as he swallowed hard while watching the scene. A trickle of light caught his attention, drawing his eyes to the cave exit. From there, a group of guards began to walk in. "What? What did you do to Milla?" He growled then stumbled back as he realized they were Queen Erma's personal guards.

The Queen then walked out from amongst them, fury in her eyes, "You lied to me. You were my most trusted adviser and confidant. You are a magi, Alberic, how could you? You will die for your betrayal." She growled at him.

"No..." Alberic gasped stumbling back. "No, this isn't real."

Ethan moved his shaking arm to aim his sword at the mass of raised dead. Alberic's words had allowed him a moment to refocus and rethink. He shut his eyes then cried out, "Regin ala megin!" A sense of calm swept through the cave and wiped out all the nightmarish visions. Milo immediately took up his hammer and stood, his eyes wide and happy at the sudden change.

The dragon's head lifted, and its long neck stretched high, "What's this?" He grumbled. He then tilted his massive head. "The familiar voice brought friends," his head then tilted in the other direction, "But not just any friends. Another Warden and..." A rumbling growl slipped from his lips, "You wish to take my heart for your own stórrhugr? I can feel your power from here. So… young and ready to be molded. You are too young and untrained to defeat me stórrhugr. Out of respect, I will allow you to leave."

Rune, who had remained hidden behind the rock wall, narrowed his eyes. Deciding the dragon must have been talking about him, "I'm not going anywhere!" He yelled out as he drew his small sword, "You are the one that needs to leave this land and never return!"

The dragon seemed to laugh as it turned its head in Rune's direction, "I am your better. I am more ancient than any of your stolen ancestors and I have been around long before your kind placed these foul ward stones to keep me out. I knew your pathetic wards would fail someday and now I have my vengeance before age takes me." His mouth opened, and a gurgling sound rose from his throat.

Alberic's eyes widened. In all the stories told of dragons a gurgling sound was always followed by the dragon spitting fire. He yelled to the others, "Get out of the way!" and he darted behind the wall. The other two followed swiftly as the dragon spit its acid out and sprayed it across the ground where the three stood not moments before. The acid sizzled and bubbled, then evaporated, leaving only hot melted stone behind.

"I will give you one chance," the dragon spoke, now seeming angry, "Leave this place stórrhugr, take your precious friends and do not return."

Rune grinned faintly and looked to the others, "He's scared," he whispered. The three nodded in agreement, so Rune continued. "Hah! Bargaining is a sign of fear and weakness. You know we've come to destroy you and you fear us. But we do not fear you, dragon."

There was another spray of acid followed by a large growl, "So be it, stórrhugr. I will melt your flesh and devour your friends." The dragon slowly raised up onto its feet.

Ethan spoke with an urgent tone to the others, "Right. With its size, it won't be able to maneuver well in this space. Avoid the spit and get in. Milo, try to distract it to the far end of the cave. Alberic, you and I will try to get an angle toward the heart. Rune," he turned a stern expression to him as he continued, "Your chance will come soon. Be ready and be cautious." Rune nodded sharply and swallowed, his own expression a mix of fear and anticipation.

"You are a young and untrained fool, stórrhugr!" the dragon yelled out as the group hopped over the molten rock and moved to position themselves.

"Why do you keep calling me that? My name is Rune," he yelled out.

"If I were a younger dragon, oh, the things I could teach you, stórrhugr. You and I could rule this land," he started, but was distracted as Milo ran out in front of him yelling. Eilifatli gurgled and let out his spit but just missed, as Milo hid behind a distant wall.

Alberic, seeing the dragon had turned to a perfect angle, charged out pointing toward the dragon's heart. Seeing this, Rune quickly moved up, ready to act but stumbled and hesitated as he now finally laid eyes on the towering beast. "Regin ala-" Alberic started but was halted as Eilifatli let out a roar as ear piercing as it was deep and earth-shaking. All inside covered their ears then collapsed as the ground trembled so fiercely that it was impossible to stand. As the roar stopped, Eilifatli swiped out with his massive clawed hand and sent Alberic sliding across the room and striking the distant rock wall.

"Alberic!" Rune cried out as he stood.

The gurgling started in the dragon's throat again as he prepared to finish Alberic off, but he was interrupted as Milo charged out from hiding in a blind rage. The large man roared with fury as he bolted forward, holding his hammer high. Before Eilifatli could react, Milo's heavy hammer struck down on one of its clawed fingers with a cracking force. The dragon screamed out, then with a swift motion, knocked Milo back with the same hand. Milo recovered quickly and charged again. As this small battle ensued, Ethan positioned himself and pointed to the dragon's heart, but before he could speak a word, the dragon reared up and slammed its front legs down to crush Milo beneath. Milo rolled out of the way of the stomping claw but stumbled with the others afterwards, as the earth shook beneath their feet. Rocks and boulders began to tumble from above, just missing the aspiring dragon slayers, though several struck Eilifatli. He roared out as he shifted and cowered backwards, awaiting an end to the small cave-in. "Enough!" he then thundered. Milo quickly took that opportunity to check on the unconscious Alberic as the dragon continued, "A deal then." Eilifatli grumbled.

"We'll make no deals with you, dragon!" Ethan bellowed.

"Not with you Warden, I wish to make a deal with the stórrhugr," Eilifatli clarified.

"You have nothing I could possibly want," Rune barked.

"Oh, but I do," the dragon chuckled. "For as you know, your kind is prone to madness. I sense this as your greatest fear. It is a madness that only we dragons can stop. Were you aware of this, stórrhugr?" A silence fell. Milo took this time to lift the unconscious Alberic and carry him out of danger's way toward Ethan and Rune. "Is it not tempting, stórrhugr? Not only for you, but those who know you. A lesser seer would pose no threat, but all here are keenly aware of the threat you pose. Perhaps even equal to my own?"

"Just spit out your offer!" Ethan demanded.

The dragon chuckled again, "My offer is this. You allow me and the stórrhugr to leave together, to another land. I will teach him to master his powers and avoid the madness. In return, he will be removed from your land, and I will have an apprentice to help lengthen my life."

Another silence fell as Ethan turned his eyes to Rune. He finally spoke quietly, "Do you think it's worth the risk?"

Eilifatli continued, "If you do not accept, you may perhaps destroy me," he paused, "but in my death, the stórrhugr's power will increase and madness will consume him. All of your lands will be at his mercy. You all fear the stories of the one you call the Great Seer? This boy's power is already greater."

Rune swallowed and looked to Ethan, "It's me the Thane was talking about. Killing the dragon gives me the power to destroy our world. Don't you see?" Ethan frowned deeply and looked off.

"Come to me, stórrhugr. Have your friends leave this place. You and I will prepare for our journey to distant lands and extraordinary greatness." The dragon continued.

"It could be a trick," Ethan warned, "He might just be looking to kill you."

Rune thought that over a moment then called out, "You say I can lengthen your life? Is that what you get out of this?"

"Indeed," Eilifatli answered, "The relationship between dragon and seer is symbiotic. I am ancient, and my days are numbered. I should like to live several more of your generations, and in doing so, you would live as long as I."

Rune frowned then let out a sigh, saying to Ethan, "Go, get the others out."

"Rune," Ethan started, "If this is a trap-"

"I know. Just go, I can handle it" Rune demanded, "If we fail, this dragon will still be a threat. If we succeed, I will be the threat. Let's at least try the only option that has a happy ending."

Ethan frowned deeply. He hesitated then said, "Rune, let me say this. I do not think you capable of such madness and evil as to destroy our world. I want you to know that. But I will do as you ask. I trust you." He then turned and made his way out with Milo in tow, still carrying Alberic.

Once Ethan was out of view, Rune placed his sword on the ground and made his way toward the dragon, slowly and carefully revealing himself from behind the cave wall. The moonlight illuminated him as he stepped below the large opening above and spoke, "We have a deal then. Where will you be taking me?"

Eilifatli's long mouth turned up in a grin as his long body swayed towards Rune, each step shaking the ground lightly. He listened a moment, to be sure no others remained. "It is indeed true that you could have lengthened my life, stórrhugr," the dragon began as he then stepped between Rune and the exit. With a swift motion, he swiped his massive tale towards the exit, crushing down a piece of the wall and blocking Rune's escape. Rune fell to the ground from the tremor, his eyes wide as Eilifatli continued amongst the sound of crumbling walls and rolling boulders, "But it is too late for me. I intend to continue my path of destruction. This accursed land, that dared banish me after destroying all that I loved will pay in kind. Until my dying breath, all will know the wrath of Eilifatli. But first," he sneered, "I will end you."

Rune stood with wide eyes, "I knew it! I knew I shouldn't have trusted you!" Eilifatli chuckled, followed by a gurgle emanating from his throat. Rune snarled, "If I go, you go with me." With that an explosion of force emitted from Rune, so great that it sent the dragon crashing against the wall. The cave quickly collapsed inward in a devastating roar of crumbling rocks.

CHAPTER 40

Ethan and Milo made their way out of the cave to the expectant gaze of Milla, which then turned to concern, seeing Alberic unconscious over Milo's shoulder, "What happened?"

"Alby was hurt," Milo said sadly.

Ethan frowned. "And a deal has been made. Rune will-" a thundering crack sounded from behind him and they all jolted and turned to the cave entrance with shocked concern. A rush of dust sped past them forcing them all to turn away and guard their faces. Once the worst was over, Ethan turned and charged back into the cave. "Rune!" he cried out, but it didn't take long for him to notice that the tunnel was now blocked. He ran back out, saying with urgency, "There was a cave in. We should-" the three were then thrown off their feet as a deafening explosion shook the ground, followed by a shower of dust and small rocks. They all twisted and covered their heads from the rocky onslaught, Milo also being sure to guard Alberic from the harsh downpour. Even as the dust settled, the sound of rolling rocks and boulders could be heard where the cavern used to be.

Milla quickly stood as she rushed over to the collapsed entrance, "Rune!" she cried out then began pulling the rocks away, "We have to see if he's alright!"

Ethan regained his senses and shook his head in an attempt to clear the ringing from his ears. He then pushed himself to stand and rushed to Milla, grabbing her arm to stop her. "We won't be able to do that from here." He turned to Milo, "Get Alberic out of here to safety, but see if you can find help for him. Be careful though, who knows what attention we drew to this place." Milo swiftly complied after a nod and Ethan turned back to Milla and continued, "You and I will head around to see if we can get to where the hole at the top used to be. It will give us a better idea of Rune's survival odds."

Milla followed Ethan up to the crater that was once a cavern. As they moved over the cracked and broken rock, they carefully examined the area for any sign of life. Milla covered her mouth as she began to tear up, "Oh, poor Rune."

Ethan bowed his head in sorrow as he stopped where he assumed the large hole had been, "We shouldn't have left him."

"Is it dead then?" Milla asked after a sniff, her tears darkening the dust covering her face, "Is the dragon dead?"

Ethan thought that over a moment as he looked over the rubble. "Can a cave-in kill a dragon?" They both remained silent for a long while as they continued to scan. Ethan then perked up and moved toward Milla, "Listen."

She did just that, listening carefully. Her eyes widened and filled with horror as she turned them to Ethan, "I can hear it breathing."

"We no longer have a seer," Ethan added, also looking highly concerned. The ground beneath their feet then began to shift and rumble. "Run," Ethan ordered. "We failed. Get out of here. I'll try to slow it down."

"I won't leave you!" Milla cried out, then held onto him, steadying herself as the ground shook more fiercely. Ethan grabbed onto her as well and they used each other to keep balance while the rocks now shifted and pushed away from a central spot nearby. No matter their desire to run now, it would have been impossible. A hole then opened as the final stones and boulders lifted into the air, floated above for a moment, then fell to the side as the quaking stopped. Milla and Ethan both raised their brows and froze in spot, confused at the bizarre spectacle. Even more-so as Rune raised himself from the hole, seemingly guarded by an invisible sphere that pushed all rock and dust away from him. He floated himself above solid ground, then collapsed to his knees as the sphere dissipated.

The two onlookers gazed at Rune with silent wonder. "I'm not sure if I should be happy or terrified," Ethan finally said.

Rune took in several steadying breaths before he stood and looked at the other two, "I have no idea what that was, but I'm going to go with happy, if you don't mind."

"I thought we lost you," Milla said with an overjoyed smile as she moved toward him, "What about the-" she started again but the ground began to rumble again.

They all fell to the ground as nearby rocks raised up and rolled away from an extensive mound that slowly formed. "Get around it!" Ethan yelled as he steadied himself, "Avoid the rocks!" Rune and Milla stumbled over the shaking and shifting ground as they followed Ethan's orders. After several close calls with rolling boulders, Ethan readied his sword and Milla readied her bow, widening her stance to keep balance as she pulled out an arrow. Blue scales then emerged near Rune and he stumbled away from it, falling backwards. The dragon's arm then raised and whipped out to brace onto the stone, knocking him back further.

"Rune!" Milla cried out, her eyes darting from the emerging dragon to Rune, who rolled holding his chest as he coughed, and blood began to trickle from his nose.

Seeing Rune was at least still alive, Ethan focused on the dragon, his stance wide and his sword held steady in front of him. Finally, the nose emerged, leaking the putrid mist over the rocks. Ethan and Milla resisted covering their noses from the smell as they waited for their chance to strike. Finally, an eye was seen raising from the rubble and without hesitation Milla fired an arrow. The dragon let out a scream as it flung its head and emerged even faster, causing the rocks above to fly off in random directions, crashing to the ground soon after. The sudden movement shifted the rocks from under Ethan's feet and he fell back, then struggled to stand as the dragon now emerged fully, it's head whipping back and forth as it shrieked in pain. Rune struggled to stand as he watched the dragon flail. As Eilifatli pulled himself from the rubble, it was clear that he was heavily injured and struggling to stand. He swung out his tale blindly as he still whipped his head to shake the arrow loose. Rune was almost hit but was able to roll away and just avoid the tip of the tail in time. Ethan rushed towards the dragon to strike, but Eilifatli had just stopped his flailing and peered out of his good eye in time, swiping out with the back of his talons, knocking Ethan back. After a few rolls, he stopped on his side and regained his senses.

"Ethan!" Milla shrieked, then fired another arrow at the dragon, though this one struck the scales of the dragon's neck and failed to penetrate.

Eilifatli turned his attention to Rune and began to chuckle. That chuckle soon turned to a hearty laugh as he slowly laid down to rest, billowing his chest heavily with wearied breaths. "So, the old ways truly have been forgotten completely in this land, have they? How wonderful." His long lips stretched again in a grin, as his head fully faced Rune. Rune trembled as he prepared to have to dodge the acidic spit of the dragon, but instead it spoke. "This is good news indeed, very good news. You and your friends did have me concerned, but it seems you only held a scrap of knowledge, the true purpose now lost. A young stórrhugr seeks to destroy me with sword and arrow, how amusing," he laughed out again then tried to force himself to stand, only collapsing soon after.

Ethan took this opportunity to point toward Eilifatli's heart, "Regin ala lysa!" he called out. A blaze of light formed around the dragon, then dissipated. The group of three all visibly lost heart at the failed spell. Milla strung another arrow, firing it toward the dragon's heart, but it only bounced off. Ethan then charged again as frustration consumed him, this time reaching the beast and striking its chest. The sword hit, and bounced off the dragon's flesh, sending Ethan stumbling back.

Eilifatli let out another rumbling laugh, "You can not destroy me, and you will not be able to destroy the hordes of dragons that will soon appear on your shores. Neither you, nor your friend have the strength to penetrate my flesh, and you do not have the knowledge needed to destroy my kind. We will rule you again, like days long past. As it should be."

Ethan breathed heavily as he snarled, tightening his grip on his sword. His eyes drifted as he thought over everything Alberic had said. In an instant, he turned his eyes up to the dragon and yelled out, "Not while I still breathe dragon!" He then charged again at the dragon yelling, "Regin ala megin!" Eilifatli's eyes widened and it pushed itself back while it watched Ethan charge. It opened its mouth and gurgled as it prepared its acidic spray.

"Stop!" Milla ordered in a desperate voice, and to her surprise the gurgling stopped as the dragon turned his gleaming blue eye angrily toward her. Ethan's sword penetrated the dragon's chest amongst the confused hesitation. A shadow seeped from the now open wound, and Ethan's eyes grew wide with accomplishment and fear as he tried to yank his sword free from the ruptured flesh.

The dragon grabbed at Ethan and threw him flying across the stones, then faltered as it looked down at the sword penetrating his chest. Eilifatli then snarled at Rune, "This is far from enough to kill me stórrhugr!" He raised his clawed hand and lurched forward to strike at Rune.

Still feeling strength from his last incantation, Ethan quickly pushed himself to his knees. He pointed at the shadowy wound before yelling out, "Regin ala lysa!" The wound ripped open further and the dragon screamed out as the sword fell from the opening and light beamed from inside. Eilifatli roared again in an enraged growl and with fury and purpose in his eyes, set to drag himself toward Ethan. Rune rushed towards the distracted dragon and ducked past the closest leg to get in front of the opened chest. Reaching up, he grabbed hold of a glowing orb that seemed to hover inside. Eilifatli's eyes widened in shock and realization as he swiftly grabbed hold of Rune, then violently threw him away. In doing so, the orb was ripped out of his chest. Rune continued to hold tightly to it while his body soared away. The dragon then collapsed as Rune's body collided with the ground, and there was silence.

Ethan breathed heavily and watched the dragon fall, his mind in shock while Milla rushed over to check on Rune. Ethan continued his steadying breaths through the silence until his eyes finally turned to where Rune lay motionless with eyes closed, his hands still grasping the orb of light. He limped towards him as he asked Milla, "Is he alright?" She turned sad eyes up to Ethan as he approached. He dropped to his knees next to Rune as he ripped the glove from his own hand. Placing that hand on Rune's shoulder, he shook him gently, "Rune, wake up. We did it!" Rune remained motionless, his face pale and lifeless as blood slowly trickled from his nose, across his cheeks. Ethan placed his fingers on Rune's neck to feel for a pulse, then laid his head on his chest and listened. "Damn it." He whispered then bowed his head.

Tears fell from Milla's eyes, further wetting her dusty cheeks as she gently brushed the hair from Rune's forehead, "Oh Rune. You were so brave."

A quiet buzzing approached the two and a small surly voice spoke, "Sae close," Feagan said sadly.

Ethan and Milla both flinched and looked to Feagan with shock, "Where did you come from?" Ethan blurted out.

"This is the trickster faerie?" Milla asked as she examined the scruffy little winged man.

Feagan frowned at Rune's lifeless body, "Th' one an' only an' th' one ay many," He sighed as he moved closer to Rune's face to look him over.

Milla looked to Ethan, "What did he say?" Ethan shrugged, his eyes remaining on Feagan.

"Ah only jist got haur. Tay late it seems. He didne hae a chance tae absorb it. It will eventually return tae th' dragon, an' th' dragon will live again." Feagan continued.

Milla shook her head, "I don't understand. The dragon will live again?"

"We need tae gie it ay haur quickly," Feagan said through tears after a noisy sniff, still looking at Rune, "Afair it wakes."

Ethan shook his head, "You want us to leave?"

Before Milla could protest Feagan spoke, "Thaur is naethin' ye can dae fur heem noo, sae yerself."

"You're going to have to speak slower," Ethan then said with slight frustration, "So we can understand you."

Feagan sighed, "Yoo're a sexy cheil if nae a wee dense." He continued with more urgency speaking slower, "We hae tae lae. Gang. Rin. Th' dragon will bide again."

They were all distracted as the orb rapidly began to glow brighter. "What's happening?" Ethan said as he and Milla both stood.

"Ah - ah dunnae ken," Feagan said, "Mebbe it awreddy begins tae return tae th' dragon."

"He's warning us that the orb will return to the dragon and it will come back to life. Maybe it's to do with Rune not finishing what he's supposed to do with the orb," Ethan explained as he stood and turned to the dragon, "You must run Milla. Warn everyone that you can. If this beast was telling the truth, there are a lot more of his kind coming."

"There's nothing you could say to make me leave you here alone to fight that thing," Milla growled indignantly as she stood and faced him.

Ethan let out a frustrated grunt as he put his hands on her shoulders, "Milla, please. Let me save at least you."

Milla instead moved in to hold him around his chest, then turned her head to watch the orb. Ethan let out a slow breath as he wrapped his arms around her and also watched the orb grow brighter. The orb then began to absorb into Rune's body. "Ethan," Milla peeped, "I don't think it's returning to the dragon."

Within that moment, Rune took in a gasp of breath and opened his eyes as the light dissipated. He looked up at Milla and Ethan, then winced before saying, "Ow."

Ethan laughed and sighed out in relief as he and Milla released each other. He reached down to help Rune up, "You had us worried there."

"Feagan!" Rune cried out with joy as he noticed him while painfully attempting to stand with Ethan's help, "You're alive!"

Feagan widened his eyes fearfully then said loudly before he zipped away, "Rin!"

Ethan looked to him with confusion and called out, "Run? Why?"

"Jist dae it!" Feagan cried back as he zipped off.

The three looked at each other and decided not to question further as they began to run in the direction that Feagan flew. Rune and Ethan both had a harder time than Milla staying upright as they made their way down the rocky slope, due to their injuries, but finally they all made their way down. They then rushed up the grassy hill, towards the road, hearing a sizzling sound behind them. Rune looked back, just able to see the dragon's body slowly collapsing in on itself. He tripped but was quickly righted by Ethan as they all continued to run. Soon after, there was a violent bursting sound, followed by the noise of rushing fluids, bubbling and sizzling. They all looked back in unison to see the dragon's body gone and a pool of green fluid rising and rushing towards them. Ethan returned his eyes forward and ran even faster, forcefully dragging Rune and Milla to keep up with him. They continued to run up the hill until they were a good distance away and the sound of boiling pursuit dispersed. All three turned to look back, seeing the ground behind them was now blackened and bubbling, but there was thankfully no more green liquid flowing toward them. They panted heavily, and Ethan fell to his knees as he asked, "What just happened?"

"Not sure," Rune said between pants.

Feagan flew back to them and said with relief, "Guid tae see ye aw gart it. That's th' first time Ah hae seen a dragon die. Ah almost forgot abit th' mess they make."

Ethan let out a noise, "What?"

Rune piped in, "That's normally what happens?"

"Aye it is," Feagan answered. "Wa dae ye hink there's sic' a lack ay dragon parts?"

After a long silence, Ethan laughed then said, "We killed a dragon."

Milla smiled brightly, "That's not something anyone has been able to say in a long time."

"We killed a dragon," Rune said then grinned. He paused as he looked over the black mass again, reality finally starting to sink in, "We killed a dragon." He repeated, then jumped up and cheered loud, "We killed a dragon!"

Ethan laughed, "We celebrate after we get to safety and see to our wounds." The joy was short lived as a large company of guards approached briskly from the road. "With our injuries, we won't be able to get away in time," Ethan said sadly as he stood to face them. Milla moved to his side and held onto his arm.

Rune sighed and shook his head as Feagan zipped off to the nearby trees. He then sat down taking in a slow breath, "We did good."

Ethan smiled slightly and nodded, placing a hand on Milla's, "Yes, we did good."

CHAPTER 41

The approaching southern guards marked clearly by their blue, black, and yellow uniforms looked over the three cautiously. They slowed their advance as they neared, taking note that the would-be prisoners chose not to run. Ethan moved in front of the other two to stand between them and the armed group, staring at them expectantly. Rune eyed them sideways, noting that many had their eyes on the black mass that steamed and bubbled nearby.

"What happened here?" the forward guard asked in a tired and bewildered tone.

"Oh that?" Rune asked in a sarcastic manner, "We ran into a dragon in there and had to kill it. Sorry about that."

The guard that spoke took a staggering step backwards, "You... killed it?"

Ethan grinned and copied Rune's sarcastic tone, "Yes, we do apologize. You should really have put up signs," he said as he made the shape of a sign with his index fingers.

The guard didn't respond to that. He seemed confused and lost in his own thoughts for several moments before ordering, "Get on your feet. We're taking you to the king."

"Or," Rune piped in, "You could let us go and say you didn't find us. We did do you a favor by killing that dragon I think."

The forward guard turned his gaze to the other guards behind him. He still seemed lost in thought. He finally shook his head, saying to the three, "I'm afraid I can't do that." He then ordered his troop, "Seize them." The guards complied and moved to the three with pointed spears. Rune was forced to his feet, and the three had their wrists bound before being led to the castle.

The walk down the road and through Regintun was slow and quiet. It seemed none of the party were in a rush to reach the king's throne room.

Even after they entered the castle and approached the massive throne room doors, the pace slowed. The forward guard gave a silent nod to the two men guarding the doors and they moved to open them with grave expressions.

A repulsive smell poured out of the grand chamber as the over-sized doors edged open. The iron odor of blood, old and new, mixed with the stench of stomach and intestinal contents hovered in the air. Drying blood seemed to seep into every crevasse of the stone floor. As they were led inside, only the forward guard followed them into the dark chamber. The only light emanated from two large braziers next to an empty throne at the center of the vast room. Each sticky step they took echoed off the towering walls, and as their eyes adjusted, they were welcomed by the sight of countless bodies and body parts lining those walls. It was clear, none of the victims had swift or easy deaths. Milla's face turned a sickly color as she averted her eyes and looked to her companions. Rune shared her expression, though Ethan's remained hard and grim. The head guard cleared his throat and spoke up, "Your Majesty, three more for you. They claim to have killed the dragon." Only then did the three notice the king standing as if a statue to their right, facing away from them in front of several bloody and broken bodies. He didn't respond or even show a sign that he was aware of anyone being there. The guard swallowed hard but dared not repeat himself. The silence grew long.

"Unbind them," the king finally spoke. Without even the slightest hesitation the three were unbound and the guard then returned to his silent wait. Again, the king said nothing and did not move.

"Your, uh, Majesty," Rune spoke up and several worried eyes turned to him. Despite this, he continued, "Not to rush you or anything, but is this standing around and waiting part of the torture?"

Ethan widened his eyes at Rune, seeming to be caught in between disbelief and amusement, but the other's expressions turned to horror as the king finally turned to see his new guests. "Leave us," he said to the guard, who hesitated only a moment, then marched out of the room.

The silence grew again as the king examined the three. His bloodshot eyes bore dark circles and showed a man who seemed beyond the brink of exhaustion. His long, frizzy hair was matted in several places with dried blood, though his braided beard was clear of the grime. He stood, not as a proud King, but with his shoulders slumped forward, seeming unable to bear the weight of the heavy furs wrapped around them. This time Ethan spoke, "Your Majesty, King Brandr of the South and all its people, Lord of Swords; I greet you with respect and a heavy heart. I am Prince Ethan of the North, captain of the Second Sons. My mother is Queen and High Queen Adva of the North and all its people, Lady of Light. My father is King Nero of the North and all its people, Lord of Strength. Your people have taken me and my companions prisoner, as is your right in times of war. I tell you this now; If harm should befall me or my friends, my mother will see to it that all your armies are destroyed and that you and your Queen's fate are the same as mine. We have killed your dragon. Without it, you have no chance against us. I offer truce on behalf of the North. See to it that my friends and I-"

"My Queen is dead," the King interrupted, his voice loud but strained.

Ethan stopped his long-winded speech. His brows furrowed, and he finally spoke, "My condolences, King Brandr."

"I killed her with my own hands," the King continued quieter as he looked off, his eyes becoming distant, "Right over there." He pointed to where the dissected naked body of an unrecognizable woman was strapped to a tilted iron bed. "I tortured her first, like the others."

Ethan and Rune looked to each other with disbelief, but Ethan seemed to keep his cool. He asked cautiously, "Why?"

The King shrugged limply and shook his head. His eyes unblinking. "Curious things, dragons. They seep into your mind. Draw out parts you did not know were even there. Or," he paused and moved to a nearby table. Taking up a chalice, he drank from it before continuing, "Perhaps I knew, but I kept it well hidden. They have you do things that feel to be of your own free will. They make you feel as if you enjoy what you are doing. It is shameful, the secret knowledge that part of you enjoys war... killing. The power you feel over the lives you take... the horror in their faces," He paused a long moment, "Then, when the dragon is gone, so is that feeling. It leaves you with all the memories of what you have done, and none to blame but yourself." He then moved to the wall and pulled a sword from a stand nearby, immediately turning back towards the group.

Ethan moved himself between the King and his friends defensively, "Your Majesty-"

"How long has it been? How long have I been causing such horror?" the King continued as he turned the blade on himself, aiming towards his own heart.

Ethan seemed speechless at this point, but Rune quickly stepped forward and spoke, "It wasn't you. It wasn't you at all. It was the dragon. It's dead now."

The King looked to Rune, his eyes filling with tears and his lips quivering, "I killed my Roshan. I killed my beloved. I tortured her until she died. I made them all watch."

Rune moved forward more and calmed his voice, "No you didn't. The dragon did, and he made you watch. You are a victim, as was your Queen."

Tears flowed down the King's cheeks, "I can not live with those memories. I can not."

"Yes, you can," Rune said in a demanding voice, "You must. Your people need to know it wasn't you. They need to see that you are not that man that terrorized them. This war needs to end, and you need to stop it."

"If the dragon is gone, then the war will end on its own," the King growled, and with that, he slid the sword up into his own heart.

"No!" Rune cried, and they all watched with wide helpless eyes as the King dropped to his knees, then fell dead.

Ethan let out a slow breath and spoke solemnly, "It's time we all went home I think." He then called out, "Guards!" Several guards entered and screeched to a halt seeing their King dead. Rune, Milla and Ethan turned to them expectantly as Ethan spoke, "He took his own life." The guards remained speechless for a time longer. The forward guard from earlier then stepped out of the way, as if bidding them to pass and the others followed suit. Ethan dipped his head in a bow as he moved to walk between them, Milla and Rune following in tow. He watched carefully for any aggressive movements as they continued out.

As they made their way down the quiet halls, and out of the castle, they remained silent. Finally, as they crossed the castle bridge to the mainland, Milla spoke, "That was horrific. What will happen to the South now?"

Ethan shrugged lightly, "I'm not sure. I imagine whoever is next in line will take the throne, if he allowed any of them to live in his state. The South do things a little differently than we do in the North, so I am not completely sure of the steps they take. Perhaps Thane Od will take the throne for himself." He let out a sigh, "Either way, with the current Queen and King dead and the dragon gone, I think the war will end very soon, as he said. Word travels quickly in times of war."

"So, it's done," Milla said solemnly, "The darkness is lifted. We succeeded."

Rune nodded, "Seems that way," he spoke with a hint of sorrow, "Do you still regret dragging me along?"

Milla smiled warmly as she shook her head at him, "Of course not." She then sighed as she released him, "I suppose we all just... go back to our homes now?"

Ethan nodded firmly, "I need to head back quickly. I must see to the damage done and help bolster our defenses just in case. There will be a lot of work to do to heal from this war."

"And I will need to head back to my-," Milla spoke gravely after a pause, "home I suppose. Now that what I set out to do is complete I have to see if my... my omi left me any hints to my next step."

"Why the glum faces?" Alberic then piped in, as he and Milo approached from the other side of the bridge. They both sported long hooded cloaks, clearly in an attempt to disguise themselves, though with Milo's size it wasn't very effective.

"King Brandr is dead," Ethan answered, and Alberic offered an understanding nod. Ethan then continued, "It's good to see you still live."

"The feeling is quite mutual," Alberic returned. "I'm almost sad I missed the rest of the party. And the dragon?"

"Dead," Rune piped in.

Alberic nodded slowly then spoke up again, "I suppose it really is over then. I can't imagine the Southerners will care much about us as they scurry around to fill in the void. With their dragon gone, I would guess that the alliance with the East will end. There will be infighting and backstabbing... quite entertaining no doubt." The group smiled lightly but offered no response. "Come now! Don't be so glum! We were victorious! Few victories come easily and without cost. We all yet live, and that is something to celebrate." He paused, "After we get you all cleaned up. You're filthy." The three looked around at each other and laughed lightly at their appearance; Being covered with dirt and dust from head to toe. "Let us be off then," Alberic then continued dramatically, "perhaps the Thane will allow us passage now."

***

The heroes made their way through Regintun together. Those in the city payed them little attention as they cautiously emerged from their homes and took in the new air. A mixture of sounds from relief to sorrow emitted through the streets as the sun offered a new light to the residence. The gloom, stench and mist were all but a memory now.

The five met up with the refugees at the edge of the city who welcomed them with cheers and embraces. Many set off back to their homes soon after, now feeling safe enough to do so as word spread of the dragon's death.

After receiving their share of heartfelt thanks and farewells, the five took a quick moment to retrieve their horses and started their steep journey up to Steinnborg. There, they were yet again all welcomed into the city with many cheers and congratulations as the news of the dragon's death had already reached them. Despite this, there was no sign of the Thane to give his approval or advice. The city dwellers happily provided food, shelter, and supplies as they readied for their imminent journeys back to their homes.

The group had spent some time washing up and getting a great deal of much-deserved sleep and healing. By the next day, Alberic and Milo set a time to meet the other three near the northern gate to make final preparations for their upcoming departures. Alberic and Milo leaned on a nearby wall as they waited patiently for the others with idle conversation.

"Ethan," Alberic declared as he approached with Milla and Rune in tow, "There are several that wish to join you on your journey north and wish to swear fealty to Northern rule. Do you accept?"

Ethan seemed confused at first by the sudden and abrupt declaration. He then nodded. "Yes, I do, of course. In fact, after all of this I can hardly blame them."

"Good then," Alberic said with a smile, "They will escort and protect you on your journey home." He then said to Milla, "We found our companion Wulf. Once he gave up trying to kill me, we were able to come to terms. He and several others will be heading to Gottswai and I would like you to go with them. It is a faster route to your home, and you will be able to visit the shining city before your remaining journey home."

Milla smiled brightly, "I'm glad he still lives. And thank you for arranging that. It is greatly appreciated." She then turned her eyes to Ethan, and her expression became somber.

Alberic approached Rune, "Mind if I have a word with you?"

Ethan piped in, "I should finish my other preparations as well. I will see you all later I'm sure." He moved off after a few farewell nods and motioned Milla to follow, which she did without delay.

Alberic quickly moved in to speak with Rune, as Milo hovered over them, "I think Milo and I should join you when you return to your town."

"Why?" Rune asked, genuinely curious.

"I will get into the details on the trip back, but let me say, now that..." he paused as he thought over his words, "I think you will need some help and guidance in the coming years. I am well studied in both magik and... other powers," he explained, "If you would allow it, I would like to impart my knowledge to you."

"And why would you even want to help me? What would you get out of it?" Rune asked, with some suspicion.

Alberic thought over his words then spoke, "I have a strong feeling... times are changing. That change will not come smoothly, and I think, whether it be fate or coincidence, your powers are..." he stopped again as he considered his wording, "You have a great deal of power for someone so young. I'm not even sure you realize how great. I am in possession of ancient forbidden books. With my help, you can cover up your natural abilities and come off as a powerful magi which is far more... accepted in our land than... well..."

Rune raised a curious brow, "Won't people hear about what I am, after today, anyway?"

"Who would tell them so?" Alberic said with a shrug. "Only our group truly knows what happened and how. Besides, I doubt the Thane would share knowledge such as that and as far as I can see, he is the only one outside of our group that knows."

"So," Rune added with slight annoyance, "this is the part where you try to convince me that you want to help, when really you want to keep an eye on me in case I crack and decide I want to destroy the world?"

Milo grinned and smacked Rune on the shoulder, "No, it's 'cause we like you."

"That and," Alberic said with a chuckle, "Yes, I would like to keep an eye on you. You can understand why we should be concerned, I hope? With my help, we may be able to slow or avoid any... cracking. There are some tricks I have that, with Feagan's help, will keep your mind unburdened by the curses that tend to follow one with your powers. Something we can both benefit from as it falls into my field of study, among other things. Besides all of that, Milo and I will need a place to... stay... now that my own powers have been revealed."

Rune shrugged, "I understand, I don't see why not. I warn you though, there are some boys in my village that will probably want to, at least, give me a good beating as soon as I return."

"Milo and I will deal with them, don't you worry," Alberic said with a grin as he put his arm over Rune's shoulders.

"Now you're talking," Rune smirked. "You can really make it seem like I'm a powerful magi when I return then?"

Alberic nodded with a smile, "Oh yes, trust me. Your town will not even question your abilities when we enter."

"You won't hurt anyone though, right? There's no need to hurt anyone, I think," Rune quickly added.

"There will be no need for that, young friend," Alberic said with a chuckle, "Just some grand displays to fill their minds with awe and a little bit of fear. So, it's agreed then. We will go prepare." With that, Alberic and Milo wandered off.

Rune smiled gleefully as he watched the two leave. He turned and walked in the other direction. After making his way towards a nearby warehouse to find a private spot to let Feagan stretch out his wings. He climbed a thin set of stone stairs, leading to the ramparts just above. As he emerged, he noticed Milla, standing on her own a short distance away, staring out into the grasslands beyond. He approached her with a smile, "I suppose we'll be saying goodbye then?"

Milla blinked out of her daydream then looked to him, returning the smile, "I suppose we will. Thank you, Rune," she said as she turned towards him, "I owe you everything."

Rune's smile brightened, "Nah, you don't owe me anything. This was...," he sighed and shrugged, "If I didn't do this, I don't know what would have become of me. I know who... what I am now." She smiled at that then pulled out her pouch of Dregs and lifted it toward him. He shook his head with a smile as he gently pushed it away, "Keep it. I already have my payment."

Milla teared up lightly then moved to him, wrapping her arms around him, "I hope we see each other again. We are friends now, I hope."

Rune blinked several times before returning the embrace, "Right, of course we are. If you need help finding your sister, you know where I am. I'll always be ready to help you."

Milla wiped her eyes after she released him, "I might hold you to that." She sniffed then gave him a friendly push on the arm. "Please don't go insane. I like you like this and I sort of don't want the world to be destroyed."

"Yeah, yeah," Rune said with an impish grin, "This is where you say, 'I told you so', isn't it? After that lecture you gave me about Seers."

Milla laughed then pushed him again, "I told you so."

Rune chuckled then looked down, unsure of what else to say.

"Well, I hate goodbyes so..." she let out a breath, smiled sadly at him as she gave him another quick hug, then walked away.

Rune returned the hug and teared up as she wandered away, down another set of stairs and out of sight.

***

As Milla walked down the final few steps, she heard Ethan calling her name. She stopped breathing a moment as he approached, and she swiftly wiped away the tears in her eyes. "Milla," he said softly, "What's wrong?"

Milla shook her head and forced a smile, "Nothing. I was just saying my goodbyes to Rune," she sniffed and wiped her eyes again. "It was great traveling with you. Thank you for all you did. I hope your trip home is safe. Goodbye," she pushed the words together then stepped away to pass him.

Ethan placed his hand on her shoulder to stop her. "Milla," he said faintly as he gently pulled her back and turned her to face him. He tenderly placed a finger under her chin and raised her head until her eyes looked at him. After a warm smile, he opened his mouth as if to speak but the words seemed stuck in his throat.

Milla gave him a moment to find his words, but after the moment dragged on, she casually moved his finger away from her chin, then looked down as she spoke, "It's alright. You don't have to say anything. It really was very nice knowing you."

Ethan let out a sharp sigh, remaining silent for a few more moments. He finally spoke, "I just- I want-." Clearly frustrated with himself he started again, "I wish life were not so complicated." Milla nodded and tried to turn away but he stopped her again. "I hope we see each other again, truly," he said, then dropped his hands to his sides.

Milla bowed her head further as tears filled her eyes. She sniffed then quickly stood on her tiptoes and reached up to wrap her arms around his neck, holding him in a tight embrace. Ethan seemed shocked at first, then wrapped his arms around her thin waist and held her tight. After holding him for a good amount of time, she finally began to release, but he continued to hold her for several more moments. Finally, he released her and took a step back, then reached up and wiped her tears away with his thumbs, cradling her chin in his hands afterwards. They gazed into each other's eyes for a few long moments before Ethan moved in - but stopped before their lips touched. After closing his eyes and resting his forehead on hers, he moved his mouth to her ear and whispered, "We will see each other again, I promise." He then released her, and she backed away with a half smile. He returned her smile and turned around to walk away, giving her one final glance before moving out of sight. Milla kept a silly grin on her face as she watched him, then turned on her heels, in a brighter mood as she moved towards her own destination.

***

Rune had watched the two, from a safe and discreet distance away on the ramparts. Feagan sat next to him, but out of sight from anyone who might look up. " Sae hoo diz it feel tae be a hero?" Feagan asked happily.

"Don't heroes usually get the girl?" Rune asked wistfully.

Feagan moved to a better position to see Milla then grunted, " Eh, she's nae 'at pretty anyway."

"I disagree wholeheartedly."

"Rune," Feagan said after a laugh, "Wi' th' tales an' fame 'at will come frae whit ye jist did; ye will hae plenty ay pretty lassies kissin' yer feit an' beggin' ye fur yer attention. Yoo'll forgit aw abit Milla."

"I doubt I will ever forget about her," Rune said with a sigh as he began to move towards the stairs, "I should finish packing."

"Nae only prettier, but a much better disposition. 'at lassie was colder than an ice river."

Rune made his way down the thin stairs and shook his head, "Quiet now, someone will hear you. Get back in the bag."

As Feagan flew to the bag and opened it, he said, "Nae only prettier an' a better disposition, but mebbe ye will fin' one wi' a comely faerie companion!"

Rune scoffed then laughed, now moving along the warehouse wall, "Just be quiet until we get to the room."

"Ah will be quiet if ye at leest admit it's possible," Feagan returned indignantly.

Rune stopped as he reached the edge of the warehouse and peaked around to make sure no one was watching. He then turned his eyes to Feagan who snugged himself into the bag, "Feagan, we just defeated a dragon. At this point, I'd have to say anything is possible." Feagan let out a laugh and they made their way back onto the road, more than ready to start their journey home.

ABOUT THE AUTHOR

Mel D. MacKenzie was born on May 30th, 1980. Growing up as a child with a highly overactive imagination, she spent much of her youth writing stories as a hobby. Despite having notebooks and folders filled with stories, she always feared publishing her "babies". Writing is, and was, a very personal process for her - as most of her stories were taken directly from dreams and nightmares. She looked into publishing many times over the years, but it took a personal tragedy for her to finally take the leap - when her husband of 11 years passed away from prostate cancer, on June 5th, 2013. After spending a few years mourning, she finally decided to fulfill her promise to him, and publish a book.

Rune's Magik is Mel's first published book, and she is currently working on finishing the three-part series.

Made in the USA
Middletown, DE
19 June 2018